THE FOURTH FIGURE

THE FOURTH FIGURE

A PIETER VAN IN MYSTERY

PIETER ASPE

TRANSLATED BY BRIAN DOYLE

Excerpt from *Song of Egidius* translated by Francis Jones

Cover design by Mauricio Díaz

978-1-5040-3230-8

Published in 2016 by Open Road Integrated Media, Inc.
180 Maiden Lane
New York, NY 10038
www.openroadmedia.com

THE FOURTH FIGURE

It was the best of times, it was the worst of times, it was the age of wisdom, it was the age of foolishness, it was the epoch of belief, it was the epoch of incredulity, it was the season of Light, it was the season of Darkness, it was the spring of hope, it was the winter of despair, we had everything before us, we had nothing before us, we were all going direct to Heaven, we were all going direct the other way . . .

—Charles Dickens, *A Tale of Two Cities*

Ten people in a room in two rows of five, a choir at first glance. Gregorian chant drifting from a tiny speaker: an ethereal legato melody, its tempo artificially slow. A macabre ambiance. Candles flickering in bronze stands at the front, leaving those present engulfed in semidarkness at the rear unrecognizable. Shadows gliding like tongues of darkness across the room's bare walls, forming freakish silhouettes.

The inconstant candlelight illuminated a painter's easel draped in coral red, supporting a gilded picture frame. A charcoal etching was imprisoned behind glass: a traditional depiction of the devil, complete with horns, goat hooves, and forked tail. Venex, the Master, the Father, had purchased the "artwork" for a pittance at a flea market. All that mattered was that the decor seemed authentic; no one could argue the contrary.

The ceremony started with a gong struck three times in succession. The mallet was felted, and each beat reverberated long and deep. The assembled faithful lifted their heads and turned to look at the solid oak door as it slowly swung open. A young man marched into the room, his stately gait worthy of a true high priest. Richard Coleyn was dressed in a black satin shirt and velvet pants, an upside-down pentagram dangling from a silver chain around his neck. He had touched up his eyes with mascara, his lips with blood-red lipstick, and his face was buried under a heavy layer of white foundation. Venex suppressed his desire to smile, but only just. The entire spectacle amused him immensely. People would believe anything if you made it look real enough. Magicians and illusionists had been earning a living that way for centuries.

Richard took his place in a handsome chair, a neo-Gothic antique Venex had borrowed for the occasion from a friend in the trade. A hefty tome bound in leather was perched on a lectern. Richard opened it at the place marked by a purple ribbon and invoked the first incantation. The seventeenth-century book was full of sermons by a long-forgotten Jesuit, but it had been appropriated for a different purpose: as the bible of Satan. Typed sheets containing the text of the ceremony had been slipped between its original pages.

"I turn to you, Azael, master of the forge, guardian of the secrets of metal. I bow my head before you, Semyaza, Armaros, Barachiel, Kokabiel, Ezechiel, Arachiel, Shamshiel . . ."

Richard recited the names of the twenty-seven demons, and when he was finished he gestured to the young man with the gong. Jasper Simons struck the gong once again with the felted mallet, and the assembled adepts broke into a hymn. Its melody sounded suspiciously like "Dies Irae." Unfortunately the faithful were off-key, something Venex considered an utter disgrace. *They should at least have rehearsed*, he thought.

Frederik Masyn had been sitting in the kitchen for more than half an hour. To stop his sweating buttocks from sticking to the leatherette seat, he lifted one cheek, then the other, every five minutes, creating a vulgar sucking sound each time. Frederik was exceptionally nervous. He had prepared assiduously for three full months, and now the time for his initiation had come. He was soon to be accepted into the Church of Satan, in which a leading role had been set aside for him. After a youth of oppression, the time had come to embrace the task for which he had been born.

At the third stroke of the gong, the kitchen door opened. Frederik stood and folded his hands in front of his underbelly. Even as an adult, he wasn't exactly good looking, and he felt a twinge of embarrassment standing there naked in front of his brothers and sisters. They used to call him pimple-face at school, the grim reaper, oddball, dickhead, the mange, cigar-butt (in the shower), banana, meringue. Richard, by contrast, described him as Prince, Savior, Redeemer, Hidden Master, Son of Lucifer. Richard had evidence to prove it, so he said.

Frederik straightened his back, shuffled into the room, and fell to his knees on a cushion made ready for him and him alone. The singers fell silent as Richard got to his feet. The ceremony, which had started at midnight, was approaching its climax.

"Brother Masyn, do you swear fidelity to Lucifer, our Lord and Master, Creator of this world, and to all His works?"

Frederik didn't dare look up. An uncanny tranquility descended upon him. He could hardly believe he had come this far. His scrawny frame trembled with excitement.

"Yes, I swear."

"Do you swear to obey your Master and Creator without condition?" Richard continued.

"Yes, I swear."

"And do you swear unconditional obedience to His earthly representatives, on pain of excommunication and death?"

"Yes, I swear."

At this third vow, Frederik felt a tear run down over his left nostril. Tears of joy for the first time in his life. Things could only get better.

Venex gave Richard a flat box containing a silver chain with an upside-down pentagram. Richard stepped forward, opened the box, and adorned the neophyte with the sign of Satan. He then dropped his pants, turned, and offered Frederik his buttocks. Kissing the buttocks was mentioned in all the books on satanism and was thus an indispensable part of the ritual. The same went for spitting on the crucifix. When this tradition had been fulfilled—everyone present was invited to spit on the crucifix—Frederik was dressed in a black garment and the group offered their congratulations.

The solemnity of the occasion suddenly degenerated into a convivial gabfest. Jasper switched on the lights and swapped the Gregorian chant cassette for a pop compilation entitled *Hit Parade 1995*. Cigarettes appeared. Like most Catholics, satanists were happy when the service was over. Richard interrupted: "Time to raise a toast to our brother Frederik." Venex nodded and fetched an antique cut-crystal carafe from a sideboard that had been draped in red for the occasion. Frederik might be convinced he was about to be offered a cocktail of blood and wine and that its consumption would make him a full member of the Church of Satan, but the carafe contained only a mixture of cheap wine, tomato juice, black currant cordial, and a splash of Tabasco. Venex filled the glasses and served Frederik first. Their brand-new member was engaged in an animated discussion with Jasper Simons. The two seemed to be getting along exceptionally well.

When everyone had been served, Richard sought Venex's company. His legs were trembling; an animal gnawed deep inside him, refusing to leave him in peace until its hunger had been sated.

"So what do you think, Father?"

Venex nodded approvingly. "I'm satisfied, Richard."

Richard bowed his head in deference. "That pleases me, Father."

Venex raised his glass to his lips and sipped at the cocktail. The concoction wasn't bad, all things considered. Richard tossed it back, as if to encourage his master to hurry.

"So you think I did well, Father?"

Venex inspected the pale twenty-seven-year-old man who longed for his reward like a well-trained dog. He knew that every postponed second was sheer torture.

"You did well, Richard."

Venex rummaged in his pockets and produced a tiny plastic bag containing what looked like sugar. A sudden flash of light filled Richard's dull eyes. He grabbed the bag and scurried into the kitchen. Venex turned his attentions to Frederik Masyn, treating him with tenderness and calling him "my son."

1

It wasn't the first time Pieter Van In had been late for work, but it was the first time he had a good reason. Hannelore had felt her first labor pains in the course of the night. The baby wasn't expected for another three weeks, but he had called a taxi just to be on the safe side. They had rushed to the hospital, where a young trainee doctor told them that it was a false alarm. The man refused point-blank to call a gynecologist. Mrs. Martens should take things a little easier, he had said. When Van In protested, the brat treated him to a lesson about the descent of the fetus, the breaking of the water, and the dilation of the womb, all of which were signs that the baby was on its way and none of which were even remotely evident in his wife's case. Mrs. Martens was free, of course, to have herself admitted. Then they would . . .

While the doctor was summarizing the pros and cons of an early admission, Hannelore got dressed and asked Van In to call a taxi. The doctor directed them to the public phone in the foyer. Van In hated hospitals: squeaky-clean temples where people were left at the mercy of medics and their antics.

It was four thirty when the drowsy cabdriver dropped them off at the Vette Vispoort. At home, Van In and Hannelore chatted for a while in the kitchen—he with a Duvel, she with a glass of juice—and it made little sense to go back to bed. He installed himself on the sofa around six and was dead to the world in a matter of seconds. Hannelore had a fight on her hands when she tried to wake him at eight forty-five.

"What's the coffee situation, Guido?" Van In inquired as he closed the door to Room 204, took off his jacket, and lurched toward the nearest radiator to warm his frozen hands. He felt awful and looked worse. A glance in the mirror that morning had taught him that a sleepless night and twenty-four-hour stubble could turn a fortysomething into a fiftysomething.

"With or without?" asked Guido Versavel. The sergeant grinned from ear to ear. Van In hadn't seen Guido in such a perky mood for months.

"With is good."

"White or brown?"

Van In pulled a pensive face, as if he were being asked to make an important decision.

"Brown is excellent, Guido."

Guido tugged open the bottom drawer of a filing cabinet, produced a bottle of rum, filled a mug halfway, and topped it up with jet-black coffee.

"Enjoy, Commissioner."

Van In grasped the mug with both hands and deeply inhaled the rum-and-coffee vapor, hoping it might help unblock his nose. "What about you, Guido?"

"Never in uniform, Commissioner. You know me better than that."

"Then take if off."

"Only if you insist, darling," Guido quipped in English with an outrageously French accent, like the gendarme in *'Allo 'Allo* and his now legendary "I shall say zis only once." It always made them laugh. Van In raised the lukewarm rum-coffee cocktail to his lips and emptied the mug in a couple of gulps. The expected response was: "Your tie will suffice, Guido," but instead, Van In returned the mug to his grimy desktop, stretched his legs, and waited for the warm salutary glow that the rum was about to pump into his chilled legs. A pleasant silence filled Room 204. The second hand on the clock above the door turned and turned again.

Guido stood by the window and looked outside. Things had changed in the last twenty-four hours. He was a happy man again, and he enjoyed the way nature seemed to share his good humor. The sun played an absorbing game with the passing clouds, which cast capricious, intangibly gray shadows across the rooftops below.

Both men cherished these precious and invigorating moments of silence. Then curiosity got the better of Van In. He wanted to know why Guido was in such good spirits.

"So what's the story, Guido? Big lottery win?"

Guido turned, his face beaming. "Three guesses," he said.

Van In raised his eyebrows. His friend probably had a thousand reasons to be cheerful. "A tax rebate?"

"Shall I give you a hint?" Guido suggested.

Van In nodded. "But don't make it too difficult."

"Okay, here it comes." *What the hell,* he thought. Nothing could ruin his day . . . "'Egidius, where dost thou hide? Companion true, for thee I pine.'"

The sergeant declaimed the opening lines from the "Song of Egidius," a poem by the medieval Bruges poet Jan Moritoen. He had repeated these words countless times to himself in the preceding months, muffled, under his breath, but this time his tone was upbeat and lilting.

Van In didn't have to guess any further. "Don't tell me Frank is back."

Frank was Guido's boyfriend. He had left him six months earlier for a younger lover, leaving Guido deeply hurt and unhappy.

"Not quite, but close, Pieter, close. We met yesterday in the Chopin . . ."

"A moment, Guido."

Van In scrambled to his feet. A potential reunion with Frank was good news indeed. "This is a moment to be remembered," he said theatrically, "and not to be consumed like any other banal event. I suggest we celebrate it in style."

He held out his mug and Guido provided a rum-and-coffee refill. It promised to be a pleasantly lazy morning.

"Now the details, Guido, from start to finish."

Guido beamed, took a seat, and launched enthusiastically into his story. "A fortnight ago I got a card from Ron. He's just turned fifty and he was planning a celebration at the Chopin. I wasn't in the mood at first . . ."

Van In closed his eyes and unconsciously tuned Guido out. He couldn't keep his thoughts from returning to the night before. Back in the day, men were condemned to earn their living from the sweat of their brows and women were doomed to suffer when they gave birth to their children. But that was *then*. Nowadays, they still had to work themselves into the ground, just to pay the mortgage and the monthly installments on the second car. If God was as just as they claimed he was, he could at least have done something about the birthing business. Van In couldn't bear the thought of walking around with another living being in his belly preparing to force its way out.

The Singel was a remarkable street in the neighborhood of the Smedenpoort, one of Bruges's four remaining city gates. It ran in parallel with the old city moat, petered out at both ends, and could only be reached via a stone bridge. The Singel was a desolate island hidden behind a cheerless row of trees. Visitors felt as if they were stepping into another world when they crossed to the mysterious enclave in which time had stood still for forty years. The dilapidated and neglected state of the houses was partly to blame, but the almost complete absence of cars also had something to do with it. A grimy ditch full of murky water and dead, stinking leaves running the length of the street completed the picture. A better name for the Singel would be *Finis Terrae*: End of the Earth.

Karel Breyne lived in a tiny attic room on the fourth floor of one of the ramshackle town houses. The Singel didn't inspire him to poetry. He lived there because the rent was low and because the majority of social workers preferred to leave him to his own devices rather than hunt him down in the place. Some didn't even know the Singel existed. Breyne didn't care. He survived on benefits and had enough over to pay for a bottle of cheap Jenever every four days. He was happy with that, more or less. Every morning at ten thirty sharp he headed out to the local supermarket on Gistel Road, lowest prices guaranteed. It took him an hour and a half—there and back, of course—but he was happy with that too. After so many years of loneliness, he had learned the knack of killing time. One of his strategies was to walk slowly, which was probably why he immediately noticed the corpse in the black water of the ditch.

Breyne's first thought was to keep walking, but then his curiosity got the better of his indifference. The dead deserved respect, he thought, especially these days, when some people's pets were better off than people like himself. Breyne hesitated no longer. The police station was just around the corner, and the supermarket was open all day.

As he scurried across the bridge, an emaciated female figure watched him from the fourth-floor window of her filthy apartment, opposite the place where the corpse bobbed up and down against the bank of the ditch.

"That's good news about you and Frank, Guido. I'm happy for you," said Van In, suppressing a yawn and stretching his legs and arms at one and the same time.

Guido shared what was left of the rum between his own cup and Van In's. He figured he'd earned the right to sin a little. But just as Saint Anthony managed to escape temptation at the very last minute, Guido alas was robbed of the opportunity to savor the rum-coffee combo. A phone call from the duty officer changed the course of the morning.

Van In asked him a couple of questions and hung up. "Sorry, Guido, but I'm afraid our easy morning just croaked. They found a corpse in the Singel."

He crossed to the coat stand and put on his jacket. A siren wailed in the distance.

At least seven vehicles were already parked at the Singel when Van In and Guido arrived: a federal police MPV, two fire service vehicles, a Renault Espace emergency trauma vehicle, Leo Vanmaele's yellow Audi, the forensics team's gray Ford, and the police physician's BMW convertible. The locals were enjoying the spectacle from their window vantage points, exchanging noisy commentary. The emergency services' ostentatious display led some to think they were in the middle of a US police series.

"I just heard the public prosecutor's on his way," said Guido.

Van In lit a cigarette and watched Leo take photos of the victim. The young woman was lying on a tarpaulin at the side of the road. She wore a black, short-sleeved blouse and jeans. A couple of firemen were setting up a screen to hide her from the curious.

"Then you can bet your bottom dollar the press is on its way too," Van In said, grumbling.

"You should have shaved." Guido grinned.

Van In shrugged. Journalists were only interested in magistrates these days. As soon as the prosecutor stepped out of his car, the cameras would be all over him. Van In had nothing to fear.

"I wonder who called the federal boys."

"They were tipped off before us, apparently," said Guido.

"I don't get it. Breyne informed the local police, didn't he?"

Guido didn't respond. It was a public secret that his boss wasn't on the best of terms with the federal police. "D'you think it's a suicide?"

"Wouldn't be surprised," said Van In. "Winter gets people down, and if we're to believe the statistics, some people think that's reason enough to end it all. Remember the guy who hung himself last year because he didn't have enough money to buy a computer game for his son?"

Van In bent his knees and slipped under the red-and-white tape that marked off the scene. A sergeant gave him a suspicious look and continued to cordon off the street while an officer Van In recognized as First Sergeant Cuylle was wrapped in animated conversation with a middle-aged woman, probably one of the local residents. Van In ignored the federal gendarmes and headed straight to Leo Vanmaele. The two friends greeted each other with a warm handshake.

"I've done my bit," said the diminutive police photographer. He unclipped the flash from his Nikon and stored his material in a sturdy aluminum case.

"You're on the ball, Leo. This is the first time you beat us to it."

"Times are changing, Pieter. *Speed* and *efficiency* are the buzzwords these days. Public opinion can be merciless."

Van In glanced at his watch. "But I still don't get it. A crime was reported only ten minutes ago. The police station's just around the corner and we drove here right away."

Leo lifted his aluminum case and draped its carrying strap over his shoulder. "Ten minutes?" he asked. "That's strange. They called me on my beeper half an hour ago."

"Jesus H. Christ." Van In grimaced, suddenly realizing what was going on. Someone—probably the woman talking to the first sergeant—must have discovered the corpse earlier and called the competition in a moment of madness. "Now we have to work with those federal jerks."

"Looks like it," said Guido. He winked at Leo, and they both burst out laughing.

"Commissioner Van In, Special Investigations," Van In introduced himself. "A word if you don't mind, First Sergeant."

In spite of the fact that the police services had been reorganized and the ranks made uniform, Van In still used the old military titles. First Sergeant Cuylle's official title was Inspector, First Class, and he disliked it as much as Van In did. Cuylle was familiar with the slovenly commissioner's reputation and he limited himself to a surly nod.

"About the investigation," Van In added.

"The investigation's in full swing, Commissioner, as you can see."

"Of course it is," said Van In, his irritation level already beginning to rise. "I just wanted a quick word with that woman you were talking to." He pointed in her direction. "Was she the one who called in the incident?"

Cuylle reacted as a federal gendarme would be expected to

react: according to the book. "The official report will be ready by tomorrow."

While First Sergeant Cuylle savored the taste of victory, Van In had the feeling someone was holding a burning candle under his bare feet. He had to work hard to keep his voice down. "May I remind you, First Sergeant, that I hold the rank of officer in the judicial police? As long as the gentlemen from the public prosecutor's office are still here, I suggest you behave yourself."

While Van In vented his gall on the first sergeant, Guido ambled unnoticed to the place where the victim had been found. With all the commotion, just about everyone had forgotten that they had a dead woman on their hands. Even the firemen who had hauled the girl out of the water were having a smoke nearby. They'd done their job, just like the police physician who had filled in all the necessary forms and scurried off in his flashy convertible. Guido gazed at the motionless body and tried to imagine what the young woman had been thinking as the ice-cold water filled her lungs. Had she tried to save herself at the last minute or had she welcomed death like an old friend with open arms? The serene expression on her face, a common enough feature of suicides, suggested the latter. The unbearable lightness of being seemed to be claiming more and more victims with every passing day.

Guido examined the place where he imagined the girl had entered the water. Two men from the forensics team had marked it off and were scouring the canal bank in a rubber dinghy. They had to presume evil intent until the suicide theory had been verified. When the men caught sight of Guido, they waved. They looked like they were freezing. Guido waved back, then turned and inspected the dead girl anew. Not much older than thirty, he figured. Her eyes were closed, supporting the illusion that she had died in peace. She was slim and her face wasn't unpleasant. He discounted the strings of wet hair clinging to her cheeks, making her less attractive than she must have been when she was alive, and pictured a pair of bright and cheerful eyes behind her closed eyelids. It softened his judgment.

Van In appeared at his side. First Sergeant Cuylle had yielded to his arguments. When the radio announced that the prosecutor wouldn't be putting in a personal appearance—coincidentally, the local TV camera crew had also decided to call it a day; suicide wasn't news—the federal police officer consulted with his immediate superior and informed Van In that he had no further objection to the local Bruges police taking over the case. Cooperation at its very best.

"Her name is Trui Andries, and she lived here opposite at number seven," Van In said to Guido. "They didn't find keys on her, but I called Tuur. He promised to be here in fifteen minutes."

Every little victory against the "legion of darkness"—as Van In liked to call the federal police—cheered him immensely. He beamed like a self-satisfied toddler.

Number seven was one of the better maintained houses in the Singel. The copper nameplate next to the bell had been polished, so much that the letters had almost disappeared. Van In had to step back to decipher them. WID. ANDRIES, it read. The woman who had called the feds had told him that Trui Andries's mother had been taken to the hospital a couple of days earlier with a blood clot in the brain. Widow Andries was completely paralyzed, and the chances that she would ever leave the hospital were extremely slim. According to the neighbor, the elderly woman had been seriously ill for almost ten years. Her devoted daughter had taken care of her all that time. Apparently Trui Andries lived on benefits and her mother's pension and rarely left the house beyond her daily visits to the hospital.

Van In brought Guido up to date.

"Worth a little praise, if you ask me," was the sergeant's spontaneous reaction.

Van In nodded in agreement. Guido had experienced the same thing five years back. His mother had died of a stroke after a long illness, and he had nursed her at home to the very end.

"Maybe that's why she committed suicide."

"I don't think so," said Guido.

A small Suzuki van rattled across the bridge.

"That'll be Tuur," said Van In.

Guido nodded. He had a serious look on his face, worried that the commissioner was moving a little too fast.

Arthur "Tuur" Swartenbroeckx was a burly thirty-year-old. He wore his hair in a ponytail and was dressed, as usual, in spotless overalls. Locks had fascinated him all his life and he had decided to turn his hobby into his profession. His one-man business was flourishing, enough to pay for a couple of assistants, but he preferred to work alone. His motto: You do best what you do yourself. Van In liked Tuur's philosophy, and the two got on like a house on fire.

The locksmith stepped out of his van, waved, and headed to the back to get his tools.

"Tuur. How's the little one?"

"Teething."

It was clear from the tiredness in his eyes that Tuur's infant had cost him a few sleepless nights.

"Another delight to look forward to." Van In grinned.

Tuur grabbed his electric drill, bored the barrel out of the lock, and replaced it with a new one so Van In could lock up after he had finished checking the apartment. The job only took a couple of minutes, and he charged 2800 Belgian francs for the trouble. He knew doctors who had to get by on less. "Voilà, Commissioner."

"Thanks, Tuur. Next Friday at l'Estaminet?"

"Depends on the little bugger's teeth."

Most Belgian town houses had the same layout: a long corridor with stairs going up and two or three connecting rooms with doors giving out onto the corridor. Widow Andries's town house was no exception: a floral-pattern rug running the length of the corridor, a wooden chest in the middle holding an "antique" copper pot, and a couple of paintings gracing the wall, the kind they counterfeit in Taiwan by the square meter. A huge oak coat stand with brass hooks was struggling to stay upright under a mountain of winter coats.

Van In opened the first door, which gave access to what the Flemish like to call "the best room." It usually contained all the good furniture, giving the impression to nosy passersby that the people who lived there were well off.

"Kitsch," said Van In.

The second room contained a hospital bed that had never been used. The smell of old age and medicine was unmistakable. Paper diapers were stacked in piles on a metal rack, intended for adult use if their size was anything to go by.

The last room was the kitchen: cold, tiled floor; old-fashioned sink; and cheap Formica furniture. A tiny porch led out to a seriously neglected garden.

"Reminds me of my aunt's place," said Van In, the summer afternoons he spent in Aunt Clara's garden flooding his memory. That jungle was a secret paradise back then, a place where he could let his imagination run wild. Most of the time he pretended to be Davy Crockett, whiling away the hours building an improvised camp or keeping a lookout from the branches of an old pear tree. Then he would picture himself as a pirate scanning the horizon from the crow's nest in search of three-masters loaded with gold and silver. Perhaps Trui Andries had spent the happiest hours of her childhood playing on this abandoned patch of ground.

"What d'you think, Guido?"

Guido shrugged his shoulders and made a move to leave. "I'm not so sure that we need to be here. I feel like I'm trespassing."

"Understandable," said Van In. "But a quick look around the rest of the house wouldn't hurt now that we're here."

They returned to the corridor and climbed the narrow oak stairs. The upper floor was completely different. The walls had been painted white and the floor was carpeted from wall to wall in high-quality beige pile. Trui had removed an interior wall and transformed her part of the house into a spacious apartment.

"She had taste, I'll give her that," said Guido. He liked simple interiors, and the pine furniture, colorful prints, and copious plants met with his complete approval.

Van In nodded and ran his fingers over the surface of a fine, highly polished refectory table. Trui was clearly well organized. Everything had been neatly tidied, and the plants were in perfect shape. Van In poked his finger into one of the pots. The soil was still moist. Most victims of suicide tended to be depressed when they did the deed and were more inclined to neglect their surroundings. Not so here. He made his way to the window, stopping to examine a framed photograph on the wall. The girl in the photo was Trui's double, only older and with an aura that made her irresistible.

"Don't you think it's strange that she jumped into the water opposite her own house?" Van In asked.

"Doubts, Commissioner?"

Guido had pushed the suicide theory to one side when Van In told him that Trui had spent years looking after her sick mother. People capable of that kind of engagement were generally more sure of themselves.

"Call it a hunch, Guido."

"You might be right. Your hunches hit the mark often enough," said Guido. The commissioner could be boorish at times, and inclined to do things he would later regret, but when it came to intuition, he could compete with the most sensitive.

"We can pretty much rule out an accident. If she had gone out in this weather, she'd have put on a coat. And she had no keys with her."

"Are you suggesting she was murdered?"

"I'm suggesting we should keep our options open."

"Then the killer must have taken a massive risk," said Guido.

Van In nodded. There was something about the case he didn't like, too many things that didn't seem right. "Maybe one of the neighbors saw something. Either way, I'm calling the police physician when we're done here."

"Are you going to ask for an autopsy?"

Van In nodded once again. He fished a pack of John Player Special cigarettes from his inside pocket and lit one. Guido presumed from the way he inhaled the smoke and exhaled it with a vigorous sigh that something was brooding in his boss's head.

"Shall we check the place out?"

"Without a magistrate's warrant!"

Van In smiled at Guido's concern. Everyone was terrified of making procedural errors these days, and everything had to be done by the book. At least you had some kind of answer if you got called on the carpet for negligence.

"We're inside the house, Guido. And having a poke around doesn't mean we have to wreck the place. Should we have waited until tomorrow to have the door opened? And if it was suicide, we'd have to check one way or another if Miss Andries left a farewell letter."

The commissioner's approach might have been unorthodox, but there was nothing illegal about it. It only just dawned on Guido that the law allowed an officer of the judicial police to assume the functions of a magistrate, albeit provisionally, at the scene of the crime if the latter didn't consider it necessary to be present in person. But he was pretty sure that the same thought hadn't dawned on Van In.

Van In and Guido worked quickly and systematically. They checked the cupboards first, and when they found nothing interesting, they turned their attention to the desk and the bookcase. Guido found something curious in one of the desk drawers, a marbled cardboard folder, the type artists use to store their work.

He untied the ribbons and opened the folder with care. "Take a look at this," he said.

The folder contained dozens of pages of handmade paper in a variety of different sizes. Van In turned and peered sideways at a sheet of frayed paper Guido was holding under his nose. It was full of ornate letters and strange words like *meconium, ortolan, pikestaff, caboodle, chatterbox, plaguing, smoldering* . . . "What kind of crap is that?"

"Calligraphy, Pieter, and superior quality if you ask me."

"Another one of your many interests?"

Guido leafed through a pile of loose pages. As a child, he had spent hours in the workshop of a stonemason. The old man had carefully explained the importance of beautiful letters. He had even told him a story about them that was just as exciting as any other adventure story. *Bet* was the second letter of the Hebrew alphabet and it meant "house." That's where *Alef* lived and ruled over all the other letters. They were one big family, and each had its own job to do in helping people understand God's thoughts. You could use the letters to tell the future and discover nature's deepest secrets. Every letter corresponded to a number, and wise people could solve all the problems of the world by combining numbers in different ways.

"I only wish I could do that," said Guido.

"Now I know what to get you for Christmas," Van In said. "A pen and a sketchbook."

"If only it was that simple. This girl had real talent."

"Good to know, Guido, but not very helpful under the circumstances."

Guido nodded, closed the folder, and returned it to the drawer. "Found anything yourself?"

Van In shrugged his shoulders. He was standing by the bookcase and read a few titles out loud: "*Les pactes sataniques*, *The Golden Bough: A Study in Magic and Religion*, *Liber Aleph vel CXI*, *The Satanic Bible*, *Histoire du Christ*, *The Origin of Satan*, *The Satanic Rituals* . . . Our Miss Andries apparently had other interests." Van In passed one of the volumes to Guido. "Most of the stuff here is about the devil. Hmm, to each his own I suppose. Satan seems to be in vogue these days."

"And paper is patient," said Guido as he opened the book. A scrap of paper folded in quarters fell out.

Van In lit a cigarette, his fingers blue from the cold, while Guido unfolded the scrap of paper.

"This might be something." He showed the note to Van In.

Dear Trui, it read. *I submitted your request to join our Church to the High Priest, and I'm delighted to say his response was more than positive. If everything goes according to plan, we can organize an initiation ceremony before the end of the year. Warm regards, Jasper Simons. P.S. Don't forget to transfer your contribution.* It was dated June 22.

"Are you thinking what I'm thinking?" asked Guido.

"A satanic sect," said Van In. "That's all we need."

Guido closed the book in his hand and read the spine: "*Self-Alienation and Self-Belief* by Leopold Flam."

If they were dealing with the followers of Satan, he figured it made sense to get acquainted with the subject.

"I think I'll take a couple of these books home with me, if you have no objection, that is."

"Up to you," said Van In.

This was typical Guido. He grouched about rules and procedures, but if he bumped into rare or interesting books, he was the first to junk the formalities. Van In was also partial to a good book, but compared to Guido's passion for the written word, he was an amateur.

In the absence of an ashtray, Van In stubbed out his cigarette in the saucer under one of the plants. He was reminded of the Order of the Solar Temple, a sect that made the news a couple of years earlier when its members committed collective suicide—or was it murder after all? He hoped Trui's death was a one-off. Religious fanatics and ordinary criminals maintained different sets of norms, and that made it all the more difficult to track them down.

"That's strange." Guido was opening the remaining drawers in the desk. "Somebody's been cleaning up."

The drawers were completely empty. Van In shook his head. The entire affair was beginning to stink. "Maybe we should put things on hold for a bit," he said guardedly, "wait until we know the precise cause of death."

"You're afraid we might stir up some hornet's nest."

"I'm praying we haven't already, Guido."

"Prayer sounds appropriate, given the circumstances," Guido said with a smile.

They made their way outside to find the Singel just as dreary and desolate as ever. The strips of red-and-white tape that marked the place where Trui Andries had met her end fluttered in the wind like party streamers with nothing to celebrate. Guido looked up at the sky, at the ominous clouds drifting low above the treetops, making the street even more miserable than it already was.

"There's rain on the way, Pieter."

He'd hardly finished speaking when the first heavy drops exploded on the cobblestones like liquid coins. Both Van In and Guido were soaked through by the time they reached the Volkswagen Golf.

"Looks as if Inspector Pattyn's on the job," said Guido, pointing to the police vehicle parked in front of the Golf. Pattyn was charged with the local door-to-door canvassing, and everyone in the corps knew that the ambitious inspector would do anything to get promoted. Guido started the engine and turned the wipers on full blast.

"Let him get on with it. That way he won't get under our feet." Van In took his cell phone from the glove compartment and called the police physician. It took a while before the man answered.

Van In peered through the windshield at the pouring rain. There had been no sign of a phone index or address book when they were searching the house, and two of the drawers in Miss Andries's apartment had been emptied, as if someone had been trying to wipe out any clues that might say something about her private life. The letter between the pages of the Leopold Flam book was apparently the only item to have survived the cleanup. Van In was pretty certain that the hard disk in her computer had also been "cleaned."

"Hello. Commissioner Van In here. Is the doctor available?"

A refined female voice explained that the doctor wasn't in his office. Van In left a message, disconnected, then lit another cigarette. "I'll be happy when today's behind us," he said with a shiver.

"Me too," said Guido. "Frank's planning breast of duck with red wine sauce. And for dessert . . ."

"Don't get him pregnant, Guido."

They laughed.

2

The drive from the Singel to the police station was much like a visit to the car wash. It poured so hard that the wipers were virtually useless. Even the warm air from the heat vents felt humid.

"Now I know what the back of a waterfall must feel like," said Guido.

"And we'll soon know what it's like to walk through one," Van In grumbled.

Guido drove into the police station's inner courtyard and parked the car in the only available space: farthest from the entrance, needless to say. Van In pulled his jacket over his head, ran across the courtyard, and sought shelter under the awning above the main door. The sergeant joined him a second later and shook himself like a wet dog.

"Shame we finished the rum," said Van In as they stood in the elevator. "I could use a pick-me-up."

He shivered. Lack of sleep combined with the hours in Trui Andries's unheated house were beginning to take their toll.

"Is Jenever an option?" asked Guido.

"Is there any left?"

Guido nodded and held up three fingers to indicate how much was still in the bottle. Van In made a face. He'd need more than that to drive the cold from his system.

"Fancy a shot yourself?"

Guido understood that this was a rhetorical question, but he shook his head just to be clear and, of course, to reassure his friend.

Van In draped his jacket over the back of a chair, pushed it up against the radiator, sat down at his desk, and lit a cigarette. Just as he was about to treat himself to a sip of Jenever, the telephone rang. The sudden, loud ring made him knock over the glass, and the Jenever spread across his desk like an oil slick. Before he could do anything about it, some of the stuff poured onto his pants.

He cursed and picked up the phone at the same time. "Hello, Van In."

Instead of biting the caller's head off, he grabbed an old newspaper and tried to stop the flow of Jenever. Guido saw him nodding. That was a bad sign. Suddenly Van In put down the paper and started to tap nervously on the arm of his chair. Guido was now more or less certain of the caller's identity. He grabbed a dishtowel and started to wipe Van In's desk dry.

"Okay, I'll be there in two minutes."

Van In slammed down the receiver just as Guido was finished with cleaning. The surface of the desk was spotless. The alcohol had dissolved years of coffee and nicotine into a brown sludge that the dishtowel had absorbed.

"I'm guessing De Kee."

"Bull's-eye! If you ask me, the man's lost it altogether."

Chief Commissioner De Kee and Van In weren't the best of friends. The old man, as Van In liked to call him, saw his subordinate as a blot on the corps's reputation, and Van In was convinced that his superior was as dumb as they came.

"Shall I keep the coffee warm?" asked Guido.

Van In removed his jacket from the chair by the radiator and sniffed at it. It smelled like a bar at closing time, but he put it on anyway. De Kee hated informality.

"Another Jenever sounds a lot better, Guido," said Van In as he turned and headed for the door. "Shit, my pants." He groped in panic at the Jenever stain.

"Your pants were already wet from the rain, Pieter. No one will notice."

Like Thomas, who refused to believe until Jesus invited him to place his finger in his wounded side, Van In continued to grope at the inside of his thigh.

Guido shook his head. "You don't think I would let you leave the office with a wet stain on your pants."

"You're an angel, Guido."

"I know. Now get your ass out of here."

Guido tossed the dirty dishtowel into the wastebasket and poured himself a cup of coffee. He was curious, to tell the truth. What did the old man have to report?

De Kee's third-floor office was spacious and comfortable, the place from which he directed the Bruges police force as an enlightened despot. He would have been happy to add "By the grace of God" to his job description, of course, but those days were sadly gone.

Van In straightened his wrinkled jacket and rang the bell by the door. It took a while before the little box with the red and green windows flashed to green for "enter." Van In pushed down the door handle and entered the sanctuary.

De Kee wasn't in his usual place behind his desk but was sitting in a lounge area by the window. A young woman, twenty-five or thereabouts, was sitting opposite him, her legs crossed in the only respectable position her extremely short skirt allowed.

"Let me introduce you, Pieter. This is Miss Maes," said De Kee with a jovial smile.

Van In scratched the back of his ear. When the old man used his first name, caution was advised. The young woman got to her feet and shook his hand. Her eyes twinkled.

"Good afternoon, Commissioner."

Van In looked Miss Maes straight in the eye, but she neither blinked nor blushed. "So you're the journalist who wants to investigate our little enterprise."

"I wouldn't say 'investigate,' Commissioner. I'm preparing a series of articles on cooperation between the municipal police and the federal police." She dropped the name of a prominent weekly. "It might sound a little banal, but it's still a topical issue, rest assured," she said with a laugh.

Van In took a seat beside De Kee. He felt a little awkward in his damp clothes and did his best not to dwell on what he looked like, although he was certain wet hair added at least ten years to his appearance.

"Miss Maes is keen to follow an investigation at close quarters, one involving ourselves *and* our federal colleagues," said De Kee, sniffing the air suddenly like a dog with a runny snout and shifting a little to the right, the kind of maneuver people deploy when they've broken wind and want to blame it on someone else. Van In took a deep breath and realized immediately what was going on. The alcohol on his pants had started to evaporate, giving off a thin but unpleasant bar odor. His discomfort multiplied.

"You've no objections, I imagine," De Kee snapped.

Of course Van In had objections! For one thing, he had no intention of cooperating with the federal police, and for another, he hated people looking over his shoulder. Miss Maes seemed to sense his suspicion and tried to confuse him by uncrossing her legs. Van In looked away and shifted a little to the left. Her tactics might have worked a year ago, but now he had other things on his mind. He was reminded of a verse from the Bible, the book of Ecclesiastes: "A time to make love and a time to abstain," or words to that effect. "If such a case should present itself, I'll be sure to inform you, Miss Maes."

The young woman looked at De Kee, smile freezing and eyebrows raising. The chief commissioner cleared his throat. "But aren't you working on an appropriate case, Pieter?"

Van In's penny dropped. This had all been arranged in advance. Now he knew why De Kee had been using his first name.

"The incident this morning, Pieter. That bizarre suicide . . . the Singel."

"But the federal police aren't involved," Van In gently protested. "And if it turns out to be a suicide, there won't be much to investigate."

"Do you think it was a suicide?" Miss Maes asked bluntly.

"That's not what I said, Miss. I'll need confirmation of the official cause of death before I can draw any conclusions."

Van In almost bit the tip of his tongue. Guido would have bent double with laughter. *I'll need confirmation of the official cause of death before I can draw any conclusions.* He couldn't have sounded more officious if he'd tried.

"That's what makes the case perfect for Miss Maes." De Kee's forehead shone like a polished billiard ball. "Don't you agree, Miss Maes?" The chief commissioner's thin lips morphed into a broad smile, the kind he usually reserved for intimates. Van In pressed his thighs together. The smell of alcohol had mixed with the musty smell of his clothes to produce an odor that reminded him of people who only change their underwear once a month. He was sure she could smell it too.

"But I don't see what the federal police have to do with this. Perhaps, in the not-too-distant future . . ."

"Come on, Pieter," said De Kee, shaking his head. "If I'm correctly informed, the federal police were first on the scene. Isn't it time we acknowledge that?"

"That's your opinion, Chief Commissioner."

"Don't let it worry you, Pieter. Saartje . . . I mean Miss Maes . . . is only interested in the investigation itself. She's not planning to draw attention to every little friction between the police services. Am I right, Miss Maes?"

"Goes without saying, Chief Commissioner." The journalist presented two rows of snow-white teeth and a tilted-up nose surrounded by a garland of tiny freckles.

Van In sighed deeply. He was exhausted and wasn't in the mood to fight windmills, certainly not two at a time. "Do I have a choice?"

De Kee shook his head a second time. "We have to move with the times, Pieter. Transparency and openness. They're not just meaningless words anymore. Anyway, the federal boys have already agreed to cooperate. Miss Maes will pitch tent with us for the first week, then move on to our colleagues."

Coming from De Kee, the words *pitch tent* sounded particularly ambiguous. Everyone knew his mistress had dumped him a month earlier and he'd been on the prowl ever since. Van In sighed.

Frederik Masyn closed the door to his study behind him and turned the key. In his daily life, he wasn't known as a new initiate into the Church of Satan, but rather as a respectable notary who spent most of his day witnessing the signing of important documents.

Although he heard the door's deadbolt click as it should, he grabbed the handle firmly and checked three times to be sure the door was well and truly locked. He then switched on the light, closed the shutters, pushed aside an armchair, and lifted a corner of the rug to reveal a tiny door with sunken hinges in the parquet floor. Frederik unlocked the door with a key he kept on a chain around his neck. He flipped it open, looked around suspiciously, got to his feet, walked to the door, and checked for the fourth time that it was properly secured. Having completed his usual ritual, he got to his knees in front of the hole in the floor and leaned over the little safe. A plastic bag containing white gloves was attached to the door. Frederik put the gloves on and dialed the combination, a four-letter word rarely heard on national television because of the censor. From a distance, the entire performance looked like some kind of religious event. After the final click, Frederik got to his feet, dropped his pants, and started to masturbate.

When Van In returned to Room 204, Guido was reading one of the books he had taken from Trui Andries's bookcase. The sergeant looked up, not sure what to expect, although the way Van In slammed the door was already an indication. Guido mentally prepared to handle the inspector with kid gloves, put his book to one side, slinked toward the filing cabinet, and returned with the bottle of Jenever.

Van In lit a cigarette and nervously tapped his shiny desk with the tips of his fingers. Guido served him a stiff double and then some and returned to his book. The thrumming concert came to an abrupt end, and silence descended on Room 204.

The relentless rain outside had steamed up the windows, creating an agreeable cocoonlike atmosphere. Guido read with pleasure. From age ten to age sixteen he had spent many a winter evening alone with a book and had managed more or less to clean out the school library. He later ventured into more serious literature, and that hadn't disappointed either.

"De Kee's lost his mind completely," said Van In after a minute. "Starting tomorrow we've been saddled with a journalist, a young slip of a thing, wants to write an article about cooperation between us and the federal boys. Can't see the point myself."

Guido closed his book for the second time. "I can see you're looking forward to it," he said. "How long?"

"A week."

Guido sighed. He knew Van In. If the journalist got on his nerves, he could look forward to a week of moaning and groaning from his boss.

"Don't you have three weeks' holiday time you can take? Perhaps—"

"Don't be such an asshole, Guido."

"Sorry. It was only a suggestion."

Guido returned to his book. Given the circumstances, reading was the safest option. He looked at the clock above the door. His shift was over in fifteen minutes. Good thing too.

A sudden racket in the corridor outside made both Van In and Guido jump to their feet. They heard someone cursing, and seconds later a young man in handcuffs flashed past the window, followed by Inspector Pattyn and a couple of other cops. Doors opened the length of the corridor, and heads followed the juvenile fugitive as he reached a dead end, unable to open the door to the stairwell with his hands cuffed. Pattyn threw himself at the boy like a lion attacking its prey, dragging him to the ground and pressing him flat with all his substantial weight. His victim floundered like a fish on dry land, his eyes full of despair.

"What's going on, Pattyn?"

The cops standing in a semicircle around the detainee let Van In and Guido through. Pattyn turned to them with a grin on his face, but the boy took advantage of the inspector's distraction and rolled onto his side, knocking Pattyn off balance. He started to kick out in every direction and managed to land a bull's-eye in Pattyn's crotch. The poor inspector screeched like a slaughtered pig and grabbed himself with both hands. Van In stood back and enjoyed the entertainment. His colleagues, on the other hand, seized their rubber batons in unison and set upon the prisoner like a bunch of animals. Van In didn't pause. He threw himself into the fray but had to use all his authority to put an end to the aggression. *Homo homini lupus*. The effort required to end the scuffle left him gasping for breath.

"Can someone tell me what this is all about?"

The batons were returned one by one to their owners' belts. Guido was reminded of a passage from one of the gospels, in which a crowd of people is about to stone a woman caught in adultery and Jesus says: "Let him who is without sin cast the first stone."

"You saw it yourself," Pattyn groaned.

The zealous inspector scrambled to his feet, making sure he was well out of the manacled prisoner's reach.

"All I saw was six grown men struggling to get the better of a helpless teenager," said Van In.

"Don't make me laugh, Commissioner. You should take a look at his file. What you call a helpless teenager is a notorious drug dealer, a client at the Iron Virgin. He admitted it himself."

The Iron Virgin was a bar with a reputation for drug dealing—but Van In was conscious of his reputation and didn't want to lose face in front of his men.

"Let me be the judge of that, Pattyn," he said. "Everybody back to work. We'll talk about the rest in my office."

The officers headed back down the corridor as Van In leaned down to the boy and helped him to his feet. "What's your name, son?"

The boy couldn't be a day more than twenty. He looked pretty neglected too, with his sweater full of holes and his jeans so threadbare you could almost see through them in places. His eyes darted nervously from side to side as if he was expecting another attack any second.

"His name's Jonathan Leman," said Pattyn, handing Van In a dog-eared identity card. "And he was carrying drugs."

"Pounds or ounces?" Van In inquired, patronizingly.

Pattyn fished a couple of joints from his inside pocket.

"And you arrested him for that?"

"No, Commissioner."

Pattyn was smart enough to stay polite. He was up for promotion to chief inspector, and if Van In didn't support his application, he could forget it.

"We spotted our friend here at Trui Andries's place, standing at the front door ringing the bell. When he caught sight of us, he took to his heels. Luckily, one of my colleagues managed to collar him before he got too far."

"And then you asked him what he was doing at the house?"

"Correct, Commissioner."

"And what did he say?"

Pattyn grinned maliciously. "Then he buggered off again."

Van In took a look at the boy's wrists. Pattyn had fastened the cuffs around them so tight that the flesh had turned purple.

"Give me the key."

"You're asking for trouble," Pattyn protested.

"Give him the key," Guido reiterated.

Pattyn outranked Guido, but he didn't dare cross the commissioner's best buddy. He fished the key from his pocket and gave it to Van In, who unlocked the cuffs and took the boy by the arm.

"Now back to work, Pattyn. I want a full report on the door-to-door by tomorrow morning. Understood?"

Pattyn nodded, teeth gritted, and turned.

Jonathan Leman gulped down the coffee Guido had poured for him. His identity card and the two joints Pattyn had confiscated were lying on the desk.

"So take your time and tell me what happened." Van In leaned back in his chair and stretched his legs. This was turning out to be one of those days that refused to end. Tiredness and Jenever joined forces to make him feel sluggish and listless. Every fiber of his body longed for the comfort of a soft mattress. "Unless you'd prefer a cell for the night," he added.

Jonathan stared into space. This wasn't the first time he'd had a run-in with the police. He knew their tactics. Every word he said would be used against him later.

"I don't want to pressure you, Jonathan," said Van In, pointing to the clock above the door. "But let me be honest. I hardly slept a wink last night, and under normal circumstances my shift should have finished half an hour ago. I really don't care where you spend the night."

Van In picked up one of the joints and rolled it between his thumb and his forefinger. "If you ask me, you haven't committed a crime. All I want to know is what you were doing at Miss Andries's place."

As Van In rolled the joint between his fingers he was reminded of his first smoke. How long ago was it? Twenty years? Twenty-one? He was sure it was before he tasted his first Duvel. He remembered the high, the relaxed feeling, and the philosophical conversations with friends about death and reincarnation, gods and cosmonauts, evolution and creation. Weed had been tolerated in the seventies, and it didn't seem to raise people's level of aggression. The young crowd were more into the chemical crap these days. Smoking was bad for your health, wasn't it? Van In pushed the joint in Jonathan's direction.

"Smoke it if you want. You're safe here," he said.

Guido observed the scene with increasing astonishment. Van In was well known for his special interrogation techniques, but now he was teetering on the edge. Even Jonathan was thrown for a loop.

"Trui is my girlfriend," he blurted.

"So you're in a relationship?" Van In deliberately used the present tense. If Jonathan didn't know she was dead, this didn't seem like the moment to bring him up to speed.

"Yes. We have a relationship."

"Do you sleep with her?"

"She's twenty-nine," Jonathan said, grinning.

Van In understood. When he was Jonathan's age, girls older than twenty-five were middle-aged. He offered the boy a kosher cigarette and took one for himself.

"And you're nineteen."

"That's what it says." Jonathan pointed to his ID card.

Guido listened without making a sound. It was as if Van In were talking to his own son. The familiarity between the two was almost tangible.

"Do you love her?"

"I do."

Van In offered Jonathan a light. "Can you tell me why you love her?"

There was silence for a moment. Two clouds of smoke rose into the air above Van In's desk, colliding when they reached the ceiling.

"Trui gave me the gift of truth."

If Jonathan had been a Jehovah's Witness, his words would have sounded banal.

"I was living in sin and she saved me."

He hesitated. Van In puffed at his cigarette. He was no longer tired. "I'm listening, Jonathan."

"I met Trui when she was living in the darkness. But even then, she was still a child of the light."

"I need you to explain, Jonathan."

Jonathan nodded, his eyes tranquil, devoid of their earlier wildness. Guido was more and more convinced that the conversation was getting out of hand.

"Trui descended into hell, just like Christ did."

He started to pray. "I believe in one God, the Father, the Almighty, creator of heaven and earth, and in Jesus Christ his only son, born of the virgin Mary, who suffered under Pontius Pilate, was crucified and died. Who descended into hell and rose again on the third day."

The credo brought back memories. Van In had once been a believer, a very long time ago, but like so many of his contemporaries, obligatory spirituality had been watered down by the materialist philosophy of the sixties. In those days, the scientists preached a new religion in which human beings were central. Happiness was a question of consumption, and modern technology was going to liberate us from the yoke of labor and the curse of original sin. Quotations from Nietzsche had been carved into every classroom bench. God was doomed, and so was the devil.

"So she's Catholic."

"She's Christian," Jonathan said passionately. "She believes in Christ and the love of thy neighbor. Because of her, Satan no longer has any hold on me."

Guido flipped open the book by Leopold Flam. A passage on page twenty-six had been highlighted in yellow. It read:

Satan reveals himself to us in four figures: He tempts, misleads, manipulates, and deceives. These four figures correspond with four familiar archetypes: Don Juan, Faust, Prometheus, and Lucifer. His greatest strength is his ability to convince people that he doesn't exist.

Though Guido hadn't been conditioned by a Catholic upbringing like Van In, he still didn't think the highlighted passage was ridiculous. Far from it. No one could deny these days that evil tended to be rewarded more than punished.

"Are you members of a satanic sect?"

The expression on Jonathan's face hardened, and a dull glow flickered in his eyes. "Not anymore," he said.

He didn't sound convincing. At least Guido didn't think so.

Richard Coleyn followed the rules he'd first learned from Master Venex: rubbed his forearm with an antiseptic wipe, tightened the tourniquet, prodded in search of an undamaged vein, and inserted the needle. The drug took effect in no time, a sign of quality goods. He withdrew the needle, loosened the tourniquet, and lay down on the sofa. The first flash was followed by colors, capricious blotches dancing behind his eyelids like fluttering birds of paradise. The blotches blurred after a few minutes, then dissolved into tiny dots. The picture focused. Hundreds of eyes behind the wallpaper registered his every move. His body became lighter and lighter, and before he knew it, he was floating around the room.

His senses in a whirl, Richard touched the colors in his mind's eye, tasted red and blue. Red was like liquid chocolate, blue like new mown grass and like the juices young girls exude when they're excited. His penis hardened, but he felt no need to relieve himself. His heartbeat, which was now pounding deafeningly in his ears, registered orgasm after orgasm. Then everything turned moist and wet. Richard imagined himself in his mother's womb. He saw a fetus without a body, just a head pulsating in a soft halo of peach-colored light. Then the image blurred, the spirit of the child mixed with the amniotic fluid. The ancient wisdom that had been passed down from generation to generation became visible: good and evil, life and death. Richard was mobbed by countless creatures of his own species who wanted to communicate with him. Soon Father would come, caress him, whisper sweet words in his ear. The second phase of Father's plan had started.

Venex stepped out of the shower, grabbed a towel, and dried himself vigorously. He gave only a small portion of his heroin supply to his boys; the rest was sold for pure profit. But with his drug business now under threat—he couldn't keep the federal police duped forever—his discovery of Frederik Masyn was a genuine godsend.

He'd found the unstable young man through Richard's dating agency—a fortunate coincidence of timing, since Richard was barely capable of running the dating service in his current state. Frederik, Venex was convinced, was the solution to all his problems. Venex would soon be rich, and those who had ignored him in the past would have no choice but to respect him. Money, after all, was the key that opened every door.

And this time, no one was going to screw with his plans. He was prepared to get rid of anyone who crossed him.

3

"Good morning, miss."

Officer Asaert rarely welcomed visitors with a smile. He didn't have to because he wasn't paid to be friendly. But for the young lady who had just walked in, he was happy to make an exception. "How can I be of service, miss?" he asked, almost obsequiously.

The girl had a friendly face. She leaned forward, almost pressing her nose against the bulletproof glass, but the black cowl-necked sweater she was wearing prevented potential leering.

"My name is Saartje Maes and I have an appointment with Commissioner Van In. Is he in his office?" she asked with the air of someone used to having others dance to attention.

"Commissioner Van In, miss?" Asaert glanced at his watch, an Omega worth thirty-six thousand francs he liked to show off. "At five to eight in the morning?"

The question mark was clearly audible, but Saartje paid no attention. "I thought he started at eight," she said pointedly.

Asaert's smile froze. "Take my advice, miss. If you really want to speak with Van In, I suggest you come back around noon."

Saartje wasn't about to let the officer's irritating tone intimidate her. "Then I'll wait for him in his office."

Asaert put on his strict face. Pretty girls could count on an abundance of patience from him, but they shouldn't push it. He switched back to his normal tone and manner: "Let me repeat it one more time, sweetheart."

"No need," Saartje said airily. "Perhaps this can convince you." She rummaged in her handbag and produced a document. "Take a look at the signature, *sweetheart.* Your boss! If I were you I'd open the door. . . . Now."

She took a step back and produced a cynical smile. Asaert had been on the force long enough to know there was a time to go on the offensive and a time to hold your tongue. He swallowed his frustration and pressed the button that opened the door's electric lock.

Saartje straightened her back and marched with confidence toward the elevator.

Asaert waited until the doors were closed, then called the officer on duty. He wanted to know who the black widow was. The duty officer's response was short and sweet: "Keep your paws off her."

Jonathan was wearing a pair of Van In's pajamas. They were clearly too big for him, but at the rate he was gobbling Danish pastries, he would soon fill them out. Van In had bought a dozen, and Jonathan was on his seventh.

"Taste good?" asked Hannelore, who enjoyed watching the boy eat.

She hadn't managed more than a couple of hours' sleep for two nights in a row, but she still looked fresh and full of beans. She liked the idea of being able to help someone in need. Even Pieter looked as if he'd made it through the night intact. His eyes were clear, and he hadn't complained when Hannelore woke him at seven to put out the garbage.

Van In usually did complain, but his obliging response that morning had everything to do with Jonathan. Like most people, Van In was inclined to relativize the trivial things when he was confronted with a real problem. He was sure he'd made the right decision bringing Jonathan home with him. When he'd finally told him the day before about Trui Andries's demise, the boy's sorrow had verged on hysteria. *If she's dead, then I don't want to live anymore*, he had whimpered. Van In could have called social services, of course, but his own bad experience with the medical profession inclined him not to follow that route. He felt obliged to do something himself, so he suggested Jonathan stay the night at his place, and the boy had responded positively. Hannelore had taken pity on him the moment he walked through the door, and when his initial tears had subsided, he'd told his rambling, disjointed story in fits and starts.

The smell of watery coffee drifting along the corridor made Guido suspicious. When he opened the door to Room 204 and saw the person who had made it sitting at his desk, he plucked nervously at his mustache.

"Do you mind if I ask what you're up to, Miss . . . ?"

"Maes, Saartje Maes." The woman threw back her head. "I'm working, Sergeant. Is that a problem?"

Guido shook his head. Van In's reaction didn't bear thinking about. The sight of such a svelte creature on an empty stomach! "So you must be the *journalist*."

Guido's emphasis on the word *journalist* spoke for itself, but she didn't seem to notice. She grinned from ear to ear, pearl-white teeth, the whole nine yards.

"I came a little early," she said. "First day on the job, that sort of thing."

Guido nodded. A week, Van In had said, then on to the federal boys. The prospect was a comfort.

"By the way, there's news about the death of Trui Andries."

"Oh yes?" said Guido.

"The police physician called ten minutes ago. It's clear from the autopsy that she didn't drown. There was no water in her lungs."

The sergeant didn't let on that this was important information. "And he shared this with you just like that?"

"There was no one else here to answer the phone." Saartje stuck out her chin and pulled back her shoulders. Body language, they called it. The scientists were convinced it worked.

Guido was faced with a dilemma. His first instinct was to give the child a roasting. Who did she think she was? Following a case at close quarters was one thing; meddling in it another.

"And did the police physician confide in you further?"

Saartje tried to measure the testiness of his question. She decided to change course. Sergeant Versavel was Commissioner Van In's best friend. It made no sense to intimidate him as she had done with the officer at reception. But she still wasn't ready to be pushed into a corner. "He asked if we could stop by in the course of the morning."

"We?"

"Commissioner Van In and me," she said breezily. "Unless you want to join us, Sergeant."

Guido wanted to say something ugly, but instead he crossed to the coffee machine, grabbed the pot, and turned toward the door. He was determined to stay calm. Saartje followed his every move.

"We only have one coffee machine per floor. I'll do the rounds first."

"Sorry, I didn't know." She smiled winningly. "Starting tomorrow I'll make sure everyone has coffee."

"There's no need for that, Miss Maes. The coffee is my responsibility."

"Up to you, Sergeant." Saartje spun on her chair and turned back to her work.

Guido closed the door behind him, headed to the kitchen, and poured the coffee down the drain. He had two options: return to his office and put the young journalist in her place or warn Van In and prevent him from having a heart attack. He chose the latter. This was now a murder investigation and he wanted to gauge Van In's reaction. He returned the coffeepot, put on his jacket, and made himself scarce.

"Officer Asaert already has a nickname for our Miss Maes. He calls her 'the black widow,'" said Guido, bringing Van In up to speed on their new "assistant." He plucked incessantly at his mustache, making it obvious that he wasn't happy with the situation.

Hannelore poured Guido a cup of coffee and offered him the last Danish. She was having a hard time suppressing her laughter. Two adult men struggling to get control over a twenty-five-year-old girl: Now that's what she called funny.

Van In lit a cigarette, inhaled deeply, and exhaled noisily. "And you think that's a joke? You should have seen how she twisted De Kee around her little finger. Scandalous!"

"You're not jealous because she's not courting your attention?" asked Hannelore. Guido started to chuckle. Both he and Hannelore knew how sensitive Van In was in that department.

"She did at first, but . . ."

"But you're above that sort of thing," said Hannelore. She was having fun. "I bet she's pretty!"

"Absolutely," said Van In. "And she has a bad character. You know how I fall for women like that."

Jonathan sat quietly listening to the conversation, not having a clue what they were talking about.

"Then I'd like to meet her," Hannelore said. "What would the gentlemen think if I invited the black widow over for dinner this evening?" She gestured to her belly. "I'm not expected in court."

"If you do, I'll spend the night with your mother."

"You . . . with my mother!"

Van In related to his mother-in-law like Moses to the golden calf. If you left them alone together for even a moment, furious sparks were guaranteed to fly. Hannelore juddered with laughter, grabbed her belly with both hands, and ran off to the bathroom. "I can't keep this up," she said, her laughter now out of control. "I've got to pee."

Van In shrugged and lit another cigarette. He noticed the longing look in Jonathan's eyes and slipped him the pack. The boy looked around skittishly then helped himself. Guido dutifully dusted the crumbs from the tablecloth and dropped them in the empty basket.

"Now that I'm here, wouldn't this be a good time to have a look at your new music center?"

"Music center?"

"In the den," said Guido emphatically.

Van In nodded. "Tell Hannelore we're in the den?"

Jonathan nodded. Van In closed the door behind him.

"Okay, Guido, get on with it."

Guido told him about the telephone call from the police physician. "I didn't want to say anything in front of Jonathan."

"Of course." Van In collapsed onto the sofa and threw his legs onto a side table. "After everything Jonathan told us last night, I'm not really surprised."

"Anything interesting?"

"This and that."

Guido sat next to Van In. "Tell!"

"Trui Andries used to be a member of a satanic sect. She left three months ago along with Jonathan and Jasper Simons."

"The man who wrote the letter we found in Trui's apartment?"

Van In nodded.

"And the sect wasn't happy?" asked Guido.

"The three of them have been getting threats ever since."

"From the sect leaders?"

"I assume so, but they've been smart enough to keep it anonymous. Jasper Simons couldn't handle all the intimidation and became very depressed. He's on the mend, apparently, but no one knows how he'll react to Trui's death. Jasper and Trui were planning to get married soon. Jonathan told me at the station that Trui *had* been his girlfriend, but he later admitted the truth about Jasper and Trui's relationship."

"And Jonathan?"

"Jonathan's a devout Catholic these days, Jasper the same. Jonathan turned his back on the Satan stuff and wants to be a monk. Trui supported him. . . . She was his rock."

Guido rubbed his mustache. The world was getting weirder by the day. There were extremists all over the place. What had happened to the happy medium, the golden mean? "I didn't know monks-to-be were allowed marijuana." He smirked. "But who am I to judge? If the police can do it, why not the monks too?"

Van In sensed a dig. "I was trying to win his confidence, Guido."

"So you believe his crazy story."

Van In leaned back on the sofa and put his hands behind his neck. Guido may have been a little old-fashioned, but his capacity to relativize was up there with the best. Maybe he was right. Maybe Jonathan's story was crazy. But why would Jonathan lie? He had no reason, and his sadness at Trui's death was clearly genuine.

"Stories like that have been doing the rounds quite a bit of late. It's the turn of the century. Sects are popping up all over the place. The end of the world is nigh, Guido, and everyone is trying to deal with the thought of it in one way or another. Some choose sin; others strive to be holy."

"It's because they read so much crap in the papers. If one of them publishes an article on UFOs, everyone and his mother has seen one the next day."

Van In sighed. "True or not, we now know for certain that Trui Andries was murdered, and that the murderer mixes in satanic circles."

"What are we waiting for? We have Jonathan, don't we?"

"That's the problem. It took us all night to get precious little information out of him. The boy is a closed book. Every time we mentioned a name, he broke into a sweat and started to panic."

"Then let the shrinks take care of it," said Guido, unable to muster much enthusiasm.

"He doesn't want a shrink."

"So what do we do?"

"Hannelore's been confined to the house by the doctor."

After the lousy experience at the hospital, Hannelore had consulted her obstetrician and he had advised her to take time off and get some rest. She had accepted his judgment with stoic good spirits, something Van In found strange and out of character. She usually didn't give in so easily.

"She's going to try to win him over, gain his confidence. Perhaps she's the one to break down the wall he's built around himself. She managed to get a shitload more out of him than I did, I can tell you that."

Van In scrambled to his feet and rubbed his face with both hands. Sleepless nights had left him with feet like clay and legs like lead. "I'm thinking we should contact the police physician and have a word or two with Jasper Simons."

"And what about the black widow?" asked Guido.

"Ignore her, Guido."

"And if that doesn't work?"

"Then we move in with the federal boys. If we have to live with someone, then give me the feds over a dangerous spider any day."

"That means you'll have to grow a mustache, Pieter. You know what the feds do with mustacheless men?"

"I do," said Van In. "They get to lick the colonel's ass."

Forensic medicine had evolved by leaps and bounds in recent decades, and DNA technology had been responsible for most of the advances. These days, a couple of cells were enough to identify a criminal, and they didn't always have to be skin cells. Blood, sperm, saliva, sweat, and tears also contained genetic material. Investigative techniques had made similarly spectacular advances. Ear and tooth prints, for example, were just as reliable as traditional fingerprints. Invisible footprints could now be made visible using new advanced photography, blurred video material could be digitally enhanced, and toxicologists were capable of detecting just about every poison on the planet. Van In tried to keep track of it all as far and as often as he could, which was why he was so surprised that the police physician was unable to answer his question.

"So if I'm understanding you right, you haven't been able to determine the cause of death?"

"Not for the present, Commissioner. I was hoping the toxicologist's report would fill in the gaps."

"You think she was poisoned?"

The police physician had more than ten years' experience, and this was the first time in his career that he'd been stumped. "All I know is what didn't kill her."

The case clearly bothered him. He went on: There were no signs of external injury on Trui Andries's body. She had no congenital defects, yet her heart had packed it in. The blood work had been equally inconclusive. The victim hadn't been taking medication or drugs of any kind, and there were no signs of suffocation. Death by poisoning seemed the only remaining hypothesis, but the analysis had yielded nothing. All the tests were negative.

"That's why I asked Raf Geens to do some sniffing around for me," he said.

"Is that the guy who works for criminal investigations?" Van In asked.

According to some rumors, Geens was a drunk who enjoyed the protection of a few people with influence; others—a small minority, it has to be said—swore by all that was holy that the eccentric analyst was a genius.

The police physician nodded. In spite of his professional pride, he belonged to the latter group.

"So you think he'll come up with something?"

The police physician smiled. "Passion is a machine, and no one knows what it's capable of. If you ask me, Geens worked through the night on the case. Shall I give him a call? He might have something for us."

"No need, Doctor. You've made me curious. It's time we paid a visit to Mr. Geens." Van In got to his feet and shook the police physician's hand.

The police physician accompanied them to the door. "One thing, Commissioner. Raf Geens is the sensitive type. He lives for his work. If I were you, I wouldn't make any jokes about it."

"I wasn't planning to," said Van In, a little surprised. He let Guido lead the way and pulled the door closed behind him.

The laboratory of the judicial police was located next door to the new courthouse, a modern building in which the chances of losing your way were close to 100 percent. The architect who'd designed the complex was clearly a Kafka fan and had deployed the labyrinth principle wherever he could. When he was interviewed by a journalist after the opening, he'd declared that giving concrete form to a concept like the administration of justice required a healthy dose of sarcasm. He had succeeded with honors. Lawyers could be found wandering lost in the courthouse corridors, only to plead without the least embarrassment that their cases had expired while they were searching for the courtroom.

Van In and Guido were fortunate to find a helpful attendant who pointed the way to the kingdom of Raf Geens. A sign on the door to his laboratory read: I WISH TO BE DISTURBED ONLY BY INTELLIGENT PEOPLE.

"That means you," said Guido.

Van In shrugged his shoulders and opened the door. What should have been a tidy, sterile space looked more like a dorm room than a laboratory. The walls were plastered with posters of the Rolling Stones, and a radio crackled from somewhere in the depths of the place. The center of the room had the usual laboratory island with cupboards and a work surface covered with Petri dishes, long-necked flasks, test tubes, Bunsen burners, a microscope, a centrifuge, and dozens of bottles containing a rainbow of colorful powders. The modern technical stuff was lined up on a table against the wall: a powerful computer, a spectrometer, an oscilloscope, and a string of devices Van In had never seen before.

"He's probably drinking coffee somewhere," said Guido.

"I don't think so," said Van In, nodding in the direction of a coffee machine on top of a filing cabinet. Its light was still on, and it was half full. Van In made his way to the other end of the laboratory. Suddenly he heard a sound that didn't emanate from the radio. He gestured to Guido to come closer. Next to the window, and hidden from sight by the work island, a man slept on a rickety camp bed, gently snoring. Van In cautiously shook his shoulder. "Good morning, Mr. Geens. I hope we're not disturbing you."

The sleeper opened his eyes, his lack of surprise suggesting that it wasn't the first time someone had had to wake him like this.

"I'm Commissioner Van In, and this is Sergeant Versavel. The police physician sent us. We're investigating the Andries case."

Geens's face brightened at the word *Andries*. He clambered to his feet, buttoned his white coat, and shook Van In's hand. The man had a gray Vandyke and round glasses that made him look professorial, if a little shabby.

"A magnificent case, Commissioner, and a once-in-a-lifetime experience, if you ask me. I almost missed it, to be honest. The police physician had no idea what to make of it, and pathology was at a complete loss."

Geens clearly didn't suffer from morning moodiness. Van In could hardly believe that the man had been asleep only thirty seconds earlier. "I'm intrigued, Mr. Geens."

The spritely lab technician folded the camp bed and stored it in a large metal locker. "All in due course, Commissioner. Please, take a seat. Can I offer you something to drink? A wee nip of the hard stuff perhaps?"

Geens rummaged between the distillation flasks and bottles of chemical solvent, one of which was labeled "hydrochloric acid." "Homemade," Geens said, giggling. "Seventy proof. You could fly an Airbus on it."

He grabbed a couple of beakers and filled them with a generous serving of his superfuel. Guido made a face and politely declined when Geens offered him a beaker. But the lab technician wasn't taking no for an answer. His amiable smile vanished in an instant. "Come on, Sergeant. Every cop takes a drink now and then. And did you know that this little concoction of mine can kill more bacteria than a whole bucket of antibiotics?"

Guido grunted. "I'm not sick."

It was an awkward moment. Van In didn't want the man to put his guard up, so he quickly stuck out his hand and accepted the offer, doing his best to keep a straight face. *No jokes*, the police physician had said.

"There are scandalmongers who claim that alcohol shouldn't be consumed during the hours of daylight. Are you one of them, Commissioner?"

"I always thought scandalmongering was a sin," said Van In.

Geens roared with laughter, producing enough decibels to make the glasswork in the laboratory jingle in unison. Guido had met plenty of weirdos in his long career, but Geens was lining up for a place of honor in his personal top ten. He peered knowingly in Van In's direction, but his boss didn't seem to be bothered.

"Before we get down to business, let me first propose a toast to the man or woman who committed an almost perfect murder," Geens proclaimed.

Geens raised his beaker. Van In followed his host's example and sipped at the concoction. The burning sensation that followed left him wondering if the bottle hadn't contained hydrochloric acid after all. Geens, by contrast, tossed it back as if it were lemonade and refilled his beaker without taking a breath. "It was immediately evident from the absence of water in the victim's lungs that she hadn't died from drowning. There were, likewise, no traces of violence on the body. Miss Andries hadn't suffered a heart attack or a drug overdose. In short, I was clueless. Some kind of poison seemed to be the only alternative, but when I subjected the blood samples to every test in the book and the results proved negative, I was close to desperation. And then, out of the blue, the words *tetramethylammonium pyrosulphate* flashed before my eyes. And why hadn't I thought about tetramethylammonium pyrosulphate before?"

Geens introduced a short dramatic pause, a triumphant smile forming on his lips. Showing off his knowledge was obviously something he enjoyed.

"Because tetramethylammonium pyrosulphate is highly toxic, but if it's properly and precisely administered, it's impossible to trace. So you'll understand my surprise when I found evidence of the substance in the victim's blood."

"On what basis is the dose determined?" asked Van In.

"A calculation based on body weight. I've heard it has to be on the button."

"So are you suggesting we should look for the killer in medical circles?"

"Great minds think alike, Commissioner. But if it was a doctor, why didn't he administer the correct, untraceable dose?"

Van In was forced to agree. "Was the poison injected?"

Geens shook his head. "I'm pretty certain it was ingested orally. The pathologist's report is pretty clear. There were no needle signs on Trui Andries's body."

Geens took a deep breath, stuck out his chest, and stretched his scrawny neck like the proudest peacock. "So what do you have to say, Commissioner?"

Van In was speechless for a moment. What indeed did he have to say? He turned to Guido, who did nothing but blink.

"That you deserve a promotion and a medal," he blurted. Shit! He wasn't supposed to joke with Geens.

Geens nodded. His Adam's apple bounced up and down as if he was having trouble concealing his emotions. "If only, Commissioner."

He swigged at his homemade concoction and rinsed his mouth with it, as snobs are inclined to do when they're tasting wine. "My future isn't exactly rosy, Commissioner. They're planning to close the lab in six months. The bigwigs in Brussels think it's too old-fashioned. They offered me early retirement in April. After thirty years of faithful service."

Van In raised the beaker to his lips and emptied it in a single gulp. A question of courtesy. "I'm sorry to hear that, Mr. Geens."

The analyst sighed deeply. "One more for the road, Commissioner?" he said, reaching for the bottle.

"No, thank you," said Van In.

Guido could hardly believe his ears. Either Van In was getting old or Geens's concoction wasn't intended for human consumption after all.

"That's the first time I've seen you refuse a drink," said Guido as they climbed into the Golf a few minutes later. "Are you sick or what?"

"I've hardly slept a wink for two nights in a row, Guido. Another sip and you'd have had to carry me outside."

Guido started the car and headed toward the beltway. "What now?"

Van In didn't respond immediately. He tried to order the bizarre events of the previous thirty-six hours in his head. The murder of Trui Andries was a pile of question marks. If someone had administered a poison thinking it wouldn't be detectable, why did he or she then take the risk of dumping her in a ditch? Van In realized he had thought "he or she," probably because of the murder weapon. Poison was mostly associated with women. A female satanist? Should they be looking for the killer in satanist circles? Did such circles exist? And what motive did they have to murder Trui? Because she had left them? But Jasper Simons and Jonathan had done the same, hadn't they? Were their lives also in danger? Jonathan had refused to divulge the names of the sect members. He didn't want to make false accusations, he said. Strange that someone preparing to enter a monastery was so afraid of the disciples of Satan. Or was Guido right and Van In had let the boy pull the wool over his eyes?

"Do you know how to get to Keizer Karel Street?"

Guido nodded. "Is that where Jasper Simons lives?"

"Yes," said Van In. "I'm wondering what he has to tell us."

As they turned onto Vlaeminck Street, Guido heard the city's carillon jingle and glanced automatically at his watch. It was eleven forty-five. "I could use a bite to eat," he said. "What about you?"

Guido was a creature of habit. He was used to a hot meal at lunchtime, and if he missed it, he could be seriously grouchy later in the day. Van In had to admit that he also fancied a bite, something hearty. "Then we should head for the outskirts. The tourist specials at the city center are inedible."

"Frank and I had a bit of a late-night browse in the satanic literature we found at Trui's place," said Guido, detaching a chunk of rabbit with his fork, dipping it in the dark prune sauce, and popping it in his mouth with evident delight.

Van In had already emptied his plate and was enjoying a traditional after-dinner cigarette. "Late night in bed, Guido?"

"In bed, Pieter. We didn't take pictures!"

"Thank God for that," said Van In. "Enough of the teasing. . . . Speak! I'm all ears."

"It was Frank's idea. He had apparently been interested in

the subject when he was younger. News to me. Anyway, he figures there are as many forms of satanism as there are traditional religions."

"Logical, I suppose," said Van In, lifting his hand and ordering a Duvel and a Perrier. Guido was clearly on a roll and that could take some time.

"Every god has an alter ego, they say, a shadow side that embodies everything he is not. It's all necessary because we mortals have to make a choice between light and darkness."

"Without darkness we wouldn't recognize the light," said Van In. Their philosophical moments weren't usually this serious, but there were occasional exceptions.

"Exactly. Before the Fall, humankind had no choice, at least until the serpent persuaded Eve to eat from the tree of good and evil."

Van In thought for a moment about Hannelore and the labor pains she would soon be dealing with. Suddenly the slender frame of Saartje Maes interrupted the picture. He wondered how Hannelore might change with the baby.

"As a consequence, humankind has had to struggle to recover the innocence it had before the Fall. That's basically what all the major religions would have us believe, in addition to the fact that Satan is less powerful than God and doomed to face ultimate and final defeat. The devil is a bogeyman who keeps believers from straying from the right path," Guido concluded, sipping at his Perrier. "On the other hand, plenty of people claim that God is a jealous God who only made human beings because his previous creations, the angels, got a little out of control."

Van In struggled to suppress a smile. Guido spoke with such enthusiasm that half the restaurant was now listening in.

"Determined not to make the same mistake twice, God decided to put his new creatures on probation, exposing them to the temptations of the fallen angel. If they passed the 'exam,' he would reward them with eternal life in heaven. Those who opted for the dark side were welcome to join their tempter in hell for eternity. God was sure that this procedure would make his creatures more respectful toward him than the proud angels who had betrayed his confidence. At least that's how some satanists look at it. They see Lucifer as their true master, are convinced God has treated humankind unjustly, and want to know what in heaven's name Lucifer did wrong."

"Maybe he should have snuggled up next to Adam," Van In said, grinning. "Then you and Frank would be respectable citizens."

Guido pretended not to have heard his boss's remark. "According to his supporters, Lucifer was only trying to make a career for himself. He thought it was time for his creator to hand over the scepter to someone else for a change, especially after the cock-up with the angels."

Van In ordered a second Duvel. It was only appropriate, he figured.

"So what are you trying to say, Guido?"

"How can I say what I'm trying to say if you keep interrupting me?"

"Okay, okay, I get the message."

Guido continued. "Real satanists claim that Lucifer was the one who lifted humankind out of ignorance and gave them the chance to evolve and develop. After all, *Lucifer* means 'bearer of light.' He gave humankind divine knowledge, just as Prometheus brought fire from heaven to earth."

"And faced the punishment of the gods for his efforts," said Van In. As a child, he had been plagued by nightmares of Prometheus in chains. According to the myth, an eagle flew down every day to pluck out his liver. But the liver grew back, and the eagle returned time and again to torment him for all eternity.

Guido nodded. "At least you know something about classical mythology," he said with a degree of satisfaction.

"And you think these are the people we're up against?"

"Unlikely," said Guido. "Like any other religion, melancholic satanism has problems with superstition. Think about the popular traditions within the Catholic Church: the medals, the votive offerings, the candles, praying to saints, relics with the power to heal . . . The list is endless. Satanism developed along similar lines. Real disciples of Lucifer don't wear pentagrams, don't spit on crucifixes, and don't indulge in blood-drenched rituals."

"You're almost making it sound attractive," said Van In.

"Plenty of people would agree with you. Look around. Everyone wants knowledge and possessions. Would you accuse someone of being a satanist just because they're ambitious?"

"So we're all satanists when push comes to shove?"

"That's what Frank thinks. According to him the gods—the devil included—only survive by the grace of the people who believe in them. In a world of egoism and indifference, it makes sense that Lucifer's scoring better than the God of love-thy-neighbor."

"I'll try to remember that," said Van In.

The waiter took advantage of the pause in the conversation to clear the table. "Can I interest you gentlemen in dessert?"

"I'll stick with the Duvel," said Van In.

"And for you, sir?"

Guido opened the menu and ran his eye down the list of desserts. The waiter seemed irritated by the delay: "May I recommend the passion fruit and chartreuse sorbet?"

Guido ignored the suggestion and ordered vanilla ice cream with hot chocolate sauce, a traditional favorite. "Is it only me, or are waiters losing their manners these days?" he said when the smirking waiter had turned on his heels.

“Don’t exaggerate, Guido. What if he’d suggested a cheese platter? You know you’re a sucker for cheese!”

Van In smiled. As far as he was concerned, good and evil were an essential part of the human psyche. Every individual was free to choose the path he or she preferred to follow.

Jonathan made his way down Ezel Street, his thoughts elsewhere. He was carrying a shopping bag with fruit, vegetables, and meat—he had offered to do the grocery shopping for the cop’s pregnant wife, but he had another motive for escaping her oversight. Venex lived nearby, and the need to score was getting more urgent by the minute.

The cop’s wife was okay, but how would she treat him if he told her the truth? He hadn’t used for three months in a row. That’s what he had promised Trui, but now that she was gone, there was no more promise to keep. Life was meaningless without her. Only death could reunite them.

He turned and headed toward Slede Street in the fervent hope that Master Venex would release him from his suffering.

4

Christ the King was once a respectable residential corner of the city where Bruges's nouveau riche had clearly enjoyed architectural carte blanche. Many of the buildings were nothing short of tasteless, and the streets were named after the big shots of the day. Its former inhabitants were exceptionally proud of their neighborhood and back then the upper-middle class preferred Cardinal Mercier Street to Green Street.

But Christ the King had lost much of its luster over the years. As the city expanded, the elite of old moved out to the leafier suburbs, and the neighborhood's former inhabitants made way for average two-income families who earned just enough to save their now dilapidated town houses from the wrecking balls.

"*Sic transit gloria mundi*," said Guido as he turned onto Keizer Karel Street.

He parked the Golf at number 79. The Simons family home was a product of the fifties, a brick box for which some brainless architect had probably been granted an award. The people who lived here were clearly true-blue natives who hadn't been able to afford a move to the new housing developments on the outskirts of the city.

"I wonder if he's home."

"We're about to find out," said Van In, sounding detached. In reality, he was having a hard time keeping his eyes open. Sleepless nights, Duvels, and a solid meal were a deadly combination. He grabbed his jacket from the backseat and threw open the passenger door. A cold current of air made him shiver. The dry east wind was in sharp contrast to the previous day's torrential rains. *That's Belgium for you*, he thought, *the only country in the world where the weather is crazier than the people who forecast it.*

Van In announced their presence the way the FBI boys did, leaving his finger on the doorbell until he heard footsteps in the corridor. Much to his satisfaction, it only took ten seconds before the door opened, security chain slipped into place. Van In nodded at the narrow strip of face and slippers peering at him through the crack in the door.

"Good afternoon, ma'am. Commissioner Van In. I'd like to have a word with Jasper."

The woman's reaction was short and to the point. "Jasper isn't here," she said and promptly slammed the door in his face.

When Guido saw Van In staring at the door in a daze, he couldn't resist a gibe: "Maybe she thinks you're a Jehovah's Witness trying out a new routine to get inside."

"Give me a break, Guido. You don't think I'm planning to walk away, do you?"

Van In took a couple of steps backward and inspected the monotonous facade as if he were hoping to find a secret entrance. Guido stayed in the background. The rabbit "Flemish style" they had devoured for lunch was taking its revenge: heartburn for the last half hour. He remembered Van In saying that it had to have been some kind of monkey for the price they paid and not rabbit. It didn't help.

"What next? Climb the front of the house or shoot open the lock?" Guido asked, not inclined to hang around.

"Any suggestions?"

"If *I* ring the bell, she'll probably let us in. At least I'm wearing a uniform and I took the trouble to shave this morning. If I were a middle-aged woman, I'd also think twice before . . ."

Neither man noticed as they quibbled that a tall gentleman was watching them from behind the window.

"Cut the comedy, Guido."

Van In reached for the bell, but as he was about to ring it, the door suddenly opened, the chain still on.

"Sorry," said the woman with a skimpy smile. "We've had a stranger doing the rounds here in the last couple of weeks pretending he's a policeman. My husband insists I ask for some identification."

While Van In was familiar with the reports of a police impersonator, he still didn't like being asked for an ID. The woman examined his card as if it were a winning lottery ticket. It was only when she caught sight of Guido out of the corner of her eye that she softened, loosened the chain, and opened the door.

"You can never be careful enough, gentlemen, don't you think? Please, come inside."

Van In figured Mrs. Simons—he presumed—had to be in her midfifties. She was wearing a dark brown skirt and a black blouse with a red floral pattern. *A bird of paradise in mourning*, he thought. Her gray hair had a blue sheen to it, evidence of the blue rinses that kept countless hairdressers in business the world over.

When Van In started down the corridor, Mrs. Simons loudly cleared her throat and glared back and forth between Van In's shoes and the doormat he had just stepped over. The mat was wrapped in a moist floor cloth, making it clear to every visitor that the thing had a purpose.

"Excuse me, ma'am."

Van In took a step backward and wiped his feet with enthusiasm. Mrs. Simons nodded approvingly.

"Come inside," she said for a second time.

An oak shelf ran the length of the corridor with a black telephone at one end, the old Bakelite sort with a dial instead of a keypad. People who had their telephone installed in the corridor tended to make calls standing up, keeping them short and to the point. The Simonses didn't like to waste money, Van In figured. Details like that always intrigued him.

Mrs. Simons walked ahead of them and let them into a small fusty room at the end of the corridor that functioned as an office.

"Please wait here, gentlemen. My husband will be with you in a minute."

"I was actually hoping to speak to Jasper," said Van In, repeating his initial request.

Mrs. Simons smiled cheerlessly. She seemed to be hiding behind an invisible aura of sadness, a cocoon that engulfed her completely. "My husband will explain everything," she said as she gently closed the door behind her.

Van In started to pace up and down. There was something ominous about the place, an indefinable feeling that this space wanted to say something about the people who occupied it. "At least we know who wears the trousers in this household," he said. "There aren't many families left these days where the man is still the boss."

"True." Guido smirked. "And you should know." In spite of the intermittent stomach cramps, the sergeant did his best to lighten up the situation. It was his way of escaping the pressing gloominess of the room.

Van In made his way to the window. A high wall and a line of unhappy pine trees managed to prevent whatever light the sky had to offer from filtering through to ground level. "Hardly a problem *chez* Guido, I imagine. Unless Frank dons a dress every now and then."

Guido stroked his mustache with his thumb and his forefinger. "What I *meant* to say was that bossy men tend to be boring, and you're anything but. Look around, Commissioner. Compared with this, your office is a rubbish dump. You should be honored."

Van In was forced to agree with his friend. He'd struck gold with Hannelore, who never complained when he left stuff lying around the house. He was lucky she wasn't the obsessive cleaning type. Mrs. Simons clearly belonged to the latter category. Dust and disorder were her enemy. The floor was as shiny as a puddle of water, the rolltop desk looked brand-new although it was easily antique, and the wastepaper basket was spotless and empty. The only signs of life in the place were the sansevierias on the window ledge. The room was otherwise bare and far from cozy, making the eye-catching crucifix above the fireplace stand out like a wine stain on a white tablecloth. Van In couldn't help staring up at it. An uneasy feeling started to nibble at the back of his mind, a hint that something wasn't right with it, but he didn't get much of a chance to think it over. The door flew open and a man joined them in the room. He looked like a retired tax inspector, dressed in a gray three-piece suit and wearing a tie Van In wouldn't have gifted to his worst enemy. A pair of horn-rimmed glasses framed his watery eyes.

"Good afternoon, gentlemen."

The man shook hands with Van In and Guido. He had Mickey Mouse hands—at least that was what Guido thought when Simons's hand completely swallowed up his own.

"I'm Jasper's father. What can I do for you?" The elderly man had a clear baritone voice that gave him a degree of authority.

"We were actually hoping to speak to Jasper himself," said Van In for the third time.

Guido kept a close eye on Mr. Simons. He had the impression that the man's face hardened when Van In mentioned his son's name.

"My son is sick, Commissioner. We had him admitted to the hospital yesterday, to the psychiatric ward."

"Is it serious?"

Mr. Simons nodded. He ran bony fingers through his thinning hair. A common response when people were confronted with a painful question. "Do you have children, Commissioner?"

Only parents with problem children knew how much sadness could lurk behind such a question. "My wife is expecting our first," said Van In.

Mr. Simons smiled, but even his smile betrayed more pain than words could express. "Then I hope you have better luck than we did, Commissioner. A couple of years ago, the doctors diagnosed a serious psychosis. Jasper suffers from delusions and thinks that God has chosen him to kill the incarnation of Satan."

"I'm afraid that needs a little more explanation, Mr. Simons."

The man sat down, took off his glasses, and fidgeted an imaginary speck of dust from his eye. "Jasper thinks my wife is the devil in human form. He tried to kill her yesterday." Simons sighed as the wrinkles in his face deepened into dark folds. It was hard for any parent to admit they'd failed. Simons buried his face in his hands and Van In gave him the time to get hold of his emotions.

"Did you know that your son was once a member of a satanic sect?" Van In asked, emphasizing "was once."

"He was interested in that sort of thing," said Simons wearily.

He looked up from his hands and stared at Van In. "But I know nothing about a sect. He never said anything about a sect."

"Are you sure?"

"Of course, Commissioner. I'm certain."

"Did Jasper have friends?"

"When he was admitted for the first time a couple of years ago, they all abandoned him."

"And yet he mixed with satanists," said Van In, a hint of disbelief in his voice.

"I told you he never spoke about a sect or satanists or anything of the sort."

"Does the name Jonathan Leman ring a bell?"

"No."

Van In nodded as a painful silence descended on the room. He was drawn once again to the crucifix and suddenly realized what wasn't right about it. The bottom of the vertical beam had a metal eyelet inserted in it that didn't seem to belong.

"Leman claims he's friends with Jasper. He even told us that your son had turned his back on satanism."

The elderly man was as still as a waxworks dummy. The only thing that moved were his eyelids. . . . A split-second flash, but Van In noticed it all the same. "So you did know about it?"

"We thought it was a shame," said Simons.

Van In raised his eyebrows. Had he missed something . . . lost the plot?

"It might sound strange to you, Commissioner, but while Jasper was involved with the satanists his behavior was relatively normal. The aggression only started after he met that bitch. She goaded him, turned him against his mother. He's never been the same since."

No need to guess who "that bitch" is, thought Van In. "Are we talking about Trui Andries?" he asked.

"The very one," said Simons.

Van In realized that the next step was a crucial one, so he kept a careful eye on the elderly Simons. The man was probably unaware that Trui Andries was dead. If he confronted him with this information, he would have to express surprise in one form or another, and every detective worth his salt knew surprise was a genuine reaction that was impossible to fake.

"Trui Andries was murdered yesterday, Mr. Simons."

Guido had been expecting this moment and was also keeping a close eye on Simons. A shiver ran through the man's entire body as his jaw fell open; then an almost beatific smile transformed his face.

"Are you telling me the truth, Commissioner?"

Van In looked at Guido, who shrugged in response. This was a career first. He had never seen someone react to the death of another human being in such a manner. He wondered what the man on the cross would think of it all.

"Trui Andries could have been your daughter-in-law, Mr. Simons. Your son was in love with her," said Van In.

"My son was under that creature's spell," Simons retorted. "She drove him crazy. Don't you see? It's that bitch's fault that my son is in a psychiatric ward. Of course I'm glad she's dead. Now at least I know she can no longer harm anyone."

"You said that Jasper was only admitted yesterday," said Van In. His casual words and tone were ill-chosen.

Simons got to his feet and shook his head back and forth, his eyes ablaze. "When Jasper was released from hospital last month for the umpteenth time, he seemed to be better, on the mend. The doctors gave us hope, but that witch couldn't bear the idea. She filled his head with crazy talk and almost drove him to kill his mother."

Simons's pallid face turned red with rage. He suddenly grabbed his chest and seemed to lose his balance. Guido rushed forward just in time to catch him and help him into his chair. Van In charged into the corridor. Mrs. Simons had heard the commotion and came running from the kitchen.

"Your husband's having a heart attack," Van In roared.

Mrs. Simons didn't panic. She hurried back to the kitchen and reappeared with a box of tiny pills, one of which she slipped under Mr. Simons's tongue. Van In was impressed by her calm professionalism.

"He'll be right as rain in five minutes," she said.

Van In could feel his own heart pounding in his chest. The emergency had left him a little short of breath.

"My husband needs to avoid excitement of any kind," said Mrs. Simons. The accusation in her voice was loud and clear. "Please leave us alone."

"Shouldn't we call an ambulance?" asked Van In. If anything happened to Simons, he would have to take the blame.

But Mrs. Simons was proving to be more than a match for her visitors. "I know exactly what I have to do, Commissioner. And you have no reason to be afraid. My husband isn't planning on lodging a complaint."

At that moment, Mr. Simons opened his eyes. "Please . . . leave us be," he rasped.

Guido grabbed Van In's arm and coaxed him outside.

"Odd couple," said Van In as they got into the Golf.

"Do you suspect them?" asked Guido, clicking his seat belt.

Van In popped the key into the ignition. "It wouldn't do any harm to check their story," he said. "But let's first have a word with Simons junior."

He started the Golf and drove through the gloomy streets of Christ the King. The couple's strange behavior haunted his thoughts. He was reminded of a story by Edgar Allan Poe. What was it called? He remembered as the lights turned red at the end of Ezel Street: "The System of Doctor Tarr and Professor Fether," a story about psychiatric patients who had locked up the staff of the hospital and were running it themselves unnoticed.

"Are you sure we're talking about a network here?"

Adjutant Delrue twisted a paper clip into a pair of donkey's ears. "All the information we've assembled thus far points to the existence of a complex organization, Major."

A long silence followed. On the other end of the line, Major Baudrin tapped the hefty pile of documents lying in front of him on his desk with his ballpoint. Operation Snow White should have reached a critical phase long ago. If he was to believe Delrue, they were dealing with large shipments of heroin, the origins of which were unclear. According to Delrue, the stuff wasn't intended for the Netherlands but for local dealers.

"So you think we can close this network down without wasting too much time?"

Delrue reshaped the donkey's ears into a boat. They had searched a number of suspect ships in Zeebrugge the year before and confiscated ten kilos. Not bad when you think of it. They later managed to pick up a courier who provided them with the name of his supplier: Venex. Venex apparently maintained a healthy relationship with the federal police—what other explanation was there for how such an extensive network had avoided capture for so long? But the identification of Venex was getting close. It was only a question of time.

"We're close to arresting the man behind the scenes, Major. Give me another month and I can promise results."

The courier had later died—under suspicious circumstances—but shortly thereafter, an anonymous informant had come forward who provided Delrue with drug transport details on a regular basis. They had managed to make a couple of arrests in the preceding five months, occasional couriers who hadn't helped much with the investigation. Their ignorance was genuine. All they did was take the train to various prearranged destinations and make a delivery for a couple of thousand francs. The packages were then collected by local drug dealers. Delrue had grilled the latter for hours on end, but they all made the same statement. They claimed they got a telephone call from an unknown merchant who offered them an irresistible deal: pure heroin for four hundred francs per gram.

"A month! Are you kidding me? Do you think I'm Santa? How long have you been working on the case? Six months?"

"Five, Major."

"And with six men."

"Yes, Major."

Adjutant Delrue placed the boat-shaped paper clip on his desk. The corps had been thoroughly reorganized—according to the new philosophy that they had to tackle crime at its very roots—but the highest-ranking officers still behaved like dinosaurs. They belonged to a protected species, and it was forbidden to shoot them without good reason. They faced extinction, but they had all the time in the world. The politicians were to blame. They wanted to modernize the judicial system, but they were afraid the old crocodiles would go public with incriminatory dossiers if they sensed they were being thrown out with the garbage. A federal police officer wasn't just any old laborer you could send packing with a pittance for a pension.

"You've got two more weeks, Delrue. If you can't provide solid, and I mean solid, evidence by then, I'm closing Snow White down."

Delrue wished Baudrin a pleasant afternoon, returned the receiver to its cradle, and reshaped his little paper clip boat into a large V. Venex was the only name he had, and his informant had assured him he would soon be able to reveal the man's true identity.

Jasper Simons lay on his back on a metal-frame bed staring at the ceiling, which was painted a pale green-yellow like the walls. His throat was dry as a result of the double dose of Haldol and Risperdal the doctor had administered the day before. The medication confined him to his bed and made sure he didn't bother the nursing staff, at least during their coffee break. The hospital's psychiatric ward wasn't the place for difficult patients. Those who didn't play by the rules were skillfully immobilized. But no matter what the staff tried, there wasn't a medication on the planet that could tame the human mind.

Jasper concentrated on the ceiling and tried to recall the visions that had been revealed to him the night before. The ceiling functioned as a sort of giant movie screen, and Jasper couldn't wait to replay his dream.

Hieronymus Bosch warned the audience that the images they were about to witness were not suitable for sensitive viewers. The skeletal medieval painter popped a cassette into an old-fashioned VCR. The cumbersome contraption stood on a black box, the four corners of which were buttressed by slender caryatids, young scaled female figures with twisted nails and pointed breasts. After the credits, in which Jasper's name featured in scarlet red letters, the camera zoomed in on the fire, boring its way through the flames. The image shimmered like hot air above a desert landscape, but only for a couple of seconds. The images that followed were so real Jasper could feel the heat scorching his skin. In the middle of the flames, he recognized the partly fleshless body of his mother. The old woman squirmed and flailed like a lobster about to be dropped into boiling water.

Jasper got to his feet and entered the inferno. He paid no attention to the turning spits on which unfamiliar men and women were being roasted over white-hot coals and instead made his way to the place where his mother was being devoured by the fire. She screamed for compassion, but Jasper simply stared at her without emotion. He thought she was getting what she deserved. A little farther into the flames he caught sight of Konrad, his best friend in elementary school, bound hand and foot to a slowly turning cogwheel. His open belly was overflowing with squirming worms and maggots that swarmed across his entire body, into his nose, behind his eyeballs, and even into his little piss hole. Jasper felt sorry for him. Konrad had a good reputation. He was an altar boy and had wanted to be a priest when he grew up.

In the kingdom of the impaled, Jasper encountered Martine, his first girlfriend; their lips had once brushed, albeit momentarily. He avoided her gaze and ran like a man possessed through pandemonium. A series of horrifying scenes presented themselves in quick succession. Jasper saw blind people with hollow eye sockets, cripples with shattered limbs, pregnant women devouring the fruit of their womb, nuns piercing their flabby arms and thighs with long glowing needles, respected citizens with sagging skin, crazy Sister Marie-Louise kneeling in ecstasy in front of ochre-yellow dog shit, and the prime minister sizzling in a cast-iron wok like a lump of cheap meat.

Jasper closed his eyes and stumbled farther. He left the sea of flames behind and suddenly found himself in a gently undulating landscape. The silhouette of a fortress was visible on the horizon, a fairy-tale castle with lofty pinnacles and gilded castellations. Twittering birds traversed a sky of blue, and an ancient unicorn stood grazing in a dark green meadow.

Jasper sought repose in the shadow of a verdant briar and luxuriated in the cool evening air. But not for long. His rest was interrupted by a muted rumble that made the earth shake. A black knight on an armored steed stormed toward him. Jasper scrambled quickly to his feet and ran in panic toward the fortress. The ominous clatter of hooves got closer and closer, but the black knight didn't catch up or overtake him. By the time Jasper reached the moat, he was completely out of breath. He dragged himself across the drawbridge and sought refuge in the central tower. A tall man robed in white was waiting for him. A tray with two silver goblets adorned a long wooden table at the man's side.

He offered Jasper one of the goblets and ordered him to drink from it. The pale green liquid tasted like aniseed and sulfur. When he had emptied the goblet, the clatter of hooves returned, this time emanating from one of the tapestries that graced the great hall. Four horses broke free from the tapestry and galloped across the shiny stone floor. On another tapestry, the Lamb trembled in the light of hundreds of lasers. Abraham drew himself up to his full length and planted a sacrificial knife in an overripe melon. A bull and a lion lay side by side on a plush carpet of the greenest grass. An eagle soared across a perfect blue firmament, and an angel hovered on a flying carpet in front of the throne of the Father. A kaleidoscopic wheel slowed his progress and revealed a hitherto unseen display of magnificent color. The flowers in the tapestries blossomed and wilted to the rhythm of a stroboscope. Hunters raced across the drowned land of Saeftinghe with a herd of raging buffalo at their heels. A damsel urinated in the cone of her headdress and was rewarded with applause from a crowd of unshaven louts. Putti nestled in the chandeliers and leered shamelessly at chaste Suzanna. At a wedding party, the guests spilled wine from a vat. Jesus descended from his cross and mopped the spills before climbing into a gold-colored Ferrari and driving triumphantly through the streets of a city with no houses. He was cheered on his way by goblins, Norse berserkers, flagellants, mutilated gladiators, deep-frozen SS officers, card-playing Templars, cardinals in straitjackets, the Medusa in a hall of mirrors, Tarzan with a bag of fries under an olive tree, a group of Ku Klux Klan brothers disguised as cheap cigarette lighters, and an emaciated Oscar Wilde who interrupted his conversation with Isaac Bashevis Singer for the occasion. . . .

"I've been treating Jasper for two years now," said Dr. Coleyn. "And I can't say I'm not optimistic."

Doctor John Coleyn, a heavyset man in his fifties, with wild gray hair and a set of teeth that would make a horse jealous, was a professor at the University of Leuven and head of the university hospital's psychiatric division. The man was the incarnation of hospitality, and he'd invited Van In and Guido to join him in his consultation room on the ground floor of the building. The spacious room was decorated in the English cottage style. Coleyn took his seat behind an impressive polished walnut desk. Van In and Guido sat opposite in two easy chairs with padded backs and arms. The desk was so broad two people could easily stretch their legs across it without their feet touching. The distance was symbolic of the way contemporary psychiatry functioned. In contrast to the old-fashioned confessional in which sinners whispered their frustrations into the listening ear of an invisible clergyman, patients were now expected to reveal their innermost feelings and emotions out loud and face-to-face with a well-paid caregiver. Instead of forgiveness and penance, they were given a box of pills and an invoice.

"Jasper Simons isn't an isolated case," Coleyn said when Van In asked for further explanation. "We've observed an exponential increase in the number of patients suffering from religious delusions of late."

"People these days have fertile imaginations," Van In said with more than a hint of scorn. "As soon as a disorder gets a name, the patients are lining up." He lit a cigarette, assuming permission. Coleyn was currently smoking like a chimney.

"I'm afraid I'm going to have to disappoint you on that, Commissioner," Coleyn said, shaking his head.

Van In tapped the arm of his chair with his fingers. Psychiatrists were parrots in reverse. They repeated what was said to them but in the opposite sense. "Do you think the delusions you mention might have something to do with drugs?"

Coleyn stubbed out his cigarette in a bronze ashtray, a gift from a schizophrenic artist he had treated the year before. The poor guy had cut his wrists a couple of days ago. "No, Commissioner. Jasper is deeply psychotic, but drugs are not the cause."

"Is he mad?"

Coleyn lit another cigarette. As a psychiatrist he had no need to be concerned about his own physical condition. That's what other doctors were for. "We haven't used the word *mad* for a long, long time," he said. "Jasper is sick. Schizophrenic. But recently developed therapies have fortunately given us the capacity to treat such syndromes with success."

"So you give him pills," said Van In.

"Yes, we have a certain number of chemical preparations at our disposal that tend to have a positive influence on certain dysfunctions." Coleyn pressed the tips of his fingers against one another and rested his chin in the arch formed by his thumbs. The pose was intended to give the doctor an air of authority, but Van In wasn't impressed.

"And do they work?" asked Van In.

Guido, who had yet to open his mouth, observed the verbal duel between the psychiatrist and the commissioner in silence, enjoying every second. But one thing struck him as strange:

Coleyn talked about Jasper Simons as if he'd never heard of doctor-patient confidentiality. Guido didn't dare mention it because he knew there was a good chance Coleyn would clam up and Van In wouldn't be happy.

"The human brain is one big chemical factory. Our mental well-being depends for the most part on certain chemical connections that keep the delicate system in balance. Psychoses are disorders that stem from a defectively functioning nervous system whereby certain stimuli that can affect our mood are not transmitted properly. And that's because our brains don't make enough of the substance we need to transport the stimuli." Coleyn stubbed out his cigarette and immediately lit another. "Do you follow me, Commissioner?"

Van In almost said, *Yes, Professor!* But instead he answered the doctor's condescending question with a nod.

Coleyn blew a cloud of smoke toward the ceiling and continued. "We had little choice in the old days, but a new generation of antidepressives has been on the market for the last couple of years based on serotonin and dopamine."

"Is that what you're giving Jasper?"

"I prescribed Risperdal," said Coleyn, sounding as if he'd invented the stuff himself.

"And is it working?"

"Risperdal repairs the neurotransmitters. Eighty percent of people treated with it respond positively."

"Is Jasper part of the eighty percent?"

Coleyn frowned. "In Jasper's case, we've also had to resort to traditional therapies."

"You mean knocking him out with sedatives."

Coleyn leaned back in his calf leather chair. There was little trace of the jovial smile that had welcomed the detectives. "Listen carefully, Commissioner. Jasper Simons has declared war on the Church of Satan. He thinks he's been called to eradicate evil, root and branch. The appropriate medication helps us to suppress his aggression to a certain degree, but—"

Van In interrupted. "Do you think Jasper would be capable of killing his mother?"

Coleyn joined his hands behind his neck and leaned back. A tiny throbbing vein was visible on his forehead, a sign that he was clearly irritated. *Not very professional for a psychiatrist*, thought Van In.

"Jasper Simons is capable of killing anyone who gets in his way," Coleyn said, his face grim and determined.

"In spite of the pills."

"In spite of the pills, Commissioner."

"Ever heard of tetramethylammonium pyrosulphate?"

"Tetramethyl . . ." Coleyn muttered. It was clear from the expression on his face that he hadn't a clue, but would rather die than admit it. Van In put him out of his misery.

"Tetramethylammonium pyrosulphate, Doctor, is a poison. It was used to kill Trui Andries."

"I'm not a toxicologist," Coleyn protested, clearly miffed.

Van In smiled. Intellectuals all seemed to suffer from the same ailment: They took offense at the drop of a hat. "It was just a question," he said.

Coleyn sat upright in his chair and spread his hands on his desk as if he was about to stand. "Is there anything else I can do for you, gentlemen?" The rancor on his face made it clear that he was determined to wrap up their discussion.

"Just one last thing," said Van In. "Trui Andries was killed late Tuesday night or early Wednesday morning, and according to you, Jasper Simons was admitted on Wednesday morning."

"You're not suggesting . . ."

"I'm not suggesting anything, Doctor. I want a word with him, that's all."

Coleyn knit his bushy brows. "I doubt if he'll be able to talk to you," he said.

"A moment, no more," Van In insisted.

Coleyn sighed, got to his feet, and put on his white coat. "A moment then."

Van In and Guido followed Dr. Coleyn to the elevator, which whisked them smoothly to the fifth floor, where a sign on the wall directed them to the psychiatry ward. Coleyn moved with haste, the panels of his coat flapping between his legs like a pair of slack sails.

Hospitals these days were suspiciously like American hotels: Those who had never stayed in one tended to be full of praise while those who had didn't dare admit that they'd expected better.

"Will Jasper have to stay confined for long?" asked Van In.

"That depends," said Coleyn.

With patients having more and more of a say in their treatment, doctors were terrified to tie themselves down to fixed dates, an objectionable habit they had learned from the world of politics. "A month, two?"

"At the very least, Commissioner, at the very least."

When they entered the room, they found Jasper still lying on his back, staring at the ceiling. He had been given a couple of pills intended to compensate for the unpleasant side effects of the Haldol. Now he was waiting patiently for the clatter of plates and cutlery that would soon announce the evening meal. Tucking into a couple of slices of brown bread with pastrami and mustard was the only attraction on the program that evening. After that, it was a longer wait for the new sun to rise.

"Hi, Jasper. I'm Commissioner Van In and this is Sergeant Versavel."

Jasper turned his gaze to the voice that had summoned him from his lethargy.

Dr. Coleyn moved closer. "These two gentlemen are from the police, Jasper. They want to ask you a couple of questions. You don't have to answer if you don't want to."

The medical world was convinced that pills and technical ingenuity were enough to make sick people better, but they often tended to forget that other maladies like loneliness and despair cried out for a different approach, an affectionate approach. Guido wondered if Jasper would have given his right arm for a word of encouragement instead.

"It's about Trui Andries," said Van In. "Do you remember when you saw her last?"

When he didn't answer immediately, Coleyn turned to Van In with an I-told-you-so look on his face, but Guido noticed that Jasper was trying to lift his head from the magnetic embrace of the pillow. He turned on his side, seeming intent on leaning on his elbow, but he fell back to the pillow as though he lacked the strength to support himself.

"His lips are moving," said Guido.

Coleyn leaned over him, his shadow smothering the supplication in Jasper's eyes. "I think it would be better to come back tomorrow."

Van In looked at Guido, who shrugged his shoulders. "You think he'll be in better shape?"

"I'm certain of it," said Coleyn.

"Fine, then we come back tomorrow."

As they left the room, Jasper started to cry, gently. A tear rolled down his nose, pausing just above his upper lip. He licked the teardrop and tasted the bitterness of his failure.

5

It was almost eight in the evening when Van In turned into the Vette Vispoort, shivering, the cobblestones reinforcing the dry echo of his footsteps. They always sounded more hollow when it was cold. As he turned his house key in the lock he heard the clatter of pots and pans in the kitchen, and the smell of smoldering birch and thyme wafted through the letterbox. *Good omens*, he thought. A little warmth and a tasty dinner were exactly what he needed.

Hannelore was in the kitchen. She was wearing an apron with the words *Je cuisine, donc je suis*. Van In had given it to her as a gift the month before. He had cut the strings to measure. When she could no longer tie them, it was high time to prepare for fatherhood. Luckily, today was not the day.

"I managed to pick up a couple of decent knuckles of veal this afternoon." Hannelore leaned forward for a kiss. "We haven't had ossobuco in ages."

Van In licked his lips, grabbed a spoon from the counter, and tried the sauce. Delicious as usual. No one could make ossobuco like Hannelore. "You're a treasure," he said.

She loosened the safety pin holding the strings of her apron without drawing Van In's attention, crossed to the refrigerator, grabbed an already open bottle of Muscadet, and poured a couple of glasses. Van In kicked off his shoes, sat down at the kitchen table, put his legs up on a chair, and enjoyed the moment at which his fatigue (or did the tingling in his calves have something to do with poor circulation?) flowed out through the tips of his toes and was absorbed by Mother Earth. "If there's anything I can do, say the word," he said as Hannelore put the finishing touches on what promised to be a fabulous meal.

She shook her head. Why did men always think that their *willingness* to help was enough? "You can do the washing up." She sighed as she sat down at his side and offered him a glass. "Cheers."

"Cheers," said Van In.

They both sipped at the wine. Van In didn't need much to feel content that evening. A glass of wine and the thought that someone had cooked for him were more than enough.

"Is Jonathan still here?" he asked after a moment.

"He's asleep," said Hannelore. "He took a nap this afternoon and it seemed a sin to wake him."

"Did he have anything new to say?"

It was clear from her smile that she had news.

"He's really a sweet boy when you get to know him. He insisted on doing the washing up and then . . ."

Van In listened uncomplainingly to Hannelore's story. Jonathan hadn't only done the washing up, he had also vacuumed the house and picked up the groceries.

"Did he have anything new to say?" he asked a second time, trying to mask the impatience in his voice. If her reaction was anything to go by, his efforts had been to no avail.

"Don't take your frustrations out on me, Van In," she snapped.

Van In had noticed how grumpy she had been the last couple of days. He understood, but he was so bushed he found it hard not to snap back at her. It was the pregnancy, of course, sapping her energy day after day and adding pound after pound. Was there some kind of giant growing in there? he wondered. What makes it possible for a person to be so completely happy for no apparent reason, and why was it so easy to disturb that perfect balance? This time he decided not to give in to the demon who was pushing him toward the abyss. It made no sense to start an argument.

"Sorry, Hanne. *Mea culpa.*"

She nodded a couple of times in succession, aware that his words didn't come easy. *Why ruin the evening with a stupid argument?* she thought.

"Jonathan still refuses to talk about the sect, but he did say that Trui and Jasper met each other via a dating agency run by a certain Richard Coleyn."

"Coleyn," said Van In, resting his glass on the table. The entire case was beginning to stink; too many coincidences and too many features that just didn't square. Trui Andries had been killed with a rare poison that shouldn't have left any traces. She was on the point of getting married to a psychiatric patient who had been admitted into hospital days earlier and was being treated by a Dr. Coleyn. Coincidence? A relative of Richard Coleyn? And then there was Jonathan, a friend of Trui, who had been afraid to speak up to that point for fear of reprisals from a mysterious satanic sect, but in the last analysis had provided them with a name.

"According to Jonathan, Richard Coleyn is a drug addict and an old friend of Jasper."

"Good news at last." Van In sighed.

Hannelore looked at him in surprise.

"Now at least I have an old-fashioned lead, and that might appreciably simplify the case. Did he have anything else to say?"

"That we should stay out of it."

Van In shrugged his shoulders and topped up his glass. Best let Jonathan simmer for a while and first have a word with Richard Coleyn. *A confrontation later might give us a few more names*, he thought. "Is the ossobuco ready?" The aroma was making his mouth water.

"I think so," said Hannelore, readying herself to take a look. But Van In gestured that she should stay where she was.

"You've done enough work for today," he said. "Now it's *my* turn to spoil *you*."

"As long as you don't forget the washing up," she said, resting her weary legs on Van In's chair. She would ask him later to massage her ankles and would sound him out on Saartje Maes while he was at it.

"I'd rather have had an Uzi," said Venex. "They're easier to handle."

Richard Coleyn stored the Kalashnikov in an old-fashioned chest and placed it on the floor at his feet. It hadn't been easy to get hold of a machine gun, and now Father wanted an Uzi.

"I'm assured the Kalashnikov is more reliable than an Uzi," he said guardedly.

"Let's hope it is."

Venex pointed at an open bottle of Veuve Clicquot that was almost within his reach. Richard reacted immediately and topped up Venex's glass.

"To Sunday," said Venex, raising his glass and drinking. It was his fifth in less than an hour. A sense of euphoria was slowly filling his head. "I would appreciate a shoulder rub, if you wouldn't mind."

Richard hurried to comply with his boss's request. Venex closed his eyes and purred with pleasure as Richard's fingers massaged his neck. He liked to be attended to hand and foot. Slavery had been an essential part of every self-respecting civilization. No one would ever have remembered the pharaohs if it hadn't been for the slaves who built the pyramids. Greek and Roman culture was just the same. History had always been written by the powerful, and a concept like democracy had been powerless to change it. The slaves of yesteryear had evolved into industrious shareholders who worked hard to make sure the company they co-owned stayed profitable. In exchange for their labor, they received money, and if that didn't help, they were supplied with stimulants of every kind, or the promise of a better life in the hereafter. Systems used to keep slaves, workers, and shareholders in line were childishly simple, and history had demonstrated that they were extraordinarily efficient.

"So are we enjoying our new status as high priest?" Venex asked after a moment of silence.

Richard nodded. In half an hour, Venex would give him a dose of what he needed, and the promise of that made him exceptionally submissive. As long as he kept up the ritual circus act once a month and kept his mouth shut about Venex, his future was assured and he had nothing to worry about.

When the phone rang at three thirty that morning, Hannelore and Van In were both jolted from their sleep. In spite of her ever-swelling belly, she was faster than him. The only telephone in the house was downstairs, and Hannelore had picked it up before Van In had had time to catch his breath.

"It's for you," she said, handing him the receiver. "Something about Jasper Simons."

The officer on duty at the station had been hesitant to wake Van In, but the commissioner had stated explicitly that he was to be informed right away if there were new developments in the Trui Andries case.

Hannelore pressed her ear to the outside of the phone and listened in.

"He jumped from the sixth floor," she heard the officer say. "The night staff called fifteen minutes ago."

"Have you informed Guido?"

"Not yet, Commissioner."

"Then get on to him as soon as I hang up. Tell him to meet me at the station in twenty minutes."

"I'll take care of it."

Van In hung up the phone, tidied his hair, and started to unbutton his pajamas. "That's the third night in a row we've had to sacrifice part of our sleep."

"Consider it training," said Hannelore. "When the baby's here, you can expect the same night after night."

Van In glared at her in confusion. "I thought you wanted to breast-feed the baby."

"Babies have other needs, Pieter."

Van In wasn't amused. He turned and thundered upstairs, making enough noise to wake the dead.

"Don't forget Jonathan," Hannelore shouted.

After consuming a copious dinner, they had in fact completely forgotten about Jonathan. They hadn't heard from him since he'd gone to bed that afternoon. Hannelore now rushed to the guest room and carefully opened the door. Even without switching on the light, she could see that the bed was empty. She hurried upstairs and told Van In, who was standing in front of the bathroom mirror in his underwear, brushing his teeth.

"He must have slipped out while we were watching TV."

"Maybe he listened in on our conversation," said Hannelore.

Van In rinsed his mouth and put on a clean shirt. Jonathan's disappearance was an unexpected complication. "I'll send a patrol around to his house," he said. "If we find him, we lock him up."

"Maybe he's afraid because he said too much this afternoon. If he is, then I'm to blame. I virtually interrogated him all day."

Van In pulled on his trousers and slipped on his shoes. "Don't let it worry you, Hanne. At least we did our best for him." He gave her a kiss and headed downstairs. "With a bit of luck, I'll be home for breakfast."

Hannelore heard the front door slam, then sat on the edge of the bed. She was about to lie down when the baby started to kick. She lifted up her nightdress and followed the tiny feet pushing against her belly from the inside.

Belgian hospitals tend to be even more cheerless at night than they are during the day. The silence is to blame. It accentuates the restlessness of the sleepless and reinforces the groans of the lonely. When darkness falls, their corridors become surreal Paul Delvaux railway platforms, where death is driving the last train and the passengers are waiting, tickets in hand, not caring about their final destination. Despair isn't subject to the laws of logic. It propagates like amoebas, fast and relentless.

A puddle of blood marked the spot where Jasper had crashed to the ground in the hospital parking lot. A pair of surgical gloves, a syringe, and a catheter at its side testified like a botched still life to the tragedy that had taken place moments earlier.

"The doctors probably tried to resuscitate him," said Guido.

The sergeant seemed exceptionally alert in spite of the late hour. Judging by the smell of expensive aftershave and a forehead that gleamed like buffed marble, he had managed the shave and shower in the space of fifteen minutes.

"Or they took the opportunity to milk his insurance at the last minute."

Van In had hated hospitals and doctors all his life, remnants of a childhood trauma he had experienced when "they"—as he always referred to doctors and nurses—left his father to die in a tiny hospital room as cancer devoured his body. People were careful not to mention the word *cancer* back then, and Van In understood why, to a certain extent. But the fact that the leeches had subjected the dying man to one cruel test after another until he breathed his last just because the hospital's finances were "in the red" was something he couldn't forgive. "Beds are revenue" was what they said in the business. Guido knew the story and prudently held his tongue.

Van In lit a cigarette as they made their way to emergency. His father was only forty when he died. He had never smoked, and the only times he took a drink were on New Year's Eve and on his birthday. At the time, Van In had sworn that he would settle scores one way or another. He had survived his father's death by four years thus far, and just the thought of it reassured him.

"They're reunited," said Guido. "I mean Jasper and Trui." He pointed to the heavens, where thousands of stars sparkled in the moonless night sky.

"Do you think that's why he did it?" asked Van In.

"I can think of worse reasons to commit suicide."

"That's one way of looking at it, I guess," said Van In, wondering if he would do the same for Hannelore.

In contrast to what Van In had expected, the duty doctor was a friendly and patient man. He was clearly having a hard time accepting Jasper's death, and he apologized repeatedly for failing to resuscitate the boy.

"So he was still alive," said Van In.

"Human beings can be tough, Commissioner. There are cases in the literature of children surviving more serious falls. You can compare this sort of impact with the blow a car driver can expect to take in a sixty-mile-an-hour crash. You would expect it to be fatal, but resuscitation techniques are so advanced these days that a small percentage of people manage to survive. At least if we reach the victim in time."

"Was that what happened here?"

In addition to being a skillful surgeon, the doctor was also an insightful psychologist, and he sensed the suspicion in the policeman's question immediately. "One of our security people was making his rounds when Jasper jumped. He saw the whole thing happen."

"Can we have a word with him?"

"I'm sure that can be arranged." The doctor made his way to a nearby phone and punched in a number. "A couple of police officers have just arrived. They'd like to have a word with Dieter."

Van In could hardly believe his ears. A doctor who knew the first names of the security staff and wasn't full of his own shit!

"The man is in shock," he said, hanging up the phone. "If you promise not to keep him for more than five minutes, I'll take you to him."

Van In nodded. "That's very kind of you, Doctor . . ."

"D'Hondt," said the doctor. "Maurice D'Hondt."

"Do you know Dr. Coleyn?" asked Van In as they stepped into the elevator.

"We were at university together," said D'Hondt. "He specialized in psychiatry, and I ended up in surgery."

His use of the expression "ended up" as opposed to "specialized" betrayed the fact that D'Hondt's heart was in psychiatry rather than surgery.

"I come from a poor family, Commissioner. My father was a laborer. When I was accepted for university, I was content with the opportunity to study. Becoming a doctor in those days was still a noble idea. There was a shortage of internists and I . . ."

"Am I to understand that psychiatry was your first preference?" Van In inquired.

"Well spotted, Commissioner."

"Was it a jobs-for-the-boys affair?"

The elevator doors opened and D'Hondt gestured that his two guests should walk ahead. Van In wasn't stupid. He knew that anyone with the brains could become a doctor, but when it came to specializations, different norms were maintained. Quotas limited access, and the university itself decided who got to study what. Ophthalmologists were top of the pyramid. They earned more, didn't have to work weekends or night shifts, and they were rarely, if ever, confronted with serious suffering. Psychiatrists came in a commendable second. While those with a say insisted that only objective criteria were involved in the selection procedure, everyone in the academic world knew well enough that graduating summa cum laude often wasn't enough for a candidate to be considered for one of the more prized specializations.

"Coleyn came from a family of doctors," said D'Hondt. "His father-in-law was dean of the faculty of medicine in Leuven for the best part of ten years."

Van In was familiar with the dynasty phenomenon. And for once he was aware that it wasn't an exclusively Belgian thing. Nepotism was probably the only form of corruption that was universally tolerated.

"Is Richard Coleyn also a doctor?" he asked.

D'Hondt stopped in his tracks, and a look of concern appeared on his face. "Richard is John Coleyn's son, Commissioner. He was indeed expected to continue the family tradition, but when Richard was still at school, he got involved with drugs—the so-called harmless variety."

The way D'Hondt raised his eyebrows made it perfectly clear what he thought about soft drugs.

"At university, he started to experiment with heroin and ecstasy. His father spent four years trying to get him off them."

Van In nodded. He could guess the rest. There was something doubly tragic for a psychiatrist to be unable to help his own son.

The security officer was lying on a stretcher in the head nurse's office. He seemed a little pale, in spite of being treated to coffee and cake by the night nurse. The man was fifty-five and had a son of his own roughly the same age as Jasper Simons.

"Good morning, Dieter. We're from the police. Do you mind if we ask you a couple of questions?" Van In grabbed a chair and sat down at the security officer's side. "Dr. D'Hondt gave me five minutes."

Dieter nodded, then looked anxiously at the window as if he was expecting to see another body flash past. "I heard a scream first," he said, "then a thud. That's when I realized someone must have jumped."

"What did you do then?"

"I ran toward the thud."

"And Jasper was still alive?"

Dieter nodded. "At first sight, there seemed to be nothing wrong with him. I leaned down and asked what had happened."

"Did he speak?"

"He groaned and . . ."

"And?" said Van In.

"I could be mistaken, but . . ." Dieter shook his head.

"It might be important," said D'Hondt in an unexpectedly paternal tone.

Dieter hesitated. "I thought I heard him say the word 'venex.'"

"Venex?"

"That's what I understood, officer. The rest made no sense."

"Can you remember what it sounded like?"

"Something like 'owly' or 'oly.'"

Van In did his best to keep a straight face. His interrogation was beginning to sound like one of those TV quizzes where people have to guess a word or phrase on the basis of someone else acting it out.

Van In repeated the words and Guido noted them carefully in his notepad: *venex* and *owly (oly)*.

"Sorry, officer, that's all I can remember. It all happened so fast. I ran for help right away . . ."

"And when I arrived, the boy was clinically dead," said D'Hondt. "But because Dieter had found him alive, we decided on the spot to do whatever we could to resuscitate him."

"I'm sure you did, Doctor."

Jasper's death had introduced a new dimension into the case, and Van In didn't like it. He thought about Jonathan. Was his life also in danger? And what about Richard Coleyn, the drug-addicted son of the psychiatrist who had—*nota bene*—been treating Jasper? The pieces of the puzzle seemed to fit too easily, and Van In couldn't avoid the uneasy feeling that a cocktail of satanism, drugs, and psychiatric patients was likely to be as explosive as a barrel of nitroglycerine on a roller coaster.

"If you have no further questions, Commissioner, I suggest we let Dieter get some rest," said D'Hondt.

Van In jumped. He was so lost in thought that he had forgotten where he was for a moment.

"Yes, of course," he said, still a little confused. "I think we have enough to be getting on with."

They said good-bye to Dieter and made their way to reception.

"I'll send a forensics team as soon as I can," said Van In.

D'Hondt raised his eyebrows.

"We have to be sure it was suicide, Doctor. It wouldn't be the first time someone was 'encouraged' to jump out of a window."

"Then someone else must have enticed Jasper to the sixth floor before encouraging him to jump. The windows on the psychiatric ward are permanently locked."

"We'll check it out," said Van In.

At that moment, D'Hondt's beeper went off. The dutiful doctor quickly shook hands with his police visitors and rushed to emergency.

"Thanks anyway, Doctor," Van In shouted at the man's back.

The only person on the sixth floor who knew what had happened was the night nurse. The woman showed the policemen the open window and Jasper's slippers, which had been tucked neatly under the radiator.

"He must have waited until I finished my last rounds," she said. "I'd have noticed something otherwise."

Guido took down her statement, then closed and sealed the room.

"Will the room be sealed for long?" The hospital was struggling with a shortage of beds and that seemed to bother her more than Jasper's act of despair.

"Depends on forensics," Van In grunted. "And if problems arise, you can always use Mr. Simons's room downstairs. It's free, if I'm not mistaken."

"Your place or mine?" asked Guido as they climbed into the Golf.

"I could murder a Duvel," said Van In.

His muscles were tingling with exhaustion and he had to yawn every ten seconds, but he wasn't ready for bed. He had too many troubles in his head, and troubles in the head meant no sleep.

"I still have two or three bottles in the fridge from that night you . . ."

"Let's not go there, Guido."

“That night” referred to a dinner at Guido’s place when Van In mixed too many Duvels with a couple of bottles of Château Margaux and things got a little out of hand.

“If you don’t drink them, they’ll still be there next year.”

“As long as Frank doesn’t get jealous.” Van In grinned.

As Guido steered the Golf through the abandoned streets of the city, Van In pushed back his seat, stretched his legs, and called the duty officer on the radio. He was curious to know if the patrol he had sent to Jonathan’s place had come up with anything.

“Negative, Commissioner. According to the landlord, Jonathan hasn’t paid his rent in months.”

“Does hc still live there?”

“A moment, Commissioner, let me check the report.”

The night patrol officers had done a thorough job. Van In listened to their findings with his eyes closed. The landlord’s picture of Jonathan wasn’t exactly elevating. The boy was a criminal, a profiteer, and an out-and-out liar who fooled gullible people into believing his bizarre stories. When he won someone’s confidence, he wasn’t averse to abusing it and stealing from them. Van In thought immediately about the fifty thousand francs they had taken from the bank to buy stuff for the new baby. He cursed under his breath.

“Something wrong?” asked Guido.

“I hope not, Guido. But let’s have that drink first. The rest can wait till later.”

6

"I can't help feeling you're trying to sabotage my work, Commissioner. How in Christ's name can I write an article when you and Sergeant Versavel do nothing but get in the way? I wasted an entire day yesterday sitting around waiting. I thought we had an agreement. . . ."

The lips that had already caused many a macho heart to flutter were tense with pent-up rage. Van In was at his desk and deliberately didn't react to Saartje and her critique. *Hotheads are like balloons*, he thought. *When all the air finally leaks out, they end up limp and powerless.* Guido was standing at the coffee machine, staring at the hot water with the patience of a Stoic as it trickled through the filter and emerged as black gold.

"I was told we would be working together and that I would be directly involved in the investigation," Saartje Maes insisted. She glared first at Van In, then turned to Guido. "What's with the silence?"

Van In shifted position, his elbows on his desk, his chin resting on his clenched fists. She was right, of course. There was little point in ignoring her. If she really wanted to know the truth, he was prepared to tell her. He had let her speak her mind because he was in a good mood. Earlier in the day, much to his delight, he had learned that Jonathan was not a thief. The fifty thousand francs was still in the wardrobe where he'd left it and that cheered him no end.

"It's a mystery to me, Miss Maes, how you managed to persuade the chief commissioner to let you work on a case you actually know nothing about."

Guido rubbed his mustache and concealed an emerging grin in the process. Van In lined up the heavy weapons right off and didn't beat about the bush. His opening statement was sharp as a razor and left Saartje Maes red with indignation. She took a deep breath, readying an ugly salvo, but didn't get the chance to fire it.

"Let's get one thing clear. The chief commissioner knows as well as I do that the details of a judicial inquiry cannot be disclosed. According to the law, I'm not obliged to tell you anything. The fact that you're planning to publish an article on the topic is completely irrelevant."

"But Commissioner . . ."

Van In raised his hand. Three sleepless nights had melted his innate timidity toward pretty, self-assured women like an iceberg in the tropics.

"And I shouldn't have to tell you any of this, Miss Maes. You of all people should know how important confidentiality is in a judicial inquiry, as should anyone with an ounce of professional integrity. Do you realize what kind of damage you could cause?"

Guido's heart skipped a beat. A normal person would be heading out of the room in tears at this juncture, but Saartje Maes simply gulped and headed toward the coffee machine. Van In couldn't help looking up. He wouldn't have been a man if he hadn't; her swaying hips were enough to confuse a hardened hermit.

"A cup of coffee, Commissioner?" she asked, as if nothing had happened.

Her reaction was so disarming that Van In immediately said, "Yes."

"Please understand that my articles are of the utmost importance to me. Forgive me if I seem a little pushy."

She leaned forward and placed the coffee on Van In's desk.

"We have to respect the rules of the game, Miss Maes."

"When neither of you appeared yesterday, I started to worry," said Saartje. "I didn't set out to upset you. Sorry if I overdid it a little."

Van In knew she was putting on an act, but for one reason or another, he couldn't find his winning hand.

"Let's make a deal. From today on, we make arrangements and stick to them. That means the sergeant and I follow through on the investigation and we bring you up to speed at the appropriate moment."

Saartje pouted, struggling to hide her disappointment. "Does that mean I have to hang around here all day with nothing to do?"

"Of course not," said Van In, grinning from ear to ear. "I suggest that you do some detective work for us. To tell the truth, that's the most important part of any investigation. Any journalist worth her salt should know that."

Saartje lowered her eyes. "You're the boss, Commissioner."

Van In sipped at his coffee and winked at Guido. He wondered how Hannelore would react when he told her later that day how he had handled the black widow.

"Then let's start right away."

Van In had been racking his brains since the day before, trying to find an efficient way to disarm the overactive child. The solution had dawned on him only five minutes ago. "As you know, Trui Andries was murdered with a rare poison that's virtually undetectable. I want to know more about it. Maybe there's a precedent. That's why I want you to go through the documentation on all the unsolved murders in the last twenty years with a fine-tooth comb. Who knows . . . perhaps you'll find something that will help us explain Trui Andries's death."

Guido had never heard Van In talk such unadulterated crap before, but given the circumstances, his suggestion sounded plausible enough. Taming the wildcat and keeping her out of mischief was priority number one.

"And in exchange, you'll keep me up to date on the investigation?"

Van In nodded. Now that the "problem" was solved, they could finally get on with the job at hand.

"I'll inform Inspector Pattyn," he said. "He'll be delighted to introduce you to the archives."

"Congratulations," said Guido when Miss Maes closed the door behind her.

Van In emptied his cup of coffee in a single gulp. The caffeine had little effect on his exhausted body. His muscles were numb and his toes tingled as if he'd just stood on a jellyfish.

"We don't have the time to hang around, Guido."

Jonathan's disappearance continued to worry him. In spite of the stories and the gossip, he quite liked the lad. "I've sent another couple of cops to his flat. Maybe one of the neighbors knows where he is or can tell us who he hangs out with."

"And in the meantime, I dug up some details on Richard Coleyn," said Guido. "And you're right. He's listed in the registry of corporations and has been running a dating agency since 1995."

Guido printed the details and handed them to Van In. The agency went by the name of Xanthippe.

Van In folded the paper and stuffed it into his trouser pocket. "Nice name for a dating agency," he said.

"The weirder the better," said Guido condescendingly. "Some idiot opened a hairdresser around the corner from where I live and called it Cut the Crap."

Van In laughed, and that was a good sign. Recent tensions had left him feeling as if a ton weight was resting on his chest, and the imminent end of Hannelore's pregnancy wasn't making it any lighter.

Hoogstuk Street wasn't exactly the place you would expect to find a dating agency. The narrow road between the Coupure Canal and Ganzen Street was more at home in nineteenth-century Bruges than the modern tourist factory the city had become. Until recently, it had housed the city's working class, rugged, uncomplicated types who earned their livings by the sweat of their brows, who didn't worry about cholesterol when they dug into plates of bacon and eggs, and who didn't panic when they were told their liver was swelling when they reached a certain age. Van In knew the street because his nephew had lived there.

"Heroic battles were once fought here," said Van In as they turned onto the street. "When the men came home drunk on a Friday, their incensed womenfolk would be waiting for them. Woe betide the boys who'd dug too deep into their wage packets and bought a round for the entire bar in a reckless moment. More broken noses and bruised ribs were doled out on a weekly basis than most would imagine."

Guido nodded. He'd heard the story at least ten times before.

"I think this is it," he said, pointing to a renovated laborer's house roughly halfway down the street. A heart-shaped plywood board hung above the door with the word XANTHIPPE in red letters. Wind and rain had long ago obliterated the *X*, the *T*, a *P*, and the *E*, but it was still more or less legible. From a distance, the remains of the word looked like the name of a respected bank. But a bank on Hoogstuk Street would have been even stranger than a dating agency.

The doorbell roused Richard Coleyn from a deep sleep. The window was open, and the door had been removed from its hinges to avoid aggravating his claustrophobia, but the stench in his tiny bedroom was still unbearable. A dozen empty Coke bottles were scattered across the floor, and a discarded pair of grimy jeans had landed on top of a slice of fossilized pizza. The walls were covered with spiderwebs, black with dust, like lightweight swallows' nests. Richard turned on his side and peered at his watch between the cigarette butts on his nightstand. It was nine fifteen. The doorbell kept ringing, so he threw off the blankets and sat on the edge of the bed, still half asleep. Why couldn't they just leave him in peace?

He pulled on his pants, kicked the pizza out of the way, and stumbled down the stairs. In spite of the cold—he only heated the house if he had clients, and he'd seen precious few in recent months—all he was wearing was jeans and a grubby T-shirt. Richard had learned to deal with deprivation. All that counted was the stuff he collected from Venex on a daily basis.

"I don't think he's home," said Guido.

They had been ringing the bell for the best part of five minutes, and some curious neighbors had gathered behind them.

"He's definitely in there," one of them said in a thick Bruges accent, trying to be helpful.

"She said he's at home," Van In explained, still familiar with the dialect of his youth.

He rang the bell again and kept his thumb in place. Since visiting the Simons family he'd started to behave like a door-to-door salesman.

"I'm coming, I'm coming," a voice shouted.

"He's coming," said Van In, letting go of the bell and waiting for the door to open.

"Are you Richard Coleyn?"

Junkies have a sixth sense when it comes to cops, and Richard tried to slam the door shut. But Van In was one step ahead of him and he slipped his foot forward, wriggling it between the door and the doorpost with the dexterity of a seasoned Jehovah's Witness. It hurt, but at least he'd saved face. Luckily, Guido was on hand to free him, throwing all his weight at the door. Richard lost his balance and fell backward into the corridor.

"You don't have the right . . ." he roared.

Van In stepped inside and helped Coleyn to his feet. "I hope you didn't hurt yourself," he said, smiling. "My friend here has been looking for a bride for years and when we saw the sign, we thought . . ."

"You're not fooling anybody," said Coleyn, scrambling to his feet and crossing his hands over his shoulders. The sudden surge of emotion left him shivering from the cold, but the look in his eyes spoke volumes. Van In recognized the symptoms. Junkies were just as easy to spot as cops in plainclothes. "I only work by appointment."

"Then let's make an appointment," said Van In.

The lighthearted tone confused Coleyn. "I thought you guys were cops."

"Do we deserve discrimination because we're from the police, Mr. Coleyn?"

Richard had no idea what was going on. "What do you want from me?"

"A little chat, Mr. Coleyn."

Every policeman had his own technique for setting up an interrogation. In contrast to what some outsiders claimed—most of them clever dicks who watched too many US cop series—the point wasn't to confront a suspect with evidence and force an immediate confession. Experienced interrogators first tried to gain the suspect's confidence. Once a bond was established, the rest was a piece of cake.

"I've got nothing to hide," said Richard.

"Then you have nothing to fear, Mr. Coleyn." Van In was having a hard time picturing the wreck standing in front of him running a business. "If you'll come with us, we can have a little chat in more comfortable circumstances. I'm guessing you haven't had any breakfast. What would you say to a good cup of coffee?"

Van In's friendly approach left Coleyn completely nonplussed.

"And if I refuse?"

Van In turned to Guido. "What happens if Mr. Coleyn refuses to cooperate, *Commissioner*?"

Guido didn't miss a beat and slipped immediately into his expected bad guy role, a classic technique in which the senior cop played the nasty, and Van In had just promoted him to commissioner.

"In that case, we'll have to contact the examining magistrate and ask him to issue a warrant to have you remanded into custody."

"That means we have the right to lock you up for twenty-four hours, Mr. Coleyn. But I'm thinking that won't be necessary."

"How long will this little chat take?"

Van In smiled. The trick with the warrant never failed.

"No more than an hour, an hour and a half max. Correct, Commissioner?

Guido nodded.

"Okay," said Coleyn. "If you promise I'll be home before twelve."

"Your father's just trying to help, Frederik."

Dr. Coleyn lit another cigarette and tried to blow smoke rings into the air, something he had never managed in spite of being a chain smoker for the better part of fifty years. Sometimes he managed to produce a hazy saturnal ring, but that didn't count. He wanted to blow his own kind of ring.

Frederik Masyn and his father were sitting opposite him at his desk, having just concluded a ninety-minute session without an inch of progress. Frederik insisted that he heard voices, and his father, a renowned notary with whom Coleyn had studied at university, refused to believe that there wasn't a therapy that could put an end to them. He had suggested that his son be admitted to a specialized institution, but Frederik refused to cooperate.

"There has to be something," Casper Masyn said, his desperation unconcealed.

Rich people were often convinced that the solution to a problem was directly proportional to the money they threw at it. Such a blinkered approach meant good money for many a psychiatrist, and Coleyn was the first to admit that without clients like Frederik Masyn, he wouldn't be able to maintain his luxury yacht and take vacation four times a year. Curing Frederik Masyn would be financial suicide.

"Your son is receiving the best medication on the market, Casper. And science isn't standing still. The medical world is hard at work searching for new approaches, new products. Give it a couple of years . . ."

Frederik listened to the conversation between his father and the doctor with half an ear. He wasn't sick. His father and mother were sick. They didn't understand the spirituality that was guiding him. It was beyond them . . . above them.

He had a task to fulfill, and Venex had predicted that those closest to him would persecute him for it.

Colleagues passing Room 204 and glancing inside at Van In and Guido would have been forgiven for thinking the two men looked particularly relaxed. The twinge of jealousy they were likely to experience could also be forgiven. Special Investigations was a luxury unit where more coffee and Jenever was guzzled than the authorities were usually inclined to tolerate. But one thing was completely out of place: No one had ever seen Van In *serving* it!

"So you know nothing about a satanic fraternity with Jasper and Trui among its members."

"Why ask me that?"

"Because we're curious, Mr. Coleyn."

Van In smiled and patted Richard on the shoulder. "We know that Trui and Jasper met each other through your agency. Trui was murdered and Jasper jumped out of a window earlier today. Serious business, don't you think?"

Van In studied Coleyn's reaction. He buried his face in his hands. "I didn't know . . ." he spluttered.

Young people who'd grown up with television knew exactly what to do if they wanted to appear convincing during a police interrogation. The main thing was to not get too emotional. Richard knew they were watching him, and it was of vital importance that he didn't cause suspicion. Bursting into tears would give the wrong impression.

"Jasper was a close friend. When I started the dating agency three years ago, he was one of my first clients."

He and Jasper had grown up together, attended the same high school, had fallen in love with the same girls. Jasper had introduced him to hash, and they'd later even shared needles.

"Why a dating service?" Guido inquired.

"I needed money, Commissioner."

"Didn't your father help out?"

The question made Richard blush. His father deposited twenty thousand francs in his account at the beginning of every month. "He rejected me. I wasn't good enough."

"Because you screwed up at college?"

"That's what *he* says."

Didn't they know he had been top of his class at school until the year before he left? A grade average of 83 percent and higher for math and Latin. But no, the old bastard insisted on summa cum laude at college, just to be like him.

"So none of it's true?"

"My father was never satisfied."

"So he gave up on you."

"You could say that."

"And then you got the idea of starting a dating agency," said Van In.

"I read in a magazine that young people were having more and more trouble finding partners, and when I heard they were willing to pay good money for help, I pushed the boat out."

"And did it float?"

"At the start . . ."

Van In was familiar with the phenomenon. Eighty percent of the average dating service database consisted of men looking for a one-night stand. Fifteen percent—the genuine ones—were looking for young blondes with a job and, if possible, a sense of humor. The rest were women who had exhausted all the other possibilities without success. Most of them were in their late forties and older.

Guido looked at Van In. The commissioner was playing the role of understanding sergeant with enormous conviction, but in spite of the skilled performance, the interrogation was getting them nowhere.

"So you know nothing about a satanic sect."

"Why should I?"

"Because Jasper and Trui mixed with the satanic crowd. And Jasper was your friend, as you just informed us."

"Friends don't always tell each other everything, Sergeant."

Van In also realized that they were making little, if any, progress. He sighed and turned to Guido. "I fear this conversation is completely pointless, Commissioner."

Guido nodded and pretended to call the examining magistrate. In reality, he punched in the number of the incident room and had an imaginary conversation with the officer on duty. Coleyn was then informed that he would be transferred to Bruges's main prison and was scheduled to appear in court the following day. The judge would likely remand him into custody in the interests of the investigation. Richard turned pale. He couldn't imagine a day without a fix. Guido stepped outside for a breath of fresh air after he and Van In had agreed to give Mr. Coleyn one final chance. Guido's absence was purely psychological, intended to lower the bar a little. Suspects were always more inclined to confide in subordinates and not superiors.

"Does the word 'venex' mean anything to you, Mr. Coleyn?"

Van In produced a bottle of Jenever from a drawer and poured a couple of shots. "The commissioner won't be back for a while . . ." he added temptingly.

Coleyn reached for the glass of Jenever, trying not to shake. The word Van In had mentioned made every hair on his body stand on end. "Is that some kind of drug?"

It sounded stupid, but it was the best he could do.

"I was thinking more along the lines of a person," said Van In.

Richard slurped some Jenever. "No idea."

"Jonathan Leman?"

"Never heard of him."

"Strange," said Van In. "He says he knows you."

Richard could feel the sergeant's eyes watching his every move. Lucky the commissioner had left the room. He would have noticed that he was lying right away. "Plenty of people say they know me," he said.

"Jonathan is close friends with Trui and Jasper. My guess is you know him, Mr. Coleyn."

Van In threw back some Jenever and held his tongue. Silence was now his best weapon.

"Maybe we met once," said Richard after a minute. *That asshole Jonathan must've been shooting his mouth off*, he thought. *If he's cooperating with the police, the entire operation could be on the skids.*

"Was he one of your clients?"

If Jonathan blabbed to the cops, then they have to know about the fraternity. Why then all the questions about my dating service? Something isn't right. Venex warned me. Cops bluff. . . .

"Are you all right, Mr. Coleyn?"

Richard leaned back in his chair and smiled. "Now that I think of it, Trui mentioned that name a couple of times. She used to work in an orphanage, and if I'm not mistaken, Jonathan Leman was part of a group she was given charge of."

"An orphanage?"

The question confused Richard, albeit momentarily. He'd said more than he planned to say, but it was too late to whine about it. If he backtracked now, it would only make him appear more suspicious, and that had to be avoided at all costs.

"Suffer Little Children or something like that."

Van In was familiar with the place. One of the inmates had killed an elderly man the year before. The local press went to town on it.

"So you were still in touch with Trui and Jasper."

"Of course, Sergeant."

Richard breathed a sigh of relief that Van In wasn't going to press him on the orphanage. It didn't matter what he said about Trui and Jasper. They were both dead and they couldn't contradict him. "Jasper asked me to be a witness at his wedding. We had dinner together last Friday. . . . Spaghetti."

"I imagine you have an alibi for Tuesday night, early Wednesday."

Coleyn was now certain that the cops were groping around in the dark. Venex had taken care of everything.

"I was with friends in Antwerp for a couple of days. I just got back yesterday."

"You know we'll verify everything you have to say, Mr. Coleyn?"

Guido had returned to the room and had listened attentively to the last part of the conversation. Van In pressed his fingertips together. They tingled like his toes. The hot, dry air produced by the central heating made him feel drowsy and clouded his thoughts. He yawned. Guido noticed his head bobbing up and down a couple of times as if he were dozing off, but he couldn't tell if it was real or an act. He'd seen Van In feign tiredness before to hoodwink a suspect.

"I can give you their telephone number," said Richard with confidence.

Van In started to stretch. Richard's story had its weaknesses, but there was nothing serious enough to have him taken into custody. "I hope you're aware that false statements can have ugly consequences. If it turns out that you lied to me today, we'll come and get you. And rest assured we'll require a little more of your time. Is that understood, Mr. Coleyn?"

Richard nodded. A refreshing breeze filled his mind, blowing away the tensions that had plagued him. The cops knew nothing and he had told them nothing. Father would be content. He would get his fix.

"D'you mean I can go?"

"For the time being," said Van In.

Coleyn didn't need telling twice. When he was gone, Van In called Inspector Pattyn and told him to keep an eye on Coleyn.

Saartje, who had set herself up in the inspector's office, heard the name "Coleyn" mentioned a couple of times.

"Do you get to do the dirty work, Jean?" she asked after Pattyn had hung up the phone.

The inspector grinned like an idiot as Saartje slammed a dusty dossier shut and made a cute face. He was putty in her hands.

"I had a rummage through Mr. and Mrs. Simons's closet," said Guido.

"And?"

"Neither of them has a medical background. He's an accountant for a transport company, and she works part-time in a supermarket."

"Not much chance of them getting hold of the poison then."

Guido nodded. "I sent a patrol around to check their alibi, just to be on the safe side."

"There isn't much else we can do," said Van In.

Guido sat down at his desk and switched on his computer. It was two forty-five and he had a pile of work to write up. Van In poured himself another Jenever and put up his feet on a chair. Commissioners were allowed to indulge themselves now and again and spend an entire afternoon just thinking.

7

Do you *have* to do it today?" Hannelore asked.

She shuffled into the kitchen, switched on the coffee machine, and waggled to the table, her hands perched on her hips. With every step, a searing pain shot from her lower back through her knees to the soles of her feet. She had been looking forward to a quiet Saturday at home, but now Van In had announced, all cool, calm, and collected, that he was going to work.

"I'm doing it for you, Hanne. The quicker we get this case behind us, the more time I'll have for—"

"Will Guido be with you?"

Guido and Frank had booked a weekend on the coast and were planning to celebrate getting back together with a splash.

"I promise I'll be back before noon."

"So you're on your own."

The disbelief in her voice was loud and clear.

"Of course I'm on my own."

Hannelore buttered a slice of toast. Every ounce of fat she consumed seemed to multiply on her hips, but she was beyond caring. "Still having trouble with Miss Maes?"

It sounded like an innocent remark, but Van In didn't think so. "You're not insinuating that . . ."

"Don't flatter yourself, Van In."

Sometimes he couldn't bear it when she called him Van In. "Should I flatter you instead?" The words were out before he had the chance to think of the damage they might cause. Hannelore had been complaining for weeks about her ever-expanding body and how unattractive she felt, fishing for compliments. She had even covered the mirror in the bedroom with a blanket. "Miss Maes has nothing to do with this."

"But you wouldn't mind strutting down the street with her on your arm."

Van In hesitated. Saartje Maes was a beautiful young woman, the type any man would be happy to be seen with. And he couldn't deny that a night with her, well . . . "She has her qualities."

Mistrust is a prowling predator that appears out of nowhere and strikes when it detects a moment of weakness in its prey. And Hannelore was having a bad day. "So you fancy the whore!"

"Whore?"

He missed the logic in her accusation, but logic wasn't essential at this juncture. Domestic quarrels were like hurricanes. When hot and cold air clashed, the encounter could have terrible consequences.

This was one of those encounters. Words were exchanged, and the whirlwind intensified until Van In threw his empty cup of coffee at the wall and stormed out, slamming the door behind him. Hannelore collapsed on a chair and started to sob. But not for long. Why should *she* be the one to do penance? It wasn't her fault that Van In was so touchy!

She made her way to the living room, opened a drawer in the sideboard, and grabbed his credit card, thinking of all the things she could spend his money on. When she turned onto Saint Jacob

Street from the Vette Vispoort, she was in such a snit that she didn't notice Jonathan Leman hiding behind the monumental water pump on the opposite side of the street.

Orphanage Ter Heyden had changed its name to Suffer Little Children fifty years ago. The neo-Gothic edifice—a genuine castle by all accounts—had once served as the summer residence of a renowned aristocratic family. After the death of his lordship de Spey van Haverthinge, the last in the family line, the building passed to the Sisters of the Good Samaritan, a congregation dedicated to sheltering orphans and abandoned children. The sisters had worked hard to transform their inheritance into a modern reception center for people in need. Love of one's neighbor was the watchword. At least that's what outsiders believed. In reality, the sisters had taken advantage of the generous subsidies made available by Catholic politicians in those days to keep voters happy. The drafty old castle had been completely renovated, and with the leftover cash, the sisters had built themselves a new convent with all the modern conveniences. Even nuns had the right to a little luxury, didn't they?

Van In stubbed out a half-smoked cigarette in the Golf's ashtray, his third in less than fifteen minutes. He had spent most of the journey from the police station to the orphanage trying stubbornly to ignore the pain in his chest. His ticker ticked with the regularity of a cheap watch. He thought about his father and the fact that he had outlived him a full four years. Any professional investor would be satisfied with that kind of return.

As Van In turned into the drive leading up to Suffer Little Children (the sisters had neatly paved the dirt road) he was suddenly confronted with an overwhelming urge to turn back. What in the name of God was he doing? The man who preached to anyone who would listen that work wasn't everything had walked out on his pregnant wife to chase down some vague clue. As things stood, it was quite possible that Jonathan Leman had nothing to do with the death of Trui Andries. He had also treated Hannelore unfairly. By storming out of the house, he had more or less admitted that something was going on between him and Miss Maes, and that was a mistake he had to put right before war broke out. He vowed to make this interview a quick one.

Sister Marie-Louise accompanied Van In to the parlor, a room by the front door that smelled of sour milk and Dettol. *Dickensian*, Van In thought: *subdued light, the smell of polished leather, oak furniture, and portraits of grim-faced gentlemen with mustaches and sideburns.*

"Take a seat, Commissioner."

The elderly sister was wearing a gray skirt, a sterile sheath that stopped midcalf, and a flannel blouse, the cloth of which was thick enough to black out a darkroom. Van In had once heard that nuns cut up old towels to make sanitary napkins. After use, they were soaked and boiled and reused. The very idea that Sister Marie-Louise might still need sanitary napkins made him shiver.

"Good morning, Sister. I'd like to ask you some questions about Jonathan Leman. I believe he grew up here. . . ."

"We don't make a habit of passing on information about our pupils, Commissioner."

Her brusque reply reminded Van In of his childhood. Sisters didn't like to be contradicted. They were the brides of Christ, and their behavior matched their status.

"The boy has disappeared, Sister. I just want to help him," said Van In, aware that threats made no sense. He had to get her on a point that was beyond discussion: love of thy neighbor. "His life is in danger, and it would be a real shame if we were too late a second time."

Sister Marie-Louise's pallid face hardened. She sat down opposite Van In. "What do you mean 'a second time'?"

"Two young people lost their lives this past week, Sister."

Sister Marie-Louise nodded. The death of Trui Andries had been all over the news, and it was impossible to deny that the sisters read the papers. "Trui Andries worked here for more than ten years," she said. "But what does that have to do with Jonathan?"

Van In smiled cautiously, not wanting to make the sister suspicious. "Jonathan told me they were good friends."

Sister Marie-Louise folded her arms in a conditioned and emotionless gesture. Trui's murder and Jasper Simons's suicide had dominated the conversation among the sisters for the last few days. Everyone was in complete agreement that the hand of God had manifested itself. "I imagine you know that we had to let Trui Andries go a year back."

Van In moved his head in a manner that neither confirmed nor denied the sister's statement. "Was there something between her and Jonathan?"

The sparks in Sister Marie-Louise's glare would have been enough to start a fire in a downpour. "Jonathan is an unstable boy," she said. "We did everything we could to help him stay on the straight and narrow, but when he turned eighteen and left the orphanage . . ." She hesitated, gulped, her sadness apparently genuine.

"You knew about the drug problem?" Van In asked.

Sister Marie-Louise nodded, wrapping her fingers around the cross that hung from her neck on a silver chain, as if to urge her "boss" to get involved in the conversation.

"Was Trui Andries supplying him?" Van In sensed that the sister was getting desperate. She wasn't allowed to lie, and she knew that the commissioner would exploit that fact if he needed to.

"Jasper was the supplier."

Van In raised his eyebrows.

"Jasper Simons was employed here for a year and a half as a youth worker. He led Trui astray, and both she and Jonathan paid the price."

"Was she also taking drugs?"

Sister Marie-Louise was suddenly overcome by a sense of doubt and hesitation, a gnawing disquiet that matched the struggle she had waged for years with the now-crumbling certainties that had been fed her as a young novice. Those who believed would be saved, and every prayer was a tile that paved the way to heaven. Certainties were important. That's why she'd entered the convent. The world outside belonged to the devil, and only faith in God could protect her from a life of sin. She had learned that from her teachers, but if her teachers were right, then why had Trui and Jasper been so happy?

"Trui gave in to temptation," she said. "Jasper tempted her, misled her, deceived her."

Van In was reminded of the fragment Guido had quoted from the book by Leopold Flam: *The devil tempts, misleads, manipulates, and deceives.* "Are you implying that there was something satanic about Jasper?"

Sister Marie-Louise looked him straight in the eye for the first time in their conversation. People who worked for Catholic organizations were expected to live according to the principles of the Church. No one could serve both God and Satan. Surely that was obvious. "Jasper worshipped evil, Commissioner."

Van In had no interest in pressing the subject. It was all beginning to sound a little too much like the Inquisition, a phenomenon that moviemakers had milked of all its mystery. "Were they in a relationship?"

Sister Marie-Louise could still remember the day she caught Trui and Jasper together in the supply room in the basement. She had remained by the open door and waited discreetly until the groans had ebbed away. Even now she had to admit that the pair's fleshly union hadn't left her unperturbed.

"Jasper was a disciple of Satan," she asserted. "He dragged Trui with him into the abyss. We were forced to intervene."

Van In considered lighting a cigarette. He took one from his pack and started to play with it.

Hannelore was lying on the bed, tired from shopping, when the bell rang. The spoils of her expedition were on the kitchen table: three bags full of things she really didn't need. She knew that it couldn't be Van In—he had his own key—so she hurried downstairs. The bulge, as they called it, still undecided on a name, meant that she was unable to see her feet as she descended, and she was forced to take a step back when she opened the door in the narrow hallway.

"My name's Saartje Maes. Is Pieter Van In at home?"

Hannelore looked her up and down as if she was a piece of trash. "Miss Maes. What a surprise."

Saartje managed to conceal the fact that the sarcasm in Hannelore's words confused her. *Time to put the hippo in her place*, she thought, and she came straight to the point. "I have to speak with him urgently."

"Commissioner Van In is out at the moment, Miss Maes. Can I take a message?"

"Thanks, Mrs. Van In, but it's rather personal. I'll see him on Monday at the office."

In spite of the ice-cold weather, the journalist looked glamorous and sexy. Hannelore was of a mind to treat her to a kick in the ass. Had lack of sex strained Van In's mind so much that some bit of skirt calling herself a journalist was enough to turn his head?

"I'll be sure to tell him, Miss Haes."

"Maes," said Saartje.

"Funny," said Hannelore. "I thought you said Haes."

"No, Mrs. Van In. My name's Maes."

"And my name's Martens. Hannelore Martens. Something to remember?"

She slammed the door and waggled to the kitchen. A roll of paper towels was perched on the cooker hood. Hannelore grabbed it, tore off a couple of sheets, and ran upstairs in tears. Pieter was working on his own today after all. Why had she baited him for no reason?

Van In lit the cigarette. Sister Marie-Louise grabbed a saucer from under a potted plant and placed it in front of him.

"I shouldn't really be telling you this, but . . ."

"Don't worry, Sister. Whatever you say will be held in the strictest confidence, as if I were your confessor."

The image was a simple one, but it worked. Clichés always worked, even with nuns.

"You were asking about Jonathan."

Van In nodded.

"Jonathan was abandoned as an infant. Social services entrusted him to us." Sister Marie-Louise smiled. "He was found in the restroom of a department store. His mother had wrapped him in toilet paper and left him on the floor. It was December twenty-fourth, *nota bene*."

"A Christmas Carol."

"What was that, Commissioner?"

"It sounds like a Christmas tale, Sister."

"And it was, it was. Everyone fell in love with the child. Especially Guy, who saw the baby as a sign."

"Guy?"

"Guy Deridder. The janitor. He was over the moon. He and his wife took pity on little Jonathan from the outset. They treated him like their own son."

"Is it possible to have a word with them?" Van In asked.

Sister Marie-Louise lowered her eyes, as though recounting a painful memory. "The Deridders wanted to adopt the boy. But . . ."

Van In puffed at his cigarette, and as the clouds of smoke drifted upward to the pristine white ceiling he thought of Hannelore and of the child he hadn't wanted at first but now longed for with all his heart. Blood of his blood, soul of his soul. Only children can make you immortal.

"In spite of the fact that Mrs. Deridder was infertile, the couple were still refused permission to adopt little Jonathan. The commission decided they didn't think the Deridders would offer him a decent future. They had very little room at home, and they didn't earn enough money to deal with a baby's needs."

Van In tried to follow Sister Marie-Louise's logic. "But didn't they both work for the orphanage?"

The sister brushed both her hands over the coarse cloth of her skirt, something women often did when struggling with embarrassment. "We thought they were happy with what they had. A child would only have made their work so much more complicated."

The Catholic inclination to think for others was still alive and kicking.

"Would it be possible to have a little chat with them about it?" asked Van In a second time.

Marie-Louise didn't respond right away. Mother Superior would be furious if she found out she'd been talking about the Deridder affair. But what could she do? The commissioner wasn't going to be fobbed off. She hunted desperately for a solution.

Lying was a sin that could be forgiven, but first she had to come up with a plausible story.

"Guy Deridder resigned two years ago," she said. "We haven't heard a word from him since then."

"I don't believe you, Sister," said Van In, looking her in the eye. He might just as well have said: Sisters shouldn't lie.

Marie-Louise looked down at her hands. "Guy Deridder was a thief," she admitted. "He tricked us out of millions."

Van In lit another cigarette. This was getting interesting. Marie-Louise took a deep breath and told him the entire story. Deridder had won the community's confidence and had worked his way up from janitor to accountant, a task he acquitted with exceptional skill. The monastery profited considerably from his bookkeeping creativity, and no one was the least bit suspicious, not until the adoption question arose. When the social workers turned down the Deridders' application, arguing that their financial position didn't allow them to consider adoption, the Deridders submitted a bank statement confirming that they had more than three million francs in their savings account. An investigation revealed that Guy Deridder was a cheat, but the social workers were never informed because Mother Superior insisted on drawing a discreet veil over the scandal, and the Deridders were permitted to remain employed.

"Guy's wife never recovered from the dishonor. I heard she passed away. Ovarian cancer. Guy worked in a hospital for a while after that."

Van In scratched the back of his left ear. The whole business was more complex than he had expected, and the deeper he dug into the past of those involved, the further he strayed from the murder of Trui Andries.

"Didn't the convent press charges?"

Marie-Louise shook her head. She didn't dare mention that the sisters had also profited substantially from Deridder's creative accounting, in spite of the three million loss. Their former janitor had been smart enough not to keep it all for himself. The sisters should have handed over their share of his ill-gotten gains to the appropriate government office, but they hadn't. As a result, they were just as guilty as Deridder.

"Am I correct in saying that Guy Deridder had no connections with Trui Andries and Jasper Simons?"

"That's correct," said Marie-Louise. "The janitor wasn't involved with the other staff."

Van In shook Sister Marie-Louise's cold and bony hand. The frail sister accompanied him to the main entrance, keeping an appropriate distance as they walked along the gloomy corridor. Van In thought of Saartje. *Life would be so much easier if all women looked like Sister Marie-Louise.*

He started the Golf and drove to the nearest florist's shop, where he bought a large bouquet of orchids. He had decided to spend the rest of the day with Hannelore. If she still wanted him, of course.

"I did what you asked, Master," said Jonathan.

As proof that he had fulfilled his task, he handed Venex a key. In exchange, he received a triple dose of heroin.

"I'm very satisfied, Jonathan. Go now and become one with the world on the other side. There you will see Trui and Jasper again, and you will be happy together."

Venex accompanied Jonathan to the front door. He had reasoned like a general in the heat of battle. Defeating the enemy was a question of tactics, a pliable strategy that accounted for the circumstances in which the struggle was being waged. He no longer needed to be concerned about Trui or Jasper or Jonathan, and Coleyn would keep his mouth shut as long as his supply was assured. The only remaining obstacle was Van In, and the commissioner had a pleasant surprise in store.

"You made the right decision," said Venex when Jonathan said good-bye.

"Thank you, Father." Jonathan lowered his eyes. He felt like the Nazarene on the cross. *It is accomplished.*

8

The Bible says the seventh day belongs to God. For once, Van In had not begged to differ and had devoted the rest of the weekend to the lesser known Morpheus, the god of dreams. After a stormy reconciliation, he and Hannelore had retired to bed around eight the previous evening and had slept like innocent children for sixteen uninterrupted hours. They were still in bed. It was three degrees below zero outside and a tree branch lashed the windows in the wind and roused Van In from his slumber. He sat up, took a look outside, then turned and huddled up against Hannelore's back. The warmth she radiated mingled with the memory of his last dream and he dozed off again.

The central heating in Saint Jacob's Church on Moer Street waged a one-sided battle with the ice-cold east wind that howled mercilessly through the door every time another latecomer entered the building. In the old days, pastors would complain about that sort of thing, but now that so few people attended church, they counted themselves lucky to have a congregation of sorts. The number of weekend masses had been reduced to a mere two, but even then, less than a couple of hundred diehards made the effort. Not what you would call busy for a parish with five thousand parishioners.

The eleven thirty mass usually attracted the biggest crowd. People tended to prefer the later hour.

"Go in peace to love and serve the Lord."

Numb with cold, the assembled faithful responded in haste: "Thanks be to God."

The organist pounded the keys and drove the parishioners outside with a mangled version of Johann Sebastian Bach's *Toccata and Fugue in D Minor.*

The dry cracks that followed one another in quick succession sounded like the rattle of machine-gun fire. Hannelore opened her eyes in a daze, leaned over to the window, and peered through the curtain. There it was again. . . . *Ratatatat, ratatatatat.* She pushed Van In onto his back and sat upright.

"Did you hear that?"

Van In's open mouth produced a snore that sounded like an angry growl. Hannelore glanced at her watch. Was it really twelve fifteen?

A short five minutes later, the first sirens rent the Sunday silence. They seemed to be coming from every point of the compass and increasing ominously in volume. Hannelore shook Van In to wake him. When she didn't immediately succeed, she threw off the comforter and jumped to her feet.

"Jesus," she said. "Something terrible must have happened." She scurried downstairs, leaving the bedroom door wide open. Van In groped around without opening his eyes and tried to pull the comforter over his head. When that failed, he rolled over on his side once again and fumbled fruitlessly for the warm body that was no longer there.

"Pieter! Get down here, for Christ's sake."

Now he too could hear the sirens. It sounded as if the entire Bruges police fleet had landed in front of his door. He scrambled to his feet, pulled on his pajama bottoms and slippers, and joined Hannelore at the front door. They watched the emergency services flashing past the intersection of the Vette Vispoort and Moer Street.

"I'm going to take a look." Van In made a move to go outside.

Hannelore held him back.

"In your pajamas?"

At the side door of Saint Jacob's, all hell had broken loose. A dozen police officers were doing their best to calm the hysteria and keep the road open for ambulances as they waited for reinforcements. By the time Van In arrived on the scene, the provincial disaster management plan had already been set in motion. A Medical Emergency Team doctor was assessing the wounded and handing out color-coded wristbands. Up to four additional doctors were on their way, hardly enough given the extent of the calamity. According to initial estimates, there were eight dead and seventeen wounded, three of them seriously. Van In grabbed the first officer he could get his hands on and asked what was going on.

"All I know is some crazy guy let loose with a machine gun in the church." The young officer had a lump in his throat and was having trouble holding his tears in check. "I don't get it . . ."

"Have they arrested anyone?"

"You'll have to ask Fier, Commissioner. He was first to arrive."

Van In wormed his way through the tangle of caregivers offering first aid to the wounded. A child had taken a direct hit to the chest, and one of the caregivers was trying in desperation to stop the bleeding. The entire situation was so surreal, Van In still wasn't completely sure what had happened. The blood and the mutilated victims made Moer Street look like Sarajevo after a mortar attack.

Inspector Ronald Fier was doing his level best to bring some order to the chaos. He had called in for assistance from the federal police and the Red Cross. A truck was on its way with crush barriers to close off the street, and the governor and mayor had been informed about the bloodbath. Everything was running according to plan, and no one could accuse him of screwing up, but he was still happy to see Van In emerge from the crowd. Clearing the area was going to be difficult, and he needed all the help he could get. They had simulated disasters in training, but nothing could have prepared them for this. People ran back and forth, shouting, trying to offer help, unaware that they were actually in the way.

"Did anyone see the gunman?" Van In shouted.

Fier stared at the commissioner in surprise. In all the commotion he hadn't thought about the killer.

Van In didn't push the matter. "Give me your walkie-talkie, Fier."

The order wasn't intended to be as blunt as it sounded. Fier didn't mind. He was more than content that someone was taking charge.

"Close off the street and start rounding up eyewitnesses inside the church. It's warmer in there."

"I'll do my best, Commissioner."

Fier scurried off. A choir of sirens in the distance announced the arrival of reinforcements. Van In glanced at his watch. It was twelve thirty, and Hannelore had jumped out of bed at twelve fifteen? The killer couldn't have gotten far, not even in a car. He pressed the speak button on the walkie-talkie and asked for the duty officer.

The incident room was a hive of activity, with people milling around and the telephones ringing incessantly. The officer on duty, a corpulent deputy commissioner, was out of breath from all the toing and froing. *Why on a Sunday*, he thought, *and why on my watch?*

"Rocher here," he said, ignoring the usual walkie-talkie etiquette on account of the emergency situation.

Van In said, "I want every police corps and federal brigade within a range of twenty miles placed on standby. We need as many officers on the streets as humanly possible. Try to close off the main roads and have them check every vehicle."

The duty officer took a deep breath. His blood pressure was edging higher and higher. *What's he thinking? That I've got six arms?* He wanted to say he was on his own, but Van In didn't give him the chance. He broke the connection.

Hannelore was hard at work. She had wrapped herself up against the cold and was interviewing the first eyewitnesses who had assembled at the back of the church.

"He was driving a gray Toyota, ma'am," said an elderly man who had witnessed the massacre at close quarters. He was bleeding from a wound on his forehead, which he dabbed incessantly with a cotton handkerchief. He was a war veteran and had been in worse predicaments.

"With all due respect"—a piercing female voice forced its way uninvited into the conversation—"but if you ask me it was a Ford Fiesta."

The neatly dressed war veteran grunted. "It was gray, I'm sure of that."

Hannelore turned and concentrated on the new witness. "Are you sure, ma'am?"

The elderly lady with peroxide blond hair nodded conclusively as she caressed her fur coat—a genuine mink that she had received as a gift from her husband after years of whining.

Fortunately it had been spared in the catastrophe. A bloodstain would have been unthinkable.

"Of course I'm sure. There's nothing wrong with my eyes. Eh, Eduard?" She cast a knowing glance in the direction of the man who had paid for the coat. Eduard had been branch manager of a major bank and had spent most of his private life playing second fiddle to his spouse, but in the circumstances he felt obliged to disagree with her observation.

"I thought it was a Renault, honey."

The glare with which the lady treated her husband seemed just as deadly as the hail of bullets that had initiated the bloodbath. Hannelore knew from experience that people behaved strangely in extreme circumstances—but with eight corpses on the sidewalk outside, the conversation was getting a little bizarre.

Van In had harvested a healthier crop of witnesses. A young churchgoer remembered the first three numbers on the car's license plate because they happened to be his initials. Van In scribbled the initials *PVA* in his notepad.

"And the make?"

"Sorry," he said. "I'm afraid I can't help you there. When the man started shooting, I hit the floor."

Van In understood.

"The car was definitely gray," said the young man when Van In asked if there was anything else he could remember.

Van In immediately sent out a description of the car and made his way to the church. Moer Street looked like something out of Dante's Inferno. The armada of ambulances grew larger by the minute. Doctors and nurses spread out their wares: catheters, sterile compresses, syringes, ripped packaging. Swirling lights enveloped the neighborhood in a nervous blue. Van In spotted a Renault Espace parked between the ambulances and recognized the logo of the local TV station. A cameraman was checking the reserve batteries that hung from a belt around his waist, clearly aware that batteries were more precious than gold at that moment. If his camera were to lose power, his producer would have him charged with criminal negligence. And rightly so. Something like this was a once-in-a-lifetime experience and soon his pictures would be transmitted all over the world. The public loved its daily portion of sensation, and he was going to provide it today.

Van In pushed open the church door. There wasn't a trace of the devotional silence that normally filled such buildings. The nave looked as if a hurricane had just passed through. The high-backed wicker chairs typical of most Flemish churches had been thrown all over the place. People huddled together weeping, trying to console one another. Those with minor injuries waited in the aisles on stretchers and filled the church with their groans. Inspector Fier had set up an improvised crisis center in the choir area and was desperately trying to coordinate operations on a borrowed mobile phone. Van In left him to it and joined Hannelore, who was in the middle of a heated discussion with public prosecutor Beekman.

"Prosecutor Beekman," said Van In, shaking the man's hand, which felt clammy in spite of the cold. Beekman had been through the wars in his career, but the despair on his face was almost tangible.

"I'm happy you're here, Pieter."

Van In nodded. The compliment pleased him. He leaned forward and kissed Hannelore on the forehead. "Make sure you don't catch cold," he said.

"I told her the same," said Beekman.

Van In realized only then that the prosecutor's leather jacket was draped over Hannelore's shoulders. Beekman was a modern magistrate, but deep inside he was a romantic who would have preferred to have lived at a time when *savoir-vivre* was more important than the inflated politenesses his function obliged him to maintain. In the company of Hannelore and Van In, he felt free to act like a normal human being.

"We have a description of the car," said Van In. "It's not much, but we have to start somewhere."

Beekman nodded. He would have to speak to the press later, and he was glad to have something to tell them. "I want you to lead the investigation, Pieter. You've got carte blanche, and I'll make sure you get everything you need to do your work."

Van In didn't argue. The fact that he was in the middle of another case was beside the point at the moment.

"I'm going to need all the help I can get, Prosecutor Beekman. And if you can throw in a miracle . . ." he added with a forced smile.

"We're in the right place, Pieter. Look around you," he said. "Saints and sinners everywhere."

The mayor of Bruges waited patiently while a hastily procured journalist readied himself for an interview for the commercial station. The journalist happened to be in town for a tourist program he was presenting, a fortunate accident that gave him an advantage of at least three hours over the public broadcaster. The staff at VTM—the Brussels-based commercial broadcaster—were working at fever pitch to prepare an extra news transmission and were almost ready to go on air.

"I've just been informed that eight people are confirmed dead. Three others have been taken to Saint Jan's Hospital in critical condition," said the mayor, looking straight into the camera. He had learned a lot in his four years as mayor. Without the usual scrap of paper with prewritten questions, he felt like a whale in shallow waters. Fortunately this was television, and no one expected him to say anything original. The images of the bloodbath would speak for themselves.

"I understand the disaster management plan was immediately implemented," the journalist said. "How long did it take for the emergency services to get here?"

The mayor nodded. A standard question. "The first ambulances were on the spot within five minutes."

"On the spot" was a phrase the mayor was to use many times in the course of the day.

"We've had our fair share of experience with major disasters," the mayor continued, referring to the capsizing of the MS *Herald of Free Enterprise* and the series of multiple collisions that had plagued the highways of West Flanders in recent years. "Our people are exceptionally well trained, and as you can see, they're doing an excellent job."

The interview was beginning to sound like soccer game commentary. The journalist was obliged to end it. Self-adulation was bad for audience ratings, and he had to take that into consideration. "If I'm not mistaken, the governor of West Flanders has just arrived . . ." The camera swerved in the direction of a farmer stuffed into a tailored suit.

While the politicians polished their images in front of the camera, Van In and Hannelore continued interviewing eyewitnesses undaunted, assisted by Fier and his men, Guido—who had heard the news via the radio—and Prosecutor Beekman. After more than four hours, during which each witness was questioned extensively, they managed to ascertain that a masked man or woman had opened fire on the churchgoers from a stationary gray car. One specific detail was intriguing. The shooter had waited until roughly thirty people had left the church before opening fire. Descriptions of the shooter ranged from heavy-built to skinny, and estimated age from twenty to fifty. Everything was carefully written down and passed on to the appropriate people but to no avail. The gray car with license plate PVA had not been spotted thus far.

"How does a cup of coffee back at my place sound?" asked Van In.

No one protested. The sacristan, who had spent the preceding half hour looking at his watch, produced his keys and hurried to the sacristy to lock up and switch off the lights.

"Glad to see the back of us," said Inspector Fier with a grin.

A couple of officers who had already made their way to the door laughed at the double entendre. Van In waited in the nave.

The powerful halogen lamps in the vaulted ceiling went out like a row of giant candles, engulfing the church in a cheerless half-light. Van In was reminded of something he'd heard Guido say: *Light needs darkness to justify its existence.* In the darkness, the church was suddenly sinister and eerie. The monumental rood screen behind the altar had been reduced to a vague silhouette, and the rounded arches on either side were filled with blackness, granting access to an uncanny world. The polished floor tiles reflected the streetlight that filtered through the massive windows of the building, transforming the floor into a dismal and desolate lake. The other side, where freedom beckoned, was unreachable. Hideous monsters lurked under its treacherous surface, waiting patiently for a foot to disturb the water, then snapping in an instant and dragging their prey into the deep. As a boy, Van In had had countless dreams about being locked up in a large building, terrified to move, an unutterable menace hiding in every corner and behind every door. Even when he woke up drenched in sweat, he was afraid to move a muscle for minutes on end.

"Hey, Pieter. Are you planning to join us?" Hannelore's sonorous voice tugged him back to reality. She walked toward him, took him by the arm, and said: "You're not thinking of spending the night here, are you?"

Van In shook his head, and Hannelore steered him to the door. Ridiculous as it may have sounded, he was happy to be outside again.

Moer Street was deserted. Beekman had insisted the street be closed off until the forensics team had finished their work, and they still had hours to go. They had recovered fifty-six empty shells thus far. Every bullet hole was marked with chalk and photographed, as were the positions of the victims.

"It looks as if he used a Kalashnikov," said Beekman. "At least that's what the experts are saying."

Van In put his arm around Hannelore's shoulder. In spite of the prosecutor's leather jacket, she was shivering like a reed in the wind.

The group zigzagged in the direction of the Vette Vispoort, avoiding the pools of blood that had been sprinkled with sand and the chalk lines that marked the contours of the dead.

At home, Van In installed Hannelore in front of the open hearth and ordered her not to move. Guido disappeared into the kitchen to take care of the coffee. Since the living room was too small to accommodate the entire group, the younger officers automatically assembled in the kitchen, while the senior officers remained in the living room with their superiors. Hierarchy wasn't an empty concept.

"If I'd said five years ago that this could happen in Bruges, everyone would've laughed in my face," said Van In. "Even Los Angeles doesn't have to deal with events like this every day."

"We've always understood this kind of thing as something American," said Beekman. "According to the FBI, motiveless crime is on the rise in the United States, and it's a cause of major concern."

Van In lit a cigarette, and a few of the others immediately followed suit.

"Any ideas on how you plan to approach the case, Pieter?" Beekman inquired.

Just as Van In was about to formulate an answer, the bell rang. He excused himself and made his way to the front door, hoping his in-laws hadn't decided to ruin his day completely.

When he opened the door, Saartje Maes stood there wearing jeans and a pilot's jacket lined with wool. Her makeup was restrained, and she smelled of spring flowers.

"I'm not disturbing you, I hope," she said with an inviting smile.

Van In stepped back and let her in.

"I saw the news on the TV and thought . . ." Five pairs of greedy eyes exploring her body from the living room doorway forced her to cut short her sentence. "The sacristan told me you were here."

Her voice was devoid of emotion, or better said, she sounded elated. The bloodbath had added a new element of excitement to her job. Van In helped her out of her jacket, and she headed toward the kitchen like a model on a catwalk.

"Hi, Guido," she said. Guido, who was arranging cups on a tray, pretended to smile and then treated his boss to an accusatory glare. Van In responded with an I-couldn't-send-her-packing look and followed her into the living room. Before he had the chance to offer her a seat, she had snuggled in between Hannelore and Beekman on the sofa.

"May I introduce Prosecutor Beekman," Van In said stiffly.

Saartje shook the prosecutor's hand, nonchalant, barely looking at him. It was clear that she was more interested in Hannelore.

"Miss Martens. How are you?"

Van In avoided Hannelore's eyes and the almost tangible suspicion they exuded. Guido arrived with the coffee and saved the moment.

"I suggest we get back to business after the coffee," Van In said when the clatter of cups and spoons had subsided. "I want reports on my desk tomorrow morning."

None of his colleagues complained for once, thanks to the presence of the public prosecutor, of course.

"Our first priority is to trace the killer's car. The vehicle records office staff have promised to fax a list of license plates beginning with the letters PVA. As soon as we have the list, we'll start with the gray cars. If that doesn't work, we'll move on to other combinations."

Van In briefed his men and kept an eye on the women. Hannelore was dozing off, and the look on Saartje's face didn't bode well.

"If the boys from forensics come up with new information, we check it out immediately. In the meantime . . ."

The telephone rang and everyone jumped. Van In ran into the kitchen and picked up the receiver. "Van In speaking."

The conversation lasted no more than thirty seconds. Van In scribbled a couple of illegible words on a piece of paper towel. The triumphant smile on his face when he hung up suggested good news.

"The Blankenberge police have spotted a gray Fiat in front of the train station with PVA 256 on its plates. The car belongs to a certain Bart Muylle, an unemployed metalworker with an offense record. There are traces of blood on the driver's door. What do we do, sir?" he said, turning to Beekman.

Under normal circumstances, the public prosecutor would have insisted on further investigation, but the present situation was too serious for delay.

"Go get him, Pieter. And don't take risks. The man is dangerous, and today's death toll is already too high."

9

Jeruzalem Street was located in the middle of a blue-collar district appropriately known as the Verloren Hoek, or Abandoned Corner, a part of the city where a handful of Bruges residents had somehow managed to escape the advance of tourism, a genuine little miracle in the shadow of the Church of Saint Anna. In spite of the wave of renovations and the invasion of property speculators, the neighborhood had largely succeeded in preserving its own identity. The Verloren Hoek was an oasis of calm, and its residents were proud of it.

The convoy of police vehicles that drove into the street thus caused something of a stir. Those who hadn't yet fallen asleep in front of their televisions emerged from their homes in great haste and offered noisy commentary on this bizarre display of law enforcement muscle. In less than a couple of minutes, a quick-witted schoolteacher had established a link between the police presence and the mass shooting. Her words spread like wildfire through the crowd, and the tension increased to the point of being palpable.

Van In had requisitioned four SSVs and three Golfs. The vehicles were manned by twenty-two officers in combat gear. Half belonged to the so-called Argus Platoon, Chief Commissioner De Kee's showpiece. The elite unit was deployed in high-risk situations—often at soccer matches known for their hooligan supporters—and consisted of officers who had undergone special training. Van In directed the assembled forces like an aging general. He gave his men time to ready themselves then divided the tasks to the best of his ability. When everyone was in position, he and Guido made their way to the front door of the suspect's house. A strip of light under the curtains suggested the man was at home. Van In found it hard to imagine that someone who had just murdered eight people in cold blood could be relaxing in front of the TV a couple of hours later as if nothing had happened. He announced via his walkie-talkie that Operation Condor—Beekman's idea—was good to go.

"Are we ready?"

Guido nodded. The entire neighborhood had been hermetically sealed, and every possible line of escape was manned by a couple of heavily armed officers.

As Van In rang the bell, he could hear a pair of loudspeakers in the living room blasting the Sisters of Mercy, taxed to their limit, the bass tones buzzing ominously. The suspect couldn't possibly have heard the doorbell, but Van In waited fifteen seconds nevertheless, hoping secretly that the door would open and a respectable family man would welcome him in. The fifteen seconds became twenty, twenty-five . . . His mouth was dry, and he could feel the blood pounding in the artery in his neck. His stomach tightened. The eyes of his colleagues were focused on him. He didn't dare wait another second. Anxiety had its advantages. It generated adrenaline and made people do things they would otherwise avoid. Van In took a deep breath—a potential confrontation with a mass killer wasn't an everyday event—and gave orders to break down the door. One of the officers, the pride of the Argus Platoon, charged at the door but hurt his shoulder in the collision and beat a whining retreat. No one dared laugh.

"What now?" said Guido.

Operation Condor was beginning to look like a scene from a slapstick movie. Van In had once read that antiterror units used riot guns to blow a door off its hinges. A couple of explosions, a firm kick, and the job was done. *Shit.* Why hadn't he thought about riot guns earlier? But it was too late for riot guns. He had to improvise.

Van In drew his revolver, held it by the barrel, and smashed a window. The music was loud enough to drown out the sound of breaking glass, but everyone still held their breath. Guido stared at the star-shaped hole that was barely big enough for a cat to slip through and gestured to a couple of officers to remove the rest of the glass from the frame. One of them cut himself on the razor-sharp splinters and was forced to join his fellow officer in one of the SSVs. Van In could already see the headlines: "Two Officers Injured as Police Arrest Mass Killer."

When the job was finally done, Van In squeezed through the window, and the Argus Platoon followed with weapons drawn.

Bart Muylle's living room was bathed in the light of an upright halogen lamp. Besides the powerful music system, two CD racks, and a shabby lounge chair, the room was more or less empty.

Van In turned the volume to zero and the abrupt silence somehow robbed them of their sense of cover. The officers turned and waited to see what he would do. What *should* he do? They were like figures in a waxwork museum.

Five seconds later, loud footsteps could be heard in the corridor. The troops braced themselves. When Muylle finally stormed into the living room, the first person he saw was Guido, and the two stood face-to-face for a couple of seconds. The sergeant couldn't prevent his eyes from wandering downward. The man had to be at least six three and was as naked as a wild cave dweller. He had a thick chest of hair, and his arms and shoulders were tattooed with dragons and other monsters. He was wet, like he'd just stepped out of the shower.

Muylle stood still for an instant, then looked at the broken window and started to curse.

"What the . . . Are you crazy or what?" he said, his Bruges accent as thick as they come.

Van In thought his reaction was strange. Surely the man knew why they were there. But there was no turning back. "Bart Muylle," he said with a steady voice, "I'm arresting you on suspicion of murder."

As far as he could remember, this was the first time he had used the actual arrest formula. Words that could be heard every day on TV sounded even more ridiculous in real life than he had expected. Muylle seemingly shared his opinion, given the way he looked the troops up and down as though they were getting ready for a carnival parade. He grinned from ear to ear and lumbered toward Van In. "Kiss my ass, the lot of you!" he said.

Van In took a step backward, reason enough for the Argus Platoon to throw themselves in unison at Muylle. Muylle put up a fight, taking out a third officer in the process, but he didn't stand much of a chance.

When they cuffed him and took him outside, the crowd treated them to loud applause. Hundreds of locals jostled for space behind the police barriers, honest and upright citizens who were planning to pay their overdue parking fines the following day, and with the greatest of pleasure.

• • •

"So you spent the entire day in bed?" Van In made the statement sound like a question. Muylle was sitting in front of him on a chair, grim-faced and motionless. After the altercation in his living room, the police had dressed him and dumped him in an SSV as if he were a piece of dirt. During the trip from Jeruzalem Street to the police station, he had banged his head a couple of times—so to speak—on a metal protuberance. His left eye was badly swollen, and his upper lip looked like an overripe blackberry.

"I asked you a question, Mr. Muylle," said Van In, opting deliberately for the hard approach. This was his first-ever confrontation with a mass killer. And it was late. He wasn't in the mood to spend the entire night at the station.

"I told you ten times already."

The metalworker repeated the same words time after time, and as soon as the words *mass killer* were used, he cursed his interrogators black and blue. Guido started to take pity on the man. He had spent the last two hours insisting that he had staggered home after a late night of drinking at the Iron Virgin and had slept most of the day.

"Can anyone confirm your story?"

Muylle treated his interrogators to another string of curses. Were they all out of their minds?

Van In lit a cigarette and listened patiently to the aggrieved man's tirade. Did the commissioner have someone who sat by his bed at night in case he needed a witness?

"I was thinking of a girlfriend, Mr. Muylle. A witness would help verify your alibi and make the entire affair a whole lot simpler. Don't forget that several churchgoers recognized your car."

Beekman had had the Fiat brought over from Blankenberge

to Bruges in the course of the evening, and a number of witnesses had sworn it was the same vehicle. Forensics experts had examined it and there was no sign of forced entry. In their opinion, the car had not been stolen. Whoever drove the Fiat that day used the key and started it in the normal way.

"I didn't use the car yesterday."

"Can you prove that, Mr. Muylle?"

When the suspect embarked on yet another round of protest, Van In puffed nervously at his cigarette. Surely to God they hadn't picked up the wrong man!

"Could someone else have used it?"

A Pink Panther keychain with the keys to the Fiat attached lay in front of him on his desk. The reserve key, which they had found in the suspect's wallet, was lying beside it.

"I left the car in the garage Friday night," said Muylle, his anger unabated. "Just like every other weekend."

The year before, he had failed an alcohol test and had to pay a heavy fine. Since then he walked to and from the bar.

Van In sighed. This was going nowhere.

"So you're sticking to your statement."

"Of course I am, asshole."

"Does the name Jonathan Leman mean anything to you?"

Muylle shook his head.

"Jasper Simons?"

"Trui Andries?"

"Venex?"

The metalworker shook his head again and again.

"In that case, I've no other option, Mr. Muylle. Who knows, a night in the cell might change your mind."

Van In called the incident room. No one could accuse him of not doing his job . . . not that day, at least.

After two burly Argus Platoon officers had taken Muylle to his cell, Guido looked at the clock. It was twelve thirty a.m. Van In was examining a fax that had arrived half an hour earlier with the names of those who had lost their lives.

"I bought a new bottle of Jenever yesterday," said Guido. "Fancy a shot?"

Van In kicked off his shoes and put the fax to one side. His feet were swollen, and his lower legs tingled. "Only if you join me."

Guido was wearing fashionable chinos, a lambswool sweater, and a silk scarf. He and Frank had been enjoying dinner in a fancy restaurant in Oostende when the news came through, and he hadn't had time to change.

"Why not," he said, as if it were a crime.

The first shot made Van In cough. He stubbed out his half-smoked cigarette. His lungs felt as if they were lined with sandpaper. *High time I kicked this disgusting habit*, he thought. *What if I get lung cancer?* The antismoking lobby would have a field day. "What about a visit to the Iron Virgin, Guido?"

The fact that both Jonathan and Muylle were regulars at the place might be nothing more than coincidence, but Van In wasn't convinced. And the Iron Virgin was the only concrete link he had between the Andries case and the mass shooting.

"It's on my way home," said Guido. If he let Van In go alone, he could bank on it that the commissioner would hit the Duvels big-time and be late for work the next day, which was something he had to prevent, whatever the cost.

The Iron Virgin was once just an ordinary bar, barely distinguishable from dozens of others on Bruges's Long Street. The present proprietor, known to his "friends" as El Shit, had kept the original furniture and spent less than eight thousand francs on "refurbishments." A toilet seat served as an umbrella stand—and a place to vomit in an emergency—and the headless statue of one or another saint filled the space where an antique Wurlitzer had once stood. El Shit had sold the jukebox for a small fortune and treated himself to a week of sex in Bangkok with a portion of the proceeds. He invested the rest in a West Flemish company that had recently made the news after an American electronics giant had forked out two billion francs in exchange for a minority interest.

Van In leaned against the bar door to be welcomed by a hundred-decibel wave rolling out onto the street. The foul stench of "aromatic" cigarette smoke punched him in the face. It was a public secret that soft drugs were available for purchase in the Iron Virgin. Like several other Flemish cities, Bruges maintained a policy of tolerance, although it didn't brag about it.

El Shit was standing behind the bar, and he welcomed Van In and Guido with a condescending sneer—he knew Van In from the papers. As long as the cops didn't find any hard drugs on the premises, they couldn't touch him.

"Gentleman, what can I get you?" he shouted.

"A Duvel," said Van In, and he turned to Guido.

The sergeant pointed to a table where a leather-clad heavy-metal adept was drinking a cup of coffee. "And a coffee," he said, articulating each word so that El Shit could read his lips.

Saartje Maes had spotted Van In and Guido the moment they walked in the door. It would be stupid to wait until they spotted her, so she decided to take the initiative. She wormed her way between a couple of tables, defying the groping hands of the men who happened to be in her way. The smell of leather and stale beer turned her on, and the uncomplicated interest of men who considered themselves rugged pumped her ego. Saartje knew her body and she also knew what a subtle cleavage and a tight skirt could do. She was a child of her time and wasn't afraid to exploit it.

Van In turned abruptly when he felt a hand on his shoulder and was visibly taken aback at the sight of her. Saartje smiled when she noticed the surprise in his eyes. She threw her arm over his shoulder and pulled him to her cheek. He didn't resist. Alarm bells started to go off in Guido's head.

"I figured you'd show up sooner or later," she roared in his ear.

Her breath gave him goose bumps. They were standing pelvis to pelvis, and he could feel the heat of her thighs through his pants. There was nothing special about the situation and he could have ended it with a single gesture, but he didn't. Were the marijuana fumes responsible for his weakness or did the black widow finally have him where she wanted him?

Van In pressed his lips against her ear. It looked like a kiss. At least that's what Guido thought.

"Is there somewhere we can have a quiet word?"

Saartje nodded, raised her hand, and gestured to El Shit that she wanted to ask him something.

The bar had a little hall at the back where obscure metal groups regularly raised the roof. After months of complaints from the neighbors, the mayor had threatened to serve the Iron Virgin with a closure notice if nothing was done about the excessive noise. El Shit struck a deal and brought in a firm of specialists to soundproof both the bar and the hall. Van In heaved a sigh of relief when El Shit closed the door behind him and left them alone in an oasis of silence.

"You're probably wondering what I'm doing here," said Saartje as she sat down on the stage and dangled her legs over the edge. Guido installed himself at one of the tables with his coffee, curious to hear what kind of story she would come up with this time around. Van In paced up and down, not really sure what to do with himself. Sitting next to her wasn't an option with Guido watching.

"You read my thoughts."

Saartje smiled. "A friend told me that a satanist group met here, and with everything that's happened in the last couple of days I was curious and . . ."

Van In wondered for a second where she'd picked up on the satanism link, but quickly put two and two together. The police report on Trui Andries was in the top drawer of his desk and the drawer wasn't locked. "So you decided to start your own little investigation . . ."

"Something like that."

"Results?"

"Most of the people here think the killing spree in front of the church was cool. Everyone's talking about it."

Van In shook his head. If the Iron Virgin was home base for a satanic sect and both Jonathan and Muylle were regulars, then it figured that . . .

"Is that why you're here?" Saartje slipped from the stage to the floor and straightened her skirt. Van In tried not to look. "You promised you'd keep me up to date, Commissioner."

She added a friendly smile to her reproach, leaving Van In more or less powerless. He told her what they had discovered in the last forty-eight hours, without going into too much detail.

"What do we do now?" asked Guido.

Van In wasn't sure. Everything had happened so fast that he was having a hard time analyzing all the information at a normal pace.

"I suggest we call the public prosecutor. Let him decide."

"Isn't that a bit premature, Commissioner?" said Saartje. "The satanists who meet here aren't the people you're looking for."

"Let me be the judge of that," Van In snapped.

Saartje nodded, then turned and walked away. *He better not say I didn't warn him*, she thought.

• • •

There were no records of the Bruges police ever having been ordered out en masse twice in the space of twenty-four hours, but the assistance they received from the federal police was no longer unusual. On paper, both forces worked together in perfect harmony, especially when the public prosecutor twisted the arms of both superintendents. Beekman was a man of his word. He had promised Van In he would make available whatever the Bruges police needed and he kept that promise. This was also an intervention that was likely to score highly with the general public. Everyone knew that the Iron Virgin sold drugs. Even if Van In had the wrong end of the stick, no one would blame him for ordering the raid.

At precisely one forty-five a.m., thirty-five law enforcers in combat dress burst through the doors of the Iron Virgin. Everyone present was taken to the police station for questioning, no excuses. The intensity of the raid—the federal boys were armed with machine guns—left the impression that it was all over in half an hour.

"So that's that," said Van In from behind the bar. He served himself a Duvel.

El Shit was sitting on the toilet seat surveying the mayhem. It looked as if a tornado had ripped through his bar. Chairs and tables were piled up against the wall, and there was glass all over the floor. "Can someone tell me what the fuck is going on?" he rasped.

"You'll save yourself and us a great deal of effort if you supply us with the names of the sect members," said Beekman as he lit a cigarette. Van In had known the man for at least two years and had never seen him smoke.

"Sect members? Don't make me laugh."

"So you deny that satanists frequent your bar?" Van In asked.

El Shit shook his head. "If you're talking about the Sons of Asmodeus, then I'm afraid you'll be disappointed."

"So they have a name."

"Of course they have a name. Every club has a name."

Van In gulped at his Duvel. He was so tired that the beer gave him a lift. *A bad omen*, he thought. He could expect to pay for his excesses, big-time.

"Was Bart Muylle a member?"

"Another disappointment, Commissioner. Bart Muylle hated all that business. He only came for the music and the women. The rest didn't interest him."

Van In had a nasty premonition. El Shit seemed to be telling the truth. "Tell us more about the Sons of Asmodeus."

"No problem. I can even show you their temple." He got to his feet and walked behind the bar.

"Excuse me, Commissioner." He bent down to the floor, and Van In stepped out of his way. It was only then that he realized he'd been standing on a wooden trapdoor.

Like most of the buildings in Bruges, the Iron Virgin had a reasonably spacious cellar. El Shit led the way, descending the steep stairs and switching on the light.

"This is their clubhouse," he said.

The walls of the cellar—five by eight, vaulted ceiling—had been painted black, and a pentagram had been etched on the floor. An improvised altar with a battered chalice and a pair of candlesticks with black candles graced the middle of the room. Guido, Beekman, and Saartje followed closely behind Van In and El Shit.

"Some bars have bridge clubs, we have a satanic sect. And if I'm not mistaken, they have a constitutional right to do what they do."

"Don't push it, Mr. Baels," said Beekman.

So El Shit has a name, thought Van In. Beekman had done his homework.

"I'm still trying to work out what I did wrong," said the bar owner. "You can see for yourselves that this is innocent stuff. Okay, there's a bit of monkey business now and again, but if they spill anything, it certainly isn't blood."

Van In nodded. He glanced at Saartje, who smiled as if she knew exactly what El Shit was talking about. The cellar inspection was over in a couple of minutes.

"Is that the founder of the sect?" Van In asked, pointing to a grainy photo of an elderly man with a fuzzy white beard.

Baels shook his head. "That's Father Van Haecke," he said. "Never heard of him?"

The name rang a bell with Guido, but the context eluded him.

"Lodewijk Van Haecke was chaplain to the Basilica of the Holy Blood for the best part of half a century," said Baels. "Most of the sources say he was a pious, God-fearing man, a bit eccentric perhaps but an undeniably decent priest." The sarcasm in his voice was loud and clear. "Others claim that Van Haecke was a notorious satanist, a demon worshipper, the lowest of the low. That's how J. K. Huysmans described him in one of his books. According to Huysmans, Van Haecke celebrated black masses in Paris and mixed with the upper echelons of society, mostly women. Huysmans was also convinced that Bruges was a hotbed of satanism. And history proved him right. At this moment in time there are at least four or five satanist associations in the city."

"Are you a satanist, Mr. Baels?" Beekman asked.

El Shit brushed off the question with a wave of his hand. "I'm a self-employed bar owner, Prosecutor Beekman. People expect me to know my merchandise, that's all."

Van In lit a cigarette. Smoking in a temple dedicated to Satan wasn't sacrilegious, was it? "Continue, Mr. Baels."

El Shit had studied law in a previous life, and he knew the power of a passionate plea. "Even the Old Testament talks about the fallen angel who was jealous of God's creation. Like Prometheus, Lucifer stole fire from heaven and used it to win favor on earth. He re-created the world in his own image, a world in which greed and lust for power are considered the ultimate virtues."

"A familiar story," said Van In.

"The Sons of Asmodeus are actually descendants of the Cathars. They tried to outwit the demiurge and—"

"If you could provide us with the names of the Sons of Asmodeus, Mr. Baels, that would be much appreciated. We can check the rest at the public library."

El Shit was smart enough to realize that Van In wasn't interested in the rest of his story, but he still made a final effort to get his companions off the hook. "If you're looking for real satanists, Commissioner, you're in the wrong place. The real ones are discreet about what they do. They don't flaunt their symbols and they don't have temples in bar cellars. I'm afraid you're making a big mistake. . . ."

"The names, Mr. Baels."

El Shit was exceptionally cooperative. He scribbled the names of the Sons of Asmodeus on the back of a couple of beer coasters. He listed nineteen Sons, but neither Jonathan nor Bart Muylle were among them.

"What they get up to in the cellar is meaningless," said El Shit, tired but sure of himself. "It goes with the image of the bar. You didn't expect a bridge club, did you?" He was starting to repeat himself.

"Let us be the judge of that," said Beekman.

10

Van In rarely watched breakfast television, but this morning was a professional exception. Prosecutor Beekman had managed to convince the producer of the morning news program to broadcast a description of Jonathan. The item occupied a serious chunk of time between the adverts and the rehashed news from the day before.

"Do you think anything will come from it?" asked Hannelore as she waddled from the kitchen table to the stove. Her legs were swollen, and a varicose vein slumbered on her left calf. The pregnancy was beginning to exhaust her, and she was counting the days until it was over.

"He can't hide forever," said Van In. "Someone has to spot him sooner or later."

He had just been on the phone to the station. The Iron Virgin's clients had been interrogated through the night, but the results were meager, to say the least. Even the Sons of Asmodeus—Beekman had had each of them brought in in the early hours—swore by all that was holy that Bart Muylle wasn't a member of their little fraternity. They were aware that Jonathan belonged to another satanic sect, but only because he was always going on about it. The most interesting detail to emerge from their interrogation was the fact that a couple of the Sons knew Richard Coleyn. They described him as a loner, born into money but now in the gutter, convinced he was going to be stinking rich one day soon. Van In sighed. It was going to take a while to verify all the statements, so he decided to have the duty officer get Richard Coleyn out of bed in the meantime. This time he wasn't going to let the little bastard slip through his fingers.

"Unless he's watching breakfast TV himself," Hannelore sneered.

Van In was lost in thought, and her remark made him jump.

"Who?" he asked.

"Jonathan, of course." She cracked a couple of eggs into a pan.

Van In understood what she meant. The media liked to brag about the number of crimes they helped to solve, but publicity cut both ways. It was easy to forget that the enemy might also be listening.

The eggs sizzled in the hot pan as the whites set neatly around the yolks.

"All's fair in love and war," said Van In. "The public expects action. If Beekman had done nothing, they'd be down his neck screaming bloody murder. I wouldn't like to be in his shoes right now, let me tell you."

A crispy black border formed around the egg whites. Hannelore grabbed a plate. She didn't mind playing the housewife, although she had been sure from the outset that she would hate it. It was a temporary state of affairs, of course. After the pregnancy, she was planning to give Van In a crash course in home economics. Young fathers usually fell for that kind of thing; at least, that's what her mother had told her.

"What's the next step?" Hannelore placed the plate with the fried eggs in front of Van In and joined him at the table. The thought of food turned her stomach. She had looked at herself in the mirror that morning and was convinced the sight had ruined her appetite. If the baby weighed nine pounds—which was more than reasonable—that meant she still had to lose another thirty. And what was going to happen to her breasts? What once were melons were now balloons and she had the feeling they were about to explode. She thought of pictures she had seen of African women, saddled with a pair of loose flaps for the rest of their lives after a string of pregnancies. She shuddered inside.

"First a word or two with Richard Coleyn," said Van In. "For the moment, he's the only one who can provide more information about Jasper, Trul, and Jonathan."

He prodded one of the eggs with his fork and dipped a chunk of bread into the runny yellow yolk. He had to admit that he was having trouble digesting all the information. The killing of Trui Andries raised more questions than he could answer, and the file on the mass shooting was swelling so fast that no one would have time to read all the reports and statements it contained, let alone its conclusions. He had tried without success to connect the two cases. He could put more people on the case, of course, but experience had taught him that more people meant more chaos.

"Do you still think that the killing of Trui Andries and the mass shooting have something to do with that mysterious sect?"

Van In wiped his plate clean with a crust of bread. He hadn't enjoyed breakfast this much in years. "I'm not sure, Hanne. Sherlock Holmes always had something relevant to go on, but in this case I'm struggling to separate the wheat from the chaff. If only I'd been born a hundred years ago."

Hannelore put her arm around his shoulder and gave him a kiss. "I've asked myself so many times why I fell in love with you, Van In," she said.

Van In was taken aback. He still didn't understand the female mind. "And have you found the answer?" he asked.

"Because you're an incorrigible romantic, Pieter."

Van In lit a cigarette and tried to conceal his nerves. Did women have a sixth sense when faced with potential competition, or was he just imagining things?

"Please accept my condolences, Mr. Frederik. The staff also wish to express their deepest sympathies."

Frederik's father's senior clerk was dressed in a black suit and black tie and was clearly very shaken. "Everyone here had enormous respect and affection for your father and mother. This brutal mass killing has shocked us profoundly. We are all praying that the man responsible will be brought to justice without delay."

Frederik was a little hungover. He and Master Venex had dispatched three bottles of the best Margaux the evening before, and the heavy Bordeaux was still playing tricks on him. The roof of his mouth was as dry as cork, and the excess of alcohol had left him with a blocked nose. The latter was somewhat to his advantage, however, since it gave the impression that he had spent the night in tears.

"Thank you. Your words of sympathy are a great support." Frederik stumbled, and the senior clerk rushed to help him.

"Shall I call a doctor, sir?" he asked, clearly concerned.

"No, no, no need. I didn't get much sleep last night, that's all. I'll be fine."

"But Mr. Frederik!" The elderly clerk had been in Frederik's father's employ when Frederick was born and had watched him grow up.

"I'm already feeling better," said Frederik, grabbing the handrail along the stairs. The Margaux had left him in a pretty bad way. Three bottles. 1982. If his father had known, he would've wrung his neck.

"Are you sure?"

Frederik buttoned his bathrobe. There was a box of beluga caviar in the fridge, fifty ounces of pure pleasure, ninety-five thousand francs' worth of the stuff. His parents had been planning to celebrate their silver wedding anniversary next week, a party that naturally had to be canceled given the circumstances. His father had always maintained that caviar was the best remedy for a hangover, and Frederick now had the chance to put his father's motto to the test.

"I suggest you all take the rest of the day off," he said.

"But sir . . ."

"That's what my late father would have wanted."

The clerk nodded. "I'm sure the staff will appreciate your gesture, Mr. Frederik."

Room 204 was a hive of activity, and atypically so. Police officers scurried in and out, depositing large piles of paper on Commissioner Van In's desk. Guido watched the desk fill and knew what came next. While paperwork was an inseparable part of police work, most detectives hated the administrative side of the job with a vengeance. Guido was no exception. He sat down at his desk, ignored the papers, and punched in the telephone number he had looked up the night before.

As the hot water of the shower embraced Saartje Maes's body, she wondered how Van In and Guido had gotten on at the Iron Virgin. Then her thoughts turned to her commission. The two cops were less of a problem than she had expected. Van In actually seemed competent. So why did she still have to be such an arrogant pain in the ass? Be confident, her bosses had told her during training, self-assured. Let people see you're in charge. Seduce and prevail. What a pile of crap!

Fuck the big boys in Brussels and fuck the journalist act. It was time to let the commissioner see the real Saartje Maes.

At nine thirty-five, when Van In arrived in Room 204, Guido was busy on the phone. He nodded continually, and the look with which he greeted Van In didn't bode well. At least there was coffee. Van In helped himself, sat down at his desk, grabbed a police report, and started to read.

I, the undersigned, hereby declare that . . .

Van In struggled through a couple of pages. The witness was a regular at the Iron Virgin, and you could tell from his signature that the man hadn't finished high school.

I knew people messed around in the cellar—copulated, the officer on duty had written between brackets—but that sort of thing went on all over the place. . . . I know nothing about Satanism. I went to the technical school. . . . They don't teach that kind of stuff there. Bart Muylle is a decent guy, a regular drinking buddy . . . But Jonathan's off his head . . . wants to be a priest or something. He's been driving us all crazy of late with all that horseshit about God and the hereafter. . . .

Van In sipped at his coffee. Guido was still on the phone, nodding like a toy dog in the back of a car and doodling on the back of a cardboard file. Why was he taking so long?

"Spill!" he said, as soon as Guido hung up. The sergeant smiled as if he'd just wrangled a date with one of the Chippendales.

"Praise the Lord," he said with what passed for a Bible Belt accent.

Van In tossed the report he had been reading back on the pile. He had thumbed through one report and was already sick of it. "Spare me the crap, Guido. We don't have time to piss about."

Guido shook his head, scribbled a few words on a sheet of paper, and handed it to Van In.

Saartje Maes breezed into Room 204 and greeted the men with a radiant smile. Her jacket blew open to reveal a white T-shirt that did justice to her every curve. "Good morning, gentlemen."

Van In looked at the sheet of paper Guido had just handed him and read: *Saartje Maes isn't who she says she is.*

Guido offered Saartje a cup of coffee. *Things can only get better*, he thought. After their encounter in the Iron Virgin, he had started to ask himself serious questions about the identity of Miss Maes. Her story about learning from a friend that the Iron Virgin was used by a satanic fraternity didn't hold water, and for someone who had only visited the café once or twice, she seemed to know El Shit far too well. She had raised her hand and the man had left the bar without protest to show her into the hall at the back.

"Your chief editor just called," said Van In. "He wants you to call him back. It's urgent."

Saartje took off her jacket and hung it on the coat stand.

"Something about your article," Guido added. "Did you write down the number, Commissioner?"

Van In seemed aggrieved. "I thought you had it, Guido."

"Why would I? Anyway, I'm sure Miss Maes knows her editor's number by heart. Am I right, Miss Maes?"

"I don't have to justify myself to you," she said bluntly. "I'll call the editor when I'm in the mood."

"Don't worry, Miss Maes," said Guido. "I called in your place. No one's ever heard of you!"

Her cheeks reddened, and she fiddled nervously with her nose. "Game over," she said dryly.

"This is fun," said Van In. "More games, Miss Maes?" He pushed aside a pile of reports and looked her in the eye. She seemed fragile all of a sudden.

"My name is Saartje Maes and I'm an inspector with State Security. I've been researching the existence of satanic sects in Bruges for the last six weeks." She paused, hoping their mouths would fall open in amazement. They didn't.

"Good try, Miss Bond. But surely you don't expect us to fall for a story like that."

Saartje threw back her head in a final attempt to maintain her dignity. "In October our offices received a letter from Trui Andries. She claimed that the satanic fraternity she had joined a while back was planning a terrible crime. I was ordered to start a discreet investigation and try to determine if we should take the contents of her letter seriously."

Van In and Guido were both flabbergasted.

"I called Chief Commissioner De Kee, and he guaranteed complete secrecy."

"Sounds like De Kee," Van In grumbled. He was having a hard time concealing his indignation. "Did he invent your cover too?"

Saartje nodded.

"As soon as he heard that Trui Andries was dead, he called me. I contacted my case officer, and he advised me to follow the investigation at close quarters."

Van In couldn't believe his ears. The entire country knew that Belgian State Security was led by a bunch of idiots, political buddies who couldn't find work elsewhere, but this kind of bungling bordered on insanity. "And may I ask what brought you to State Security, Miss Maes?" he inquired

The girl pouted. "My uncle is director. He's in charge of the department that deals with sects. When I lost my job last year, he suggested I sign up for the inspector's exam."

"Which you passed cum laude."

It was true that Saartje had enjoyed a carefree childhood. Her family was well-to-do, and she had finished college without too much effort. But Van In's sarcastic tone hurt her to the core. She couldn't remember ever being put in her place with so few words.

"I worked hard," she said defensively.

"Criminology?"

Saartje lowered her eyes. "I'm an accountant."

Van In nodded. A bookkeeper. The prophets of doom were right after all. The end of the world was *really* nigh! "Since?"

"I graduated three years ago."

Van In looked at Guido, who was watching and listening and shaking his head. Belgium had more unsolved crimes than any of its neighbors. Now he knew why.

"Do you realize that your silence probably cost the lives of eight people?" Van In sensed a fit of temper coming on. Was there any end to this madness?

"My job was to chart the different sects, Commissioner, and try to determine if a crime was in preparation. State Security inspectors don't have the authority to arrest people. All I can do is observe and report back to my superiors."

"Why didn't you bring us up to speed?"

"Because my case officer didn't think it was opportune. He wanted to know first if the Trui Andries killing had anything to do with satanism. That's why I wanted to get close to the investigation. If I'd known that you were following a similar line of approach, I would have revealed my true identity immediately."

Her self-confidence was returning, albeit slowly. The scores were one-all, and the ball was in his court.

"So what were you doing yesterday at the Iron Virgin?"

"Observing, Commissioner. I go there at least twice a week."

Van In sighed. The fact that she was right only made things worse. When he'd called Beekman the night before, the prosecutor had warned him not to be in too much of a hurry to intervene.

"Did you have any form of contact with Trui Andries in the last few weeks?"

"We spoke twice."

"About the letter."

Saartje nodded. She had to admit that it was partly her fault that things had gotten out of hand. The investigation into the satanic sects was her first big job. She'd thought herself superior to local police, looked down on them as dumb and naïve, and she'd clearly let them feel it. "Miss Andries told me the letter was a mistake, that she no longer wanted to have anything to do with it."

"And you didn't believe her."

"No," said Saartje. "I thought she was scared."

"Did she give a reason for her sudden turnabout?"

"She said she was seeing a psychiatrist and that the doctor had told her she'd imagined it all."

"Do you have a name for the doctor?"

Saartje shook her head. "She didn't mention it."

Van In took a pen and twirled it through his fingers. Squabbling was pointless. He needed information, and it was possible at least that Saartje Maes had discovered something that might help his inquiry.

"How many satanist sects did you manage to chart?"

"Four," said Saartje.

"Did the names Jonathan Leman, Jasper Simons, Richard Coleyn, or Venex ever come up in conversation?"

"No," she said, sure of her answer.

A knock came at the door. Inspector Pattyn waited patiently for Van In to say "come in."

"There's a problem with Coleyn," he said, coming straight to the point. "They had to cuff him to a radiator. He's causing a riot."

Saartje Maes's confession had distracted Van In so much that he had completely forgotten giving orders for Coleyn to be brought to the station.

"Sort it out," Van In snapped.

"He says the waiting room's driving him crazy. He insists we leave the door open. If you ask me, the guy's got claustrophobia."

"Put him in a cell for an hour or two and let him cool off. I don't have time for him right now."

Pattyn turned and headed for the door. Just as he was about to close it behind him, Van In called him back.

"By the way, Pattyn. Is the broom closet free?"

"I think so."

The broom closet was a tiny room on the first floor, six feet by ten and without windows. Architects were prone to the odd mistake now and then, especially when it came to public commissions. Who cared? Belgians were creative enough to find a solution for any problem.

"Good, then I'll question him there," said Van In.

Pattyn raised his eyebrows, thinking that sometimes Van In made no sense at all. First he sided with a guttersnipe who deserved a kick in the ass; now he was deciding to use an interrogation technique that Amnesty International would describe as barbaric.

Van In understood the skepticism in the inspector's face. "Eight people died, Pattyn. I don't have time to piss around."

Pattyn straightened. "Anything else, Commissioner?"

Van In peered at the pile of police reports taking up more than half his desk. There was indeed something else. "I gave orders last night for Muylle's garage to be searched. Did anyone find the time?"

Pattyn nodded. The report was somewhere in the middle of the pile, but it didn't seem appropriate to respond to the commissioner's question with a search. "There were signs of breaking and entering on the door, and the lock had clearly been forced. One of the neighbors also said he heard a strange noise that Friday night."

Pattyn's summary confirmed the misgivings that had plagued Van In since his encounter with Muylle. It was highly unlikely that Muylle would force open the door to his own garage.

"Shit," said Van In, kicking his desk out of pure frustration, bruising his big toe in the process. The string of expletives that followed was enough to shock both Saartje *and* Guido.

"I think you can go now, Inspector Pattyn," said Guido. He was familiar with the commissioner's moods. Van In could rant and rave at times, and his fits of temper were nothing short of legendary. Hannelore knew all about it.

The second Pattyn closed the door, Van In called Beekman.

"Commissioner Van In here. It's about Muylle. I think we've got the wrong man." Van In explained the new situation, keeping it as short as possible.

Beekman was calm and professional, as anyone would expect a magistrate to be. "I'll inform the examining magistrate that there are new elements in the investigation." Beekman looked at his watch. It was ten forty-five. Muylle was scheduled to appear in front of the examining magistrate in forty-five minutes. He had no reason for concern. The correct procedures had been followed. It was only when Van In then suggested that the examining magistrate might be persuaded to issue a warrant for the arrest of Richard Coleyn that his tone suddenly changed.

"I presume you have sound reasons for such a request, Commissioner."

Van In's instincts were faultless. Muylle was a mere metal-worker, but Richard Coleyn was the son of a respected doctor. That made all the difference, even for a modern prosecutor like Beekman.

"Coleyn is the only one who can tell us more about the relationship between Trui Andries, Jasper Simons, and Jonathan Leman."

A moment's silence followed as Beekman searched for an elegant way to change Van In's mind.

"Are they involved in the shooting?"

The minister of justice had called him half an hour ago. The prosecutor general was planning to retire in six months and Beekman was in line for his job if . . .

"There's a connection," said Van In, and he didn't have to be a fortune-teller to know how Beekman would react.

"Do you have hard evidence?"

Van In could have said: *Prosecutor Beekman, yesterday you gave me carte blanche on the shooting incident and now you're backtracking like a timid teenager on his first date.* But he didn't. "I'm convinced Coleyn knows more than he's been willing to divulge thus far."

Beekman weighed the pros and cons. Muylle's arrest was a mistake, and he would be held responsible, but the press wouldn't punish him for it. On the contrary, they would praise him for his bold and energetic approach. Van In, on the other hand, was far from incompetent. It wouldn't be the first time that his unorthodox methods had produced results. He opted for a compromise.

"You've got forty-eight hours, Van In."

"And you'll take care of the arrest warrant?"

A five-second silence predicted the answer. "I said you've got forty-eight hours, Commissioner. Call me if you make any progress."

"We'll manage just fine, sir. We'll be in touch." Van In hung up the phone and scratched behind his left ear.

Guido realized immediately that something wasn't right. "The broom closet?" he asked.

"Unless you can think of something smaller, Guido."

"Is there anything else I can do?" asked Saartje as Van In and Guido got up and headed toward the door. The black widow now seemed more like a harmless daddy longlegs. "Do you have a file on Trui Andries?" she asked.

Those who knew Van In were aware that he never bore a grudge. "I still have to type it up," he said, slightly embarrassed. "You would be doing us an enormous favor . . ."

She nodded enthusiastically. "And the poison killings?"

Van In looked at Guido. The sergeant didn't say a word.

"I think we can leave those old cases for the time being, Miss Maes."

Saartje beamed with joy, threw her arms around Van In's neck, and gave him a kiss. Van In felt a bit like a grandfather with a beautiful granddaughter. At least that's what he told himself.

11

Three chairs and an old-fashioned metal desk with a typewriter that had seen better days were the sole contents of the broom closet. The door was ajar, for the time being at least. The entire picture had something Hitchcockian about it, a sense of menace, the feeling that something dramatic was about to happen.

"Do you think this is the right approach, Pieter?"

Van In was reminded of Room 101 in George Orwell's *1984*. It had been a while since he'd read the book, but he'd never forgotten the cage with the rats and the terror it generated.

"Psychiatrists claim that you can cure people of their phobias by confronting them with them," he said.

"We're about to find out," Guido agreed.

What was Van In supposed to do? Admit he was at his wits' end, that the case had outsmarted him? He felt like an Internet surfer who had consulted a hundred sites but had learned nothing. Times were changing at a pace he couldn't keep up with. Unlike the old days, modern suspects rarely admitted they'd done anything wrong. They lied and deceived to their hearts' content.

It was the price society had to pay for a judicial system that forced suspects to cheat if they wanted to avoid being brought to justice. Honesty had become a sign of weakness that was punished without mercy. Perhaps modern satanism had a similar philosophy at its core? Perhaps there was a sort of connecting thread that snapped every time the knot unraveled and the way out of the labyrinth came into view, such that those who wanted to find the truth were doomed to wander forever in caves of darkness as sightless seers.

Van In had been suffering more from cheerless thoughts of late. He knew that these days you had to be able to relativize, let things go, glide off you like Teflon. Those who refused to accept the status quo were immediately labeled as right wing or stupid. Van In wondered which of the two labels he feared the most.

Two burly police officers dragged Richard Coleyn to the door of the broom closet. They had probably told him what to expect in advance, given the fight he put up. He was like a man possessed, and his appearance confirmed the comparison: hollow chest, poorly shaved, and dull, greasy skin with blackheads and pimples in profusion.

"I want a lawyer," he screamed. "You have no right to lock me up."

His screams echoed down the icy corridor. Prisoners didn't have rights. Corridors could lead anywhere. Van In signaled to the officers that they could bring Coleyn in. They succeeded, although not without a struggle. Van In then gave them the key, ordering them to lock the door and to open it only on his personal request.

Richard Coleyn turned white as a sheet. He tried to get out, to push his way past the officers at the door, but they closed it in his face. He started to tug on the door handle like a madman. When that also failed to get him anywhere, he started to kick the lower panel of the door. This wasn't the first time the broom closet had been used for interrogations, as the black smudges on the door testified.

Van In sat down at the metal desk and lit a cigarette. Guido remained standing, in case Coleyn tried something he might regret. They had agreed in advance that the commissioner would ask the questions.

"We can be out of here soon," said Van In. "It all depends on you. I've got all the time in the world."

"My father will haul you before the courts," Coleyn screeched.

"I thought your father had rejected you."

"You have no right to lock me up."

Coleyn turned. His entire body was trembling, and the empty look in his eyes reflected the desperation raging through his guts like a wildcat, its razor-sharp teeth biting into every nerve.

"You told us that already, Mr. Coleyn. I suggest you take a seat. Otherwise I'll be forced to have you immobilized."

Guido produced a pair of handcuffs and dangled them in front of Coleyn like a skilled inquisitor. "The commissioner means it," he whispered. "He's capable of leaving you here for a couple of hours if need be. He has time, and so do I."

Coleyn stared at Guido in disbelief. "I thought you were the commissioner."

Creating confusion was perhaps the most powerful weapon police officers had at their disposal. It could throw a suspect off balance, and like in judo, such were the moments that often determined who won the fight.

"What makes you say that, Mr. Coleyn? I'm Sergeant Guido and this is Commissioner Van In."

"But . . ."

"No buts, Mr. Coleyn. Take a seat and let's not waste any more time on trivial details, for Christ's sake."

Van In pointed at the chair on the opposite side of the desk. He felt like a lion tamer, only without the whip. When Coleyn finally sat down, Guido returned the cuffs to his pocket. He had to admit that the way Van In managed to impose his will on the boy was inspiring.

They say journalists are a lazy bunch because they don't always react to every anonymous telephone caller promising them the latest scoop immediately. Bert Vonck had just finished a tedious interview and was treating himself to a well-earned cup of coffee. When the telephone rang, he didn't budge. When it rang a second time immediately afterward, he answered.

"Hello, Mr. Vonck?"

"Speaking," said the journalist.

"I think I have a scoop for you."

Bert Vonck lit a cigarette, wedged the receiver between his cheek and his shoulder, and pressed the start button on the tape recorder attached to the phone. "I'm all ears."

As the conversation proceeded, Vonck puffed at his cigarette with steadily increasing fascination. If what the caller was saying was true, then every newspaper editor in chief—he meant the ones who paid big money for sensational news—would welcome him with open arms. He might even be able to buy that sports car he'd been dreaming of.

"Are you saying Jonathan Leman killed Trui Andries?" said Van In.

The limited space and the absence of an easy exit were beginning to serve their purpose. Richard was nervous, sweating like a pig, constantly looking over his shoulder.

"Isn't that what you claim, Mr. Coleyn?"

Richard nodded. The tiny room seemed to be getting smaller by the minute. They couldn't do this to him. He tried to avoid the commissioner's steely gaze as he struggled to formulate a response.

"Jonathan couldn't stand the idea that Trui and Jasper were planning to get married. He . . ."

He stopped breathing as if his lungs had collapsed. His eyes were motionless, like marbles, glassy and vacant. He gasped for air. Guido had seen this situation coming and had brought a paper bag with him, which he held over Richard's mouth. The boy seemed familiar with the procedure and gulped at the low-oxygen air. Van In waited patiently for the crisis to subside.

As the instinct to breathe won out over the call of unconsciousness, it had dawned on Coleyn that they weren't going to let him go until he'd told them what they wanted to hear. "Jonathan is an orphan," he whispered. "He's never known true love. Trui felt sorry for him, and when he turned eighteen and was released from the orphanage, she took care of him."

Van In nodded. The details squared with the information he had picked up on Jonathan. "And you got to know him through Jasper."

Richard crushed the paper bag. "Jasper was obsessed with Satan. He was hunting high and low for adepts, focusing on people who longed for some kind of spiritual anchor. Jonathan was easy prey."

"Did Jasper recruit in the Iron Virgin?"

"Among other places."

Van In glanced at Guido. Coleyn's story sounded logical enough, but it didn't line up with the version they'd heard from Jasper's parents. Doctor Coleyn also held a different opinion. According to them, Jasper was an antisatanist, determined to destroy evil in its every incarnation.

"And was it there that you met?"

Richard nodded. "Jasper and I went to school together. I bumped into him a couple of years ago in the Iron Virgin. When

I told him that my dating service was on the skids, he suggested we join forces."

"So you became a member of his satanic fraternity?"

Richard shook his head. The end of this trial was slowly coming into view. He closed his eyes tight and tried to picture himself walking along an empty beach. "Jasper was a drug dealer, and for two years I was his runner."

Van In tried to draw a link between Coleyn's statement and the information he had gathered the week before. Trui Andries knew Jonathan Leman from the time she worked in the orphanage. Jasper Simons had come up with the idea of starting a satanic sect as a cover for his drug business, and Richard Coleyn had become his sidekick for lack of money.

"Did Trui Andries know what was going on?"

Richard blinked. It was time for the most important part of his story. "Trui was madly in love with Jasper. She wanted to save him, whatever the cost."

Richard's speech was getting faster and his breathing more agitated. "She tried to share his delusions at first. Out of love. Then . . ."

Anxiety took hold once again. Guido stepped forward and flattened the paper bag with the palm of his hand, but Richard brushed him away.

"She started to study satanism. She read book after book, determined to convince him how wrong he was. He turned his back on the drug trade three months ago. They were planning to get married, live a normal life, but Jonathan couldn't deal with it."

Richard took a deep breath and looked up at Van In and Guido. The tiny hairs on his cheeks glistened like a cornfield in the sun. "He told whoever would listen that he would enter a monastery if Trui and Jasper got married. Trui was the only girlfriend he'd ever had. It drove him crazy to think he couldn't be with her."

"Just like Jasper."

"Jasper's different," said Richard. "He was born with problems. Half his family is in psychiatric care. That was his future too, and he knew it."

Van In stood, walked to the door, and asked the officer on guard to open it. Guido stroked his mustache, happy the nasty business was finally over.

The open door had the expected calming effect. Richard even smiled. Van In returned to the desk. If Coleyn was telling the truth, then they were on the wrong track. There was a serious chance that the death of Trui Andries and the bloodbath at Saint Jacob's Church were unconnected.

"One more question, Mr. Coleyn."

If Trui Andries's murder and the mass killing had nothing to do with each other, then they had wasted a lot of precious time.

"You claim that Jasper Simons was a regular at the Iron Virgin. How come nobody there had ever heard of him?"

Richard didn't have to search long for an answer. He took a deep breath and stared at the open door. "Jasper used a pseudonym. He called himself Venex."

Adjutant Delrue punched in the number of Prosecutor Beekman. It wasn't something he did every day. The federal police preferred to manage their own affairs.

"Beekman speaking." The public prosecutor had just finished a cheese sandwich and was washing down his frugal lunch with a glass of mineral water.

"Good afternoon, sir. I'm sorry to disturb you, but . . ."

Beekman listened with increasing amazement to the adjutant's story. "Are you sure your informant is reliable?"

"Operation Snow White has been running for the best part of six months now, sir. We've known our suspect must have been getting help from someone in the police, and the details we received from our informant make perfect sense."

Beekman closed his eyes tight. The headlines weren't difficult to imagine. "Thanks for the call, Adjutant. You did the right thing."

Delrue sensed that something wasn't right. With twenty years of service behind him he could tell when a magistrate was planning a cover-up.

"If you want us to proceed, we'll need a search warrant," said Delrue, his tone formal.

Beekman fiddled a cigarette from a crushed pack he kept in the top drawer of his desk for emergencies. His wife was a militant member of the antismoking lobby. He knew what the punishment would be if she caught him: two weeks on the sofa and a couple of showers every day until she was sure every trace of the toxin had vanished. Fortunately he had married into money. He expected to inherit a major fortune when his in-laws kicked the bucket. A person had to have *something* to look forward to.

"I'll discuss the matter with the examining magistrate right away, Adjutant. I'll call you back later today."

Beekman hung up the phone, lit his crooked cigarette, and hurried outside. He hated anonymous informants. In the past, he'd paid no attention to them, didn't have to, but now the public insisted that every clue should be thoroughly investigated, no stone left unturned. In spite of the separation of powers, magistrates were still appointed by politicians, and politicians had to listen to the man in the street.

The atmosphere in Room 204 was heavy, dejected. Van In was staring at the ceiling, his office chair in relax position, smoking one cigarette after the other. Guido was reading police reports and hoping to discover new evidence. Saartje Maes tapped listlessly at her computer keyboard.

"Why did that madman leave his car at the station in Blankenberge? That's what I want to know," said Van In.

Beekman had insisted that the police knock on some doors in the neighborhood, but it hadn't helped. No one remembered the driver of the gray Fiat, and the ticket clerk in the station declared that only four people had taken the five past one train that day: an elderly couple and two teenage girls. The service was reduced in the winter months to a couple of trains per hour, so he couldn't have been mistaken.

Guido perched his reading glasses on the tip of his nose. He understood that Van In had released Richard Coleyn against his better judgment, but it wasn't the end of the world. Detective work could be a painful process, and the disappointments were often more frequent than the moments of euphoria.

"Maybe he wanted us to believe that he took the train."

"I figured that already, Guido. But why Blankenberge?"

Van In concentrated on the thick cloud of smoke as it changed shape in the neon light. Strange what smoke could do, he thought. "Let me have another look at the names of the victims," he said after a moment or two.

Guido searched for the file on his PC and printed it. "They don't appear to be connected in any way, not at first sight. It looks as if the killer simply shot them at random."

"Let's have a closer look," said Van In. He studied the names on the list for a second time: Hans Moeyaert, Damien Vereecke, Anne-Marie Hoornaert, Casper Masyn, Agatha Willemyns, Robert Minne, An Beernaert, and Lucienne Debondt.

"There's a couple among them," said Guido. "Casper Masyn and Agatha Willemyns."

Van In underlined the names.

"Masyn is, I mean was, a well-known notary. Some say he was a billionaire."

The Trui Andries killing had inclined Van In to focus too closely on satanism, looking for connections that didn't exist. Now he had to start from scratch. Mass murderers were psychopaths by definition. They didn't need a motive.

"But I still think it's strange that the car used in the attack belonged to a regular at the Iron Virgin."

"Statistically speaking, there's a one in three hundred thousand chance of something like that happening," said Guido, straight-faced and pointing to his computer. "I did the math this morning."

Van In didn't want to know how Guido came up with his numbers. The man had so many qualities, some of them were best kept to himself.

"So there might be a connection between the shooting and the Iron Virgin after all," said Van In.

"Maybe someone made a copy of Muylle's key and sneaked the original back into his wallet," said Saartje out of the blue. "A customer at the Iron Virgin perhaps?"

Van In looked at Saartje.

"What do you think, Guido?"

"I think she deserves a kiss."

A persistent ringing roused Hannelore from her afternoon nap. She threw off the comforter and waggled downstairs like a drunken duck. The thermostat read 70 degrees and she was dressed up warm in a stretch wool maternity dress, but she still shivered.

"Jozef!" she said, taken aback to find Beekman standing on the doorstep. "What a surprise."

"I'm not sure if it's a pleasant one," said the public prosecutor, looking serious. "Do you mind if I come in?"

Hannelore stepped back from the door. "Of course. No one died, I hope."

She took Beekman's coat and sensed the chill that accompanied him inside. "Coffee?"

"If you show me where everything is, I'll take care of it, Hanne. You should rest."

"So it's bad news then," said Hannelore. "Don't tell me something's happened to Pieter . . ."

Beekman opened a cupboard, grabbed a pack of coffee, emptied a substantial amount into the hinged filter basket, and swung it over the glass coffeepot. "Pieter's alive and kicking, Hanne." He laughed. "You don't have to worry about Van In."

Hannelore took a seat. "So what's up?"

Beekman filled the coffee machine with water and flicked the red tumbler switch. He was about to confront her with an empty accusation and he felt embarrassed.

"The federal police have been following a drugs gang for some time now. Turns out to be a pretty complex network, and suggestions have been made that a senior police official has been protecting the gang's leader."

Hannelore rested her legs on a chair. She was happy she didn't have to worry. "Pieter will be delighted to hear it."

The coffee machine started to sputter, the first jet-black droplets plopping on the bottom of the pot. Beekman rubbed his hands together and sat down next to Hannelore. There was no point in beating about the bush. "The federal boys suspect Van In is involved."

As a little girl, Hannelore had been given a rabbit on her birthday by an uncle who lived on a farm. The fluffy creature stole her heart and she pampered it as if it were a little baby. The fact that the creature chewed everything in sight didn't bother her. When her mother told her one day that Moussy had escaped from his cage and wasn't coming back, she had reacted with the same disbelief as now. The unidentified "game" her mother served for dinner the following day only confirmed her suspicions.

She snorted. "You're not serious."

Beekman grabbed a couple of mugs from the cupboard, one with a handle and one without. "Adjutant Delrue has asked for a search warrant. If I refuse, the shit'll hit the fan."

"A search warrant!" Hannelore leaped from her chair and dragged herself to the kitchen counter. Had everyone gone crazy? "On what grounds?"

Beekman bit his bottom lip. "The federal police received a tip."

"Anonymous, I'm guessing."

Beekman nodded. He hoped she would understand the position he was in.

"Sugar?" She grabbed the coffeepot and filled both cups. The last droplets of coffee sizzled on the hotplate. The hissing sound echoed her rage. "Milk?"

"I'm just trying to prevent an escalation," he said, almost begging her to understand.

"Milk?" she snapped.

"Hannelore. I . . ."

She handed Beekman a mug of piping-hot coffee, the one without the handle. Instead of putting it down right away, he drank from it and stifled the excruciating pain. "I don't need to sign a search warrant if you give permission . . ."

"I know the law, Jozef."

Hannelore stooped for a bottle of milk in the refrigerator and the abruptness of the movement woke her slumbering baby. When Beekman heard her groan, he placed his mug on the counter. The tips of his fingers were shiny and felt as if they'd been boiled.

"Is something wrong?"

Hannelore shook her head stubbornly.

"Let the bastards come," she said, ready for a fight. "We've nothing to hide."

Van In hung up and lit a cigarette. The furrows in his forehead were getting deeper by the hour. "They let Muylle go this afternoon," he said glumly. "Couldn't hold him."

Guido wasn't sure how to react to Van In's apparent disappointment. His boss had been personally responsible for providing the evidence that got the man off the hook. He knit his brows.

"I know what you're going to say, Guido. It's a question of timing. With Muylle in custody it was easier to question him. I don't think he'll be granting interviews any time soon."

"Maybe I could talk to him," said Saartje on an whim. "He doesn't know me and . . ."

"You've got a better hand of cards," said Van In without implying anything specific. The girl had something that made men weak, softened them. He could speak from experience.

Saartje smiled. "I could use my journalist story. Everyone falls for it."

Van In liked the idea but was too embarrassed to agree right away. "Let me think about it, Miss Maes."

It had finally started to rain outside. A frail sunbeam pierced a hole in the clouds and engulfed Saartje's face in a delicate halo of light. She seemed fragile all of a sudden, and in reality that's what she was. Beauty could be a burden and Saartje was sometimes jealous of ordinary people, ugly people. They didn't have to prove themselves all the time, she thought.

Although it was forbidden to park in front of the Vette Vispoort, Adjutant Delrue didn't waste time looking for somewhere legal to leave his vehicle. He stepped out onto the sidewalk and glanced at the flowers that had piled up by the door of the church. Their bright colors had faded and their rotting stems gave off a pungent odor that only served to underline the presence of death and decay.

He wondered from time to time if there was some kind of plan at work behind all those disasters and killings. *What about the florists?* he thought. They were the winners in every tragedy. Half a lifetime in the federal police had turned Delrue into a first-class cynic. He presumed that everyone had something to answer for, no matter how well they managed to hide it.

His footsteps reverberated on the dry cobblestones with which the Vette Vispoort was paved, just like the footsteps of his colleagues behind him.

The sixteenth-century house Commissioner Van In and Deputy Martens called their home pointed, as far as Delrue was concerned, in the right direction. The restoration must have cost a small fortune, and he knew exactly how much the commissioner and the deputy earned for a living. He was also pretty sure that there was more of the same to be found inside. Rumors had done the rounds that Van In liked to collect antiques.

He rang the bell, and Hannelore opened the door. "Adjutant Delrue, Bruges Special Detective Division."

Neither Beekman nor Hannelore bothered to shake the man's hand. They returned to the kitchen table and let the detectives do their work.

12

On the outside, the police station in Hauwer Street looked like a dull concrete block with a honeycomb of square windows. On the inside, it was a hive of activity; at least, that's what passersby were led to believe when they observed shapes and shadows scurrying back and forth behind the glass. But the atypical hustle and bustle had nothing to do with the investigation into the mass shooting. It was five o'clock and everyone was hurrying to get home. The illuminated windows looked like colorful compartments in a painting by Mondrian. Then the lights went out one by one, except in Room 204 and two or three other offices on the ground floor. Five minutes later, the building looked like a government ministry: dead and useless.

"Do we have a deal, Commissioner?"

Saartje didn't dare use Van In's first name since her charm offensive had failed. Now that she'd been unmasked, there was no real reason to continue the charade. Pigheaded superbitch wasn't her favorite role, and she was happy to shed it. Why did women have to prove themselves more than men? Why wasn't it enough for them just to get on with their jobs?

"I'm not sure if I can go along with your suggestion, Miss Maes. And don't forget, you're not on the force."

Van In considered the heads of State Security to be a bunch of idiots, but he also knew it was better to let sleeping dogs lie. The bozos in Brussels could be quick to take offense, and some of the more senior officials even suffered from a sort of magpie syndrome, bedazzled by shiny objects and inclined to scream blue murder the minute an outsider entered their territory.

"A little chat with Mr. Muylle fits my mandate, Commissioner. No one can stop me doing my own thing."

She couldn't help treating the commissioner to a cute but innocent smile. Van In, on the other hand, was troubled by it. He started to imagine certain things that should have made him blush with shame. "I have no official grounds to forbid it, but . . ."

"But what, Commissioner?"

Saartje straightened her back and squared her shoulders. Van In turned toward her instinctively, although she hadn't planned it that way.

"It's a question of safety," he said. "What if Muylle gets violent?"

Guido had been listening to the conversation in silence and suddenly realized what was happening.

"I don't mind going with her, Pieter," he said, underlining his words with raised eyebrows.

Van In shook his head. "Muylle already knows you," he said.

"Muylle knows both of us, Pieter."

"I was thinking of waiting outside . . . just in case something went wrong."

Guido was now certain that Van In had something crazy in mind. "I was thinking the same," he said.

Van In ignored the look on Guido's face. "What will Frank have to say? You're only just back together, and I know how much he hates it when you work overtime."

Guido had to think twice before he answered. "Call Hannelore," he said. "Then she'll know at least that you'll be home late."

Van In was playing with fire, and Guido wanted to be sure he was aware of it.

Jonathan used a soup spoon to warm a triple dose of heroin, the reward he had received from Venex for the key. For his betrayal. A sterile disposable syringe was lying on his nightstand next to an ashtray full of cigarette butts and a half-empty bottle of Coke. The syringe was from Richard. The irony was unmistakable. Who commits suicide with a sterile needle?

He lit a final cigarette, a John Player Special from the pack he'd swiped from the commissioner. He filled the syringe and placed it on a square of paper towel at his side. He sat on the edge of the bed and watched the plume of smoke wind its way to the ceiling like a whimsical djinn. He was about to relive his life, watch it flash past in an instant, or at least that's what people said, that it was like a movie. But had anyone ever survived to confirm it?

Jonathan pulled the smoke deep into his lungs. What if the movie was a fantasy? What if he was about to disappear into a dark, bottomless pit, just another defenseless victim of his habit? No more memories, no more soul. As if he'd never existed. And if the movie was real, how long would it last? Would it be exciting? Probably not. He'd spent the best part of his life in an orphanage, where the sisters had told him he had to behave. They had told him always to sleep with his hands on top of the blankets, that he should thank the Lord with all his heart for the delicious food he received three times a day, that his future wouldn't amount to much because he was just a minuscule, insignificant fragment of the mystical Body of Christ. He remembered the sour smell in the convent, the bells, the commands, do this, do that, the endless nights, the struggle with desire.

Jonathan stubbed out the cigarette. He looked at the tourniquet, at the vein he had already selected. Dying was the most incredible adventure he would ever undertake. He lit another cigarette . . . five left in the pack.

Trui had caught him masturbating in the kitchen one day. The usual punishment was three days of solitary confinement, a crust of moldy bread, and a bowl of salt water to purify his body of evil. But Trui hadn't reported his transgression. She had explained everything to him. If humans had been created in the image of God, why was physical pleasure a sin? She talked about love and compassion, tenderness and hope. She even let him see her breasts. *You'll discover the rest later,* she'd said with a grin.

Jonathan lit another cigarette. He had seen Jasper and Trui kiss in the corridor. He remembered the pain. When he spoke to Trui about it, she kissed him too, coyly, chaste. It made him feel good, but when she went on to say that she and Jasper loved each other in a different way, he had to stifle the prickling sensation he felt at the back of his throat. Some of the older boys told him there was a remedy for his pain and initiated him in alternative pleasures. Venex took him on the moment he left the orphanage and familiarized him with the white powder. Jonathan had become his slave like so many others, and he had remained his slave until the bitter end. That was something Trui hadn't been able to change.

Adjutant Delrue and his colleagues searched Van In's house with the necessary discretion. With a couple of magistrates in the vicinity they had little choice. Hannelore refused to budge from her chair the entire time. While she understood Beekman's position, and would have granted a warrant herself under the same circumstances, the whole operation was still humiliating to say the least. She kept looking at the clock. Van In could arrive at any moment, and feathers would fly if he did.

Bart Muylle was getting ready to celebrate his regained freedom at the Iron Virgin when Saartje Maes rang the bell. He had treated himself to a long shower and a change of clothing to get rid of the foul prison smell that had followed him home: a mixture of sweat, urine, reheated coffee, and bleach. He was planning to get drunk and only come home when he was totally legless.

"Good evening, Mr. Muylle. My name is Saartje Maes. I'm a journalist, and I wondered if I could ask you a couple of questions?"

Muylle, who hadn't set foot in a church since his First Communion, murmured a quick prayer of thanksgiving. He had piles of porn magazines next to his bed full of dream babes in the most tempting poses, but this clothed example made him hornier than the two hundred pounds of glossy paper upstairs.

"May I come in?"

Muylle couldn't believe his ears. He stepped back and let her in.

Van In saw the door close. He looked at his watch and lit a cigarette.

"Can I offer you something to drink, Miss Maes?"

Muylle tried to tidy up his thick Bruges accent, determined to make an impression on his hot visitor. Saartje treated him to a smile and looked around the bare room with the enthusiasm of a Japanese tourist.

"A cozy place you have here, Mr. Muylle."

"A beer or a Coke?"

"Nice stereo."

"Four times one-fifty watts," said Muylle proudly. "Shall I pop in a CD?"

"Coke would be great, thanks."

Saartje headed toward the dilapidated sofa, swaying her hips. A grimy checkered blanket covered a tear in the imitation leather where the foam rubber stuffing was trying to escape. "Do you mind if I sit?"

The toilet was the only place the team from the Special Detective Division hadn't checked. A first sergeant unscrewed the lid of the cistern under the watchful eye of Adjutant Delrue. If nothing was found, the adjutant was going to have to come up with a fucking good excuse to explain his actions to the magistrates. Delrue pointed his flashlight into the cistern. "See anything?"

The first sergeant leaned over and ran his hand over the walls of the cistern. "Negative, Adjutant."

Delrue cursed, pushed his subordinate aside, and plunged his hand into the cistern, scraping its rough, chalk-encrusted walls with his nails like a cornered cat. "Fuck!"

The adjutant explored every inch of the cistern and it was clear from his choice of words that his determination was to no avail. The first sergeant had just stepped backward out of the way when his superior withdrew his hand and started to shake it free of water. In the process, his foot landed on a package of toilet paper sitting in the corner. The plastic wrapper was open and contained five rolls of paper.

"Are the gentlemen having fun?" Hannelore stood in the doorway with her legs spread and a look on her face that belonged in a toilet. Both Delrue and his first sergeant had no trouble guessing her thoughts. The first sergeant mumbled an apology, bent to the floor, and picked up the pack of toilet paper. He had crushed one of the rolls with his heel, so he removed it from the pack, molded it back into shape, and returned it.

Inside the bottom of the pack was a transparent plastic bag containing what looked like white powder. Hannelore spotted it only a fraction of a second before Delrue.

Van In had just stubbed out his third cigarette when Muylle and Saartje emerged from the house. Muylle threw his arm over her shoulder and whispered something in her ear. A peal of laughter echoed down the narrow street. She wriggled her derriere and treated him to a big fat kiss on the neck. Van In tried to suppress an acid belch and ignore the dull gnawing pain under his lower chest. The same pain had been bothering him a lot of late, especially when he was nervous.

The very thought of the filthy metalworker with his paws under her blouse . . . or worse . . . left him in a daze. A lot could happen in half an hour, and Saartje was clearly determined to prove herself.

Van In followed them along Pepper Street toward the Kruispoort, one of the city's ancient gates. Anyone who didn't know better would have thought they were in love.

"I presume you've no idea how this got here," Delrue said with the air of a Roman general after a triumphal return from battle.

Hannelore looked at Beekman. The public prosecutor looked away. In the past, he could have used his authority to settle something like this out of court, but nowadays, the law was much stricter. As in the days of the Inquisition, accusations tended to take priority over objective investigations. People were also greedy for tangible facts, the kind of facts you could show on TV. The plastic bag Delrue had in his hand was more important than any statement from the accused.

"Adjutant Delrue, you surely don't think I would have agreed to let you search my house if I'd known there was a half a kilo of smack tucked under my toilet rolls."

"Of course not, ma'am." Delrue tried to account for Hannelore's condition. "I'm not saying you knew anything about it." Experience had taught him that most women had no idea what their husbands got up to and vice versa.

Hannelore detested men who based their conclusions on stereotyped patterns of thinking. "So what exactly *are* you saying, Adjutant?"

Simple sentences were often a lot more effective than complicated speeches, especially when the context was right. Beekman smiled. Hannelore was holding her own, and he was sure she'd be fine.

Delrue spotted the sneer on the public prosecutor's lips and did his best to suppress a sudden sense of apprehension. Magistrates scratched each other's backs. "Was Commissioner Van In aware that we were searching his property?" he asked.

Beekman had wondered the same thing. He was willing to stick his neck out for Hannelore, but Van In's reputation complicated things. The commissioner had a turbulent history, and Delrue wasn't the only one who questioned the man's integrity.

Hannelore looked back at Beekman. The possibility that the adjutant was right didn't bear thinking about. "Let me call him," she said.

Delrue nodded. Despite the undeniable evidence he had in his hand, this was still an extremely implausible situation. Who would hide a stash of heroin in a pack of toilet rolls? Maybe his own desire to get a result had clouded his judgment. He suddenly started to doubt the reliability of his informant.

• • •

A taxi pulled up in front of the Iron Virgin at eleven forty-five. Van In lit a cigarette. After hanging around for the best part of three hours, his feet were frozen solid and he was plagued by the shivers. All he could think of was a hot meal and a Duvel. He had spent most of the time ruminating about the events of the last few days. He had tried to disconnect the murder of Trui Andries from the shooting incident but without success. The letter State Security had received from Trui Andries spoke about a horrible crime about to be committed, and her warning had been corroborated. But why slaughter eight innocent people? The only thing that linked the victims was the fact that they had attended the same church service. Van In had checked the Europol database that afternoon and searched for similar crimes. Satanic gangs had burned a couple of churches to the ground and desecrated grave stones in Sweden and Germany, and there were cases of ritual rape and animal sacrifice, but satanists had never executed churchgoers. Were devil worshippers responsible for the mass shooting at the church? The only person who could tell him more was Jonathan.

The taxi driver got out, disappeared into the Iron Virgin, and emerged again half a minute later with Saartje and Muylle in his wake. The macho metalworker was draped over Saartje's delicate frame, blustering incomprehensibly and groping at her breasts. Van In was of a mind to grab the pig by the collar and dump him in the taxi, but Saartje managed to fend off his wandering hands by herself. The taxi driver suddenly turned his head and Saartje spoke to him. He nodded, took charge of Muylle, and pushed him onto the backseat of his Mercedes.

Van In heaved a sigh of relief when he spotted Saartje handing the driver some money and slamming the passenger door.

He tossed his half-smoked cigarette into the gutter and hurried toward her.

"I gave him two thousand francs," said Saartje, straightening her bra straps and beaming at Van In.

"Did Muylle keep his hands to himself?" Van In asked. The nauseous sensation in his gut had suddenly disappeared, and the nagging pain in his chest was subsiding. His heart, on the other hand, was beating ten to the dozen. He felt like a valiant knight who had just rescued a damsel from the claws of a dragon.

"You don't need to worry, Commissioner. In that state, his hands weren't going anywhere."

They hurried side by side down Long Street like a couple heading home after visiting friends, suddenly realizing how late it was and that they had to get up early the next day. Van In sensed butterflies. "Did he say anything?"

Saartje nodded and smiled.

"Fancy a drink somewhere?"

"Why not," she said.

L'Estaminet, Commissioner Van In's favorite café, was easy to spot on the outside from the rectangular patches of light that illuminated the facade. The yellowish glow was fed by a sober art deco chandelier in the bar. Since the curtains were rarely closed and the street lighting along the side of Astrid Park didn't amount to much, the patches could be seen from far and wide. For Van In they served as a beacon, like a lighthouse to a ship's captain. He grabbed a pack of cigarettes from the vending machine in the corridor and headed inside.

The barkeeper acknowledged him with a knowing glance, the look you expect to see on the face of a hunter inspecting a fellow hunter's prey. Van In and Saartje found a table by the fire.

The place was almost empty; only three tables were occupied, and a single lonely trucker was holding up the bar, devouring a portion of spaghetti Bolognese. Van In lit a cigarette, his fingers trembling, and coughed after the first draw. Growing old wasn't easy, especially for someone whose lung capacity was half that of a normal person.

"Good evening, Commissioner, Miss . . ."

The barkeeper wiped the table with a damp cloth, flipped a beer coaster from his shirt pocket, and placed it under a frothing Duvel.

"Looks like they know you around here," said Saartje.

Van In nodded. The barkeeper offered Saartje a drinks menu and waited until she made her choice.

"I'll have what he's having," she said, pointing to the Duvel. The barkeeper poured a second in the blink of an eye.

"Muylle remembered Jonathan buying drinks for the whole bar all night long." Saartje raised her heavy Duvel glass and ticked it against Van In's. "And El Shit claims that Jonathan disappeared for a couple of hours that night. When he got back, Muylle was sound asleep and snoring at the bar. Jonathan paid the bill and they left together in a taxi."

"Is that it?"

"El Shit also told me that Jonathan and Muylle rarely hung out together."

Saartje looked at him. Muylle had spent most of the evening bullshitting about his arrest, and she'd had to treat El Shit to a big wet kiss to get him to squawk about Jonathan.

"According to El Shit, it was the first time Jonathan had ever paid for a round. He mostly scrounged from the other drinkers, but that evening, he coughed up the best part of six thousand."

"Maybe he netted a serious haul that day." Van In tugged on an imaginary fishing rod to illustrate his words and accidentally jabbed Saartje in the ribs with his elbow.

"Ouch." Saartje doubled up.

Van In turned toward her, automatically resting his hand on where he'd bumped her and rubbing it gently. She didn't stop him.

"Sorry, but that's not what I meant," he said when he felt her body stiffen. "Does it still hurt?"

When she didn't answer, Van In looked up and saw her staring blankly at the door. He followed her gaze and felt his hand wither. *This kind of thing only happens in B movies*, he thought.

"So here you are." Hannelore grabbed a chair and sat opposite Van In and Saartje. It was clear that she'd been crying, but now an icy calm had settled on her as if she was in a trance. "I scoured half the city, Mr. Van In."

Van In pulled his hand away. A jabbing pain in his chest made him dizzy. "It's not what you think, Hanne. Miss Maes . . ."

"I'm not interested in your excuses, Mr. Van In."

"Deputy Martens, I can explain everything. The commissioner and I . . ."

"Barkeep! Bring me a double whiskey and give these turtledoves here something to drink."

The smattering of guests sniggered. The trucker pushed his spaghetti to one side and lit a cigarette. This was more exciting than a TV soap.

"And bring a napkin while you're at it. Someone here appears to have been dribbling."

"Hanne! You have to hear me out."

"Have to, Van In?"

She had been standing outside l'Estaminet, peering through the window. When she saw Pieter messing around with a child young enough to be his daughter, her world suddenly collapsed. Everyone had warned her about Van In, and the backstabbers had been right all along. Their marriage had been nothing more than a bubble and now it had burst. Hannelore tried to remain calm. She had to think of her baby.

The barkeeper filled a long drink glass halfway. Pregnant or not, the whiskey would calm her down. He served it along with a couple of Duvels and felt like a prison guard bringing a condemned man his least meal.

"I'd enjoy the first night, Miss Maes, if I were you. There's a chance Mister Big Man here might be spending the next couple of years behind bars."

Van In knew Hannelore. He recognized the sarcasm when she asked for the napkin, but exaggeration wasn't her style.

"The federal police searched our house this afternoon, and guess what they found?"

Hannelore emptied her glass in a couple of slugs. Everyone, including Van In and Saartje, waited with bated breath to hear what was coming next.

"Five hundred grams of pure, uncut heroin, Mister Van In."

Before Van In could respond, she slammed the glass on the table, threw back her head, and got to her feet. "Adieu, Mister Van In."

She headed for the door. "And be careful he doesn't get you pregnant."

The whiskey worked fast. Hannelore felt a little dizzy. She hadn't eaten since lunch. When she got home, she would toss a couple of spring rolls in the fryer and then pack her bags. One more unwed mother didn't mean the world was about to come to an end.

Bert Vonck e-mailed in his article just before the deadline. The editor had promised him the front page, and that news had left him slightly euphoric. He poured himself a whiskey and collapsed on the sofa. The printout of his article was lying at his side.

The article went out of its way to put the headline in perspective. It was full of conditionals and hypotheticals, as the chief editor had insisted in the event that someone might later lodge a complaint for defamation or libel.

He read the headline again. "Bruges Police Commissioner a Heroin Dealer."

13

A home without a woman can be a lonely place to live. Van In woke up in a cold bed. He could smell his own body, sour, the smell of a bachelor who had struggled to get to sleep. It took a couple of minutes before he remembered what had happened the evening before. Saartje had walked him home and left him at the door. She'd said no when he invited her in. He had thrown his arm around her neck like a shipwrecked castaway, but she had fended him off. All he got was a chaste peck on the lips and she was gone.

Van In threw back the comforter. He hadn't undressed the night before. That explained the smell. Odors tended to combine with moods; the worse people felt, the more likely they were to stink. Now he knew why the perfume stores that were popping up on every corner were doing such good business.

He stumbled downstairs, put on some coffee, lit a cigarette—still three in the pack—and looked out of the window at the icy waters of the river Reie. A couple of gulls pranced graciously on top of a craggy strip of wafer-thin ice that meandered along the riverbank on both sides. The sight saddened him. He longed for a ray of sunlight, but even the elements seemed to have deserted him. The firmament was gray, and clouds hung like lead over the rooftops. He felt like throwing open the window and proclaiming his powerlessness for all to hear. The world was unjust. Had he been so bad to her? He sniffed. *Hannelore, my love. Why did you abandon me?*

Guido let his eggs get cold. Frank was sitting beside him, and the newspaper was open on the table in front of them, a black-and-white bird that had fluttered from the sky, its wings outstretched. "Bruges Police Commissioner a Heroin Dealer." A massive photo graced the center of the page: Van In with a five o'clock shadow and a Duvel within easy reach. It made him look like a real dealer. All that was missing were the sunglasses and the gold chain.

"What now?" asked Frank, removing the plate with the fried eggs and dumping them in the trash. Guido remained seated. Frank put the plate on the kitchen counter. Washing up was for later. He sat beside his partner. Guido needed him.

"He's your best friend, Guido. I know what you're going through." Frank wasn't jealous of the commissioner. Van In and Guido had something platonic between them, and he didn't mind at all.

"They must have planted it," said Guido. "Pieter's no saint, but he's never had anything to do with drugs. I have to help him."

Frank glanced at the clock, a modern thing without numbers that had been all the rage a couple of years earlier. "Then you better get moving. It's seven forty-five already."

Guido gave Frank a kiss and hurried to the front door buried in thought.

Although there wasn't a soul in sight, Van In couldn't help feeling he was running the gauntlet as he made his way down the corridor to his office. He could feel his colleagues staring at him through the walls. Every office had a copy of the newspaper.

Saartje Maes was standing at the window dressed in jeans and a heavy sweater that was clearly a couple of sizes too big. In spite of the slovenly outfit, she had failed to conceal her firm buttocks. On the contrary, they stood out more than ever. She turned only when Van In spoke.

"You've no reason to feel guilty, Saartje." He used her first name on purpose. She looked at him, her eyes aglow with compassion and understanding. Van In leaned forward and kissed her forehead.

"That won't make it any worse," he said softly. "Let people think what they want to think. There's nothing I can do about that."

Guido waited in the corridor until Van In sat down at his desk. He knew that the chaste kiss meant nothing, but he didn't want to embarrass his friend. They had other fish to fry. "Coffee?"

Van In nodded.

"Bracer?"

Van In nodded again.

"Jenever or rum?"

"Throw in some rum, Guido."

No one said a word about the article in the paper, as if silence could somehow change reality. Van In stretched his legs. Today was lining up to be a day like any other. The hours would pass at a snail's pace and then he would go home. A shot would help ease the pain. *Why stay sober all day when there's no one at home waiting for me?* he thought.

"We discovered something interesting yesterday," he said, turning to Saartje. "Two weeks before the shooting, Jonathan got our friend Muylle drunk at the Iron Virgin. I'm wondering why."

Van In had broken the silence in order to chase the demons from his head, but Hannelore was still there, haunting his thoughts. She had probably moved back in with her parents and it didn't look as if she was planning to come back home any time soon since all her clothes had disappeared.

Guido poured a serious shot of rum into a cup and mixed it with a dash of coffee. "In that case, logic suggests that we accept the hypothesis put forward by Miss Maes. Jonathan deliberately sought contact with Muylle, got him drunk, and took the opportunity to steal his car key and have it copied. Muylle is a regular at the Iron Virgin, and whoever was responsible for the shooting wanted us to trace the car. Muylle was the ideal suspect. He has a police record and connection with a satanic fraternity."

Guido's conclusion was simple and logical. Van In didn't understand why he hadn't come up with the same. But why had the killer abandoned the car in front of the train station in Blankenberge?

"That would explain everything, Guido," said Van In, sitting upright in his chair. He forgot about Hannelore for an instant. If Guido was correct, then they were on the right track. Jonathan had played an important role in the entire affair, and perhaps there was a link between the Trui Andries murder and the shooting after all. But who was Jonathan working for? Venex? And who was Venex? Jasper? That's what Richard Coleyn claimed, but Van In wasn't convinced. As far as he was concerned, only Jonathan could answer that question.

Suddenly the phone rang.

"Van In speaking."

He placed his cup on a paper napkin that was lying on his desk. A dribble of brown liquid trickled down the outside of the cup and formed a circle on the napkin.

"Are you certain, Mr. Geens?"

Guido cocked his ears. Van In gestured that he should listen in on the other phone.

"The rumor is doing the rounds," Raf Geens, the crime lab technician, was saying. "Maybe it's not important, but I thought you should know nonetheless."

"How long ago?" asked Van In.

"I'm guessing twenty years."

Van In took a sip at his rum-laced coffee. "Was Veerle Andries one of his patients?"

"That's precisely why the affair caused such a stir, Commissioner. Veerle claimed he raped her. The Medical Association was about to suspend him."

Van In tried to assimilate the new information, but it was a struggle. The inside of his head was like a stew that had been too long on the heat. All the ingredients had mixed and mingled until everything tasted the same. "But they didn't."

"Lack of evidence," said Geens. "The baby disappeared, and Veerle committed suicide a couple of months later."

Van In thanked Geens and hung up the phone.

Guido had scribbled a few notes in his pad and now read them aloud: "Veerle Andries, sister of Trui Andries. Pregnant by Dr. John Coleyn. Raped? Abortion? Committed suicide on October tenth, 1979. Case dismissed. What do you think, Pieter?"

Van In was deep in thought. What he really wanted to do was call Hannelore and explain to her what *didn't* happen the evening before.

"I think it's time we had another little word with Coleyn," he said emotionlessly.

The telephone rang again. Van In jumped to his feet with a spark of hope and grabbed the receiver. His face froze when he recognized Chief Commissioner De Kee's nasal voice. He listened to what his boss had to say, put on his jacket, and made his way to the third floor like a lamb to the slaughter. Guido tugged at his mustache, while Saartje remained standing by the window.

Richard Coleyn had spent the night with a girlfriend who had kindly shown him the door after breakfast. That's what she always did when she got her way. It was okay to go to bed with her, but a relationship was out of the question. His dating agency wasn't called Xanthippe, after Socrates's notoriously prickly wife, for nothing.

Richard turned into Hoogstuk Street and pulled out his key. Venex didn't expect him until seven that evening. He had plenty of time to catch up on lost sleep. He greeted his neighbor, who was peering at him through a gap in her curtains, turned the key, and pushed open the front door.

A house in which someone has died holds on to the presence of the dead person for a while. Anyone who has ever lost someone at home will confirm it. The air is heavier and the silence seems to absorb sounds before they're made, like a cemetery where even the shrillest voice sounds muffled. It was different when the reaper had somehow lost the fight and was forced to beat a retreat empty-handed. Then there was a sense of unease, the upset balance and inaudible cry for help of a victim who had escaped the scythe.

Richard had smoked a shitload the night before—his girlfriend only kicked on dope—and fatigue clouded his perception, but he immediately sensed that something wasn't right. He clambered up the stairs and threw open the spare room door without hesitation.

Jonathan was lying on the bed in the fetal position, an empty syringe jabbed into the mattress at his side. Richard stood still for a couple of seconds. He cursed himself for taking the boy in. If Jonathan was dead, he was in a serious mess. The police would ask him uncomfortable questions. Weren't they looking for Jonathan in connection with the shooting at the church? He had to warn Venex, ask his advice, and get rid of the body.

Richard had started to sweat, a cold sweat that made him shiver. Below him, a door slammed shut. He froze on the spot, paralyzed by fear. A sickly sensation in his stomach suddenly sank to his legs and turned them to rubber. The walls of the tiny room started to close in on him, threatened to crush him. There was only one way out. He threw open the window and stuck his head outside.

His neighbor had just dragged a bucket of tepid water outside and was getting ready to wash her windows. She did the same every Tuesday, whatever the weather.

The scrawny woman looked up and saw his ashen face. "Are you sick or what?" she said in a flat Bruges accent. Richard tried to speak, but his voice was hoarse and what he said sounded like the groans of someone having a heart attack.

"Stay where you are. I'll call an ambulance."

The woman hurried inside and punched in the number of the emergency services with trembling fingers. She then ran outside and started to cause a commotion on the street.

In contrast to what Van In had expected, De Kee welcomed him into his office with a warm handshake. The diminutive chief commissioner was wearing a pinstriped suit that didn't really flatter him in spite of the expensive cut. People in West Flanders had a vivid way of describing the likes of De Kee: He looked like a potato farmer.

"Prosecutor Beekman called me yesterday," he said.

No one, not even Adjutant Delrue, believed that Van In was dealing drugs. But public opinion was another thing altogether, and the newspaper article had caused a stir.

"We discussed the case and I'm thinking it might be better if you take some time to . . ." De Kee hesitated. "How shall I put it?"

Van In asked himself what the old bugger was on about.

"It would be better for all concerned if you were to disappear from the public eye for a couple of weeks," said De Kee with a broad smile. "With the investigation at this advanced stage, the last thing we want is negative publicity. If you get my drift."

Van In got his drift. This was the perfect opportunity for De Kee to sideline him.

"The federal boys will set up an investigation, pro forma of course, and Beekman has appointed an examining magistrate just to be on the safe side. So you have nothing to fear, Commissioner. Before long, the public will have forgotten your role in this nasty business and you'll be able to get back to work at your leisure."

They say rattlesnakes are deceitful creatures, but at least they made a noise when they were about to attack. De Kee, on the other hand, was like a cobra. He attacked in silence and without mercy.

"I can imagine Hannelore will be pleasantly surprised. She's about to give birth if I'm not mistaken. If I were you, I would take advantage of the situation and spoil her. You know how modern women are. When they have a baby, they like to have their husband around."

Snakes were incapable of smiling, but the chief commissioner did his best to make up for it. Van In felt the animal gnawing at his chest. The pain was getting more and more intense.

"So you're sending me home," he said flatly.

De Kee treated him to a slap on the shoulder. Van In stoically inhaled a noseful of cheap deodorant. De Kee had bought gallons of the stuff after his girlfriend walked out on him.

"Consider it an unexpected vacation, Pieter. Later, when things have calmed down . . ."

"And the investigation?"

The chief commissioner straightened his face, stuck out his chin, and rubbed his clean-shaven neck.

"I've asked Inspector Pattyn to take charge. The man has proved capable of dealing with cases of this stature in the past and . . ."

"Pattyn is an asshole," Van In snapped. "He thinks his wife's been taking an evening class in French these last three years.

De Kee raised his eyebrows. "French lessons?"

"Exactly, Chief Commissioner. She's been sampling grapes, wink, wink, not learning French . . ."

De Kee was finding Van In's point hard to follow and it irritated him. "We have no other option, Commissioner. If you refuse to go along with my proposal, I'll be forced to suspend you, and that can have nasty consequences for your career."

If Hannelore had been at home, he would probably have considered De Kee's suggestion to take a couple of weeks to let things cool off. He might even have approved of Pattyn as his replacement, but now that De Kee was using threats, Van In was more of a mind to punch him in the nose.

"Do you know what a *doigt* is, Chief Commissioner?"

De Kee stared at him wide-eyed.

"It's French for 'finger,'" said Van In.

"And what's that supposed to mean, Pieter?"

Van In took a deep breath and tried to ignore the pain in his chest. "It means you can shove it, Chief Commissioner."

He bowed like a conductor at the end of a performance and headed for the door.

"Have you gone mad?" De Kee shouted at his back.

"Rather mad than sly, Chief Commissioner. *Arrivederci!*"

The building shook when Van In slammed the door behind him. He raced downstairs to Room 204 without looking right or left.

Guido could see that something had gone wrong, big-time. "Fancy a drink somewhere?" he asked.

Dr. D'Hondt had just finished a twelve-hour shift when Jonathan was brought into emergency. A doctor from the Medical Emergency Team had managed to resuscitate him on the spot, but his condition was still critical. Just as D'Hondt was about to put on his coat and head for home, Jonathan went into cardiac arrest for a second time. The MET doctor didn't mess about, tried the defibrillator a couple of times, and when that didn't work, he injected adrenaline directly into the boy's heart.

"I think we've lost him," the MET doctor wheezed after a few moments without a reaction.

Dr. D'Hondt took off his coat and rushed to the stretcher. "We can't give up," he said.

He took the defibrillator paddles from his colleague, turned the machine to maximum, and placed the paddles on Jonathan's chest. His lifeless body convulsed and then flopped back onto the stretcher like a lead doll. The line on the defibrillator screen peaked and then flattened. D'Hondt repeated the procedure twice. When that didn't help, he clenched his fist and thumped Jonathan's chest with all the strength he could muster. A couple of ribs cracked like dry twigs, but the flat line peaked and peaked again, three times . . . four . . .

The MET doctor just stood and watched. It was the first time he'd witnessed a medical miracle. D'Hondt put on his coat and headed outside. He thanked God he wasn't a psychiatrist.

"Dr. Coleyn has an appointment right now."

The petite secretary pressed her lips together and treated the man at the reception desk to a glare that read: *Try to get past me!*

She had seen the papers, and she recognized the commissioner from the photo.

Van In was forced to lean over. Without his glasses he was unable to read the badge that was pinned to her chest.

"My dear," he said in a frosty tone. "If you don't free up Dr. Coleyn's busy schedule for me in two minutes, I'll be forced to have a word with the hospital director. He's bound to call the public prosecutor, and I wouldn't be surprised if you're making beds here next week instead of manning the reception desk. Or they might just let you go for incompetence. This is a murder investigation, and if your name also appears in the paper tomorrow because you obstructed the investigation, I'm afraid there won't be anything I can do about it."

The secretary scowled, reached for the phone, and punched in a number. Guido smiled. Van In was on a roll, and that meant fireworks.

"The doctor will see you right away," she said a moment later. She put down the phone and emerged from behind the counter. "Follow me, gentlemen."

"Of course I remember Miss Andries's allegations," said Coleyn. The psychiatrist lit a cigarette, unable to conceal his irritation, and puffed a trio of smoke rings into the air. "But I don't see why you should keep me from my work for slanderous statements that were written off as lies twenty years ago. In fact, I'm wondering if you even have the right to question me about them, or anything else for that matter."

Van In could hear the man think. The article in the paper had clearly left an impression.

"Miss Andries tried to ruin my reputation back then, but she failed. Psychiatrists are regularly confronted with accusations of that sort. Women fall in love with their caregivers. So what's new! And when their pipe dreams are unfulfilled, they try to take revenge. It goes with the job. You should know that, Commissioner."

"So you're a happily married man," said Van In casually. He had checked up on Coleyn and discovered he was already nineteen years divorced.

The psychiatrist tried to light another cigarette, but his lighter refused to light. He threw it onto his desk and grabbed a box of matches from a drawer. "What's that got to do with it?"

"So you're divorced."

"Is that a crime?"

Van In thought about Hannelore. Who was he to lecture Coleyn?

"Are you still in touch with your ex-wife?"

"That's none of your goddamn business, Commissioner."

Van In nodded. He didn't have a leg to stand on, and even if he could prove that Dr. Coleyn had raped Veerle Andries, the public prosecutor wouldn't be able to bring charges against the psychiatrist because of the statute of limitations. But Coleyn knew that too, of course.

"Perhaps Veerle Andries was your lover and—"

Van In had gone too far. Coleyn got to his feet and placed both hands flat on his desk, something he always did when he wanted to end a conversation. "If you make a public statement about this, I'll have your ass for slander, Commissioner. Then you'll have your day in court twice over!"

Van In said nothing. Now he was almost certain that Veerle Andries was once the good doctor's lover. "A last question, Doctor."

A tried-and-tested tactic. If the person being questioned got irritable, it was time to ask one last question. Most of the time the answer was honest because the word *last* brought a sense of relief.

"Do you know Jonathan Leman?"

Dr. Coleyn shook his head, his gray locks swishing convincingly back and forth. "No, Commissioner."

"Venex?"

Guido registered a momentary reaction of surprise on Coleyn's face. Van In knew exactly what he was doing.

"Never heard of any *Venes*."

"Venex," Van In repeated.

"I'm sorry, Commissioner. I can't help you."

14

While Guido was busy ordering a couple of servings of that day's special at the hospital's cafeteria, Van In called his in-laws on his cell phone. Not the easiest thing in the world. He felt like a German general sitting in front of an unconditional surrender with a pen in his hand.

"Hello, Andrea?"

Van In couldn't think of a more appropriate name for the creature he called his mother-in-law—it literally meant "she-man."

"I can't believe my ears. The nerve!"

The usual loudmouthed fishwife. Van In held his cell phone a distance from his hear. He couldn't stand her piercing voice. "I'd like to speak to Hanne."

"She's not here."

Van In didn't dare say his mother-in-law was lying. If she picked up on the slightest hint of rudeness, she would snort, hang up, pour herself a glass of port, and spend the rest of the day gloating.

"Do you know where I can reach her?"

"I might." She paused for a moment and then mercilessly extinguished the tiny flicker of hope she had ignited. "And if I did, you know I wouldn't tell you."

She enjoyed rubbing salt into people's wounds.

"Please."

Van In heard her cover the mouthpiece with her hand and shout to her husband: "Your son-in-law said 'please.'"

"Say hello from me," Gerard Martens said with a yawn.

"Gerard says you're a bum."

Van In felt sorry for Gerard. The fact that he'd survived almost forty years with this hag was close to miraculous.

"Say hello from me too."

"Is that everything?" Andrea sneered, taking full enjoyment of his temporary weakness.

"If you see Hanne, tell her I'm sorry."

It wasn't easy for Van In to confide such words to his mother-in-law, far from it, but his spontaneous apology impressed her, and when she spoke again, her words were more measured.

"I might, if I see her, but if I were you, I wouldn't build my hopes up. Forgiveness isn't in the cards."

"I miss her," said Van In.

Andrea thought about her grandchild. A child needs a father. "I can't promise anything," she said. Her voice had softened.

"That's all I have to say, Andrea. Have a good day."

Van In hung up and made his way—suitably chastened—to the table where Guido was waiting with lunch.

"The bitch says Hanne's not home."

Guido cut off a corner of the nameless meat. Hospitals were notorious for their food. They called it sterile, and that was a good fit, in several senses of the word. Van In sat down and sipped at his lukewarm Duvel. He wasn't planning to eat the microwaved mush on the plate in front of him, but he forked a couple of fries for show and dipped them in a splotch of clotted mayonnaise. The smell was better than the taste. He grabbed his Duvel and washed it all down.

"What did Gerard say?"

"That I'm a bum."

"So he said hello." Guido knew how Van In communicated with his in-laws.

"Not so loud, Guido. The hag has ears everywhere."

The hustle and bustle in the cafeteria drowned out the last part of his sentence.

"What did you say?"

"Bon appétit, Guido."

Statistics showed that the Bruges beguinage received more Japanese visitors than Flemish visitors. Van In and Guido both thought the same thing as they forced their way through a group of chattering Asians who were blocking the entrance to the interior courtyard while a balding tourist guide did his best to explain in broken English that Beguines were nuns without rules. They were now extinct and had been replaced by a group of respectable ladies who were able to rent the historical buildings for a pittance on the condition that they abstained from the company of men, at least after dark.

"If my information is correct, she lives in number 18."

Guido had looked up Mrs. Coleyn's address in the database. Her maiden name was Meerseman. Sophie Meerseman.

"I wonder what she'll have to say," said Van In. His foot still remembered Richard Coleyn's door, and he hoped she wouldn't slam hers in his face.

Sophie Meerseman was a sophisticated woman. In spite of her age—midforties—her figure was slender enough to make many a teenage girl jealous. Her rectangular face and smooth skin were graced with eyes like burnished gems. Van In wondered why Dr. Coleyn had traded such a classy chassis for a fling with Veerle Andries.

"I'm Commissioner Van In," he said. "And this is Sergeant Versavel. Do you mind if we come in?"

Sophie Meerseman didn't ask needless questions. She stepped aside and invited the gentlemen to come in. The interior of the refurbished house was a perfect match for the class that Sophie radiated. A selection of contemporary and original paintings on the whitewashed walls, polished Burgundian tiles glowing in the discreet halogen light. The place was bright and crisp. The dark oak furniture smelled of beeswax, and vases of fresh flowers filled the windows.

"Please, take a seat."

Sophie pointed to a three-seater sofa with batik cushions in flamboyant colors. She was wearing a long purple dress that rustled with her every move. Around her neck, she wore a gold chain with a modern stylized ram half concealed between her breasts.

"Can I offer you a cup of coffee?"

"That would be kind of you, ma'am." Guido smiled.

"We're here about your ex-husband, ma'am," said Van In as she disappeared into the open kitchen.

"What's he been up to now?"

She placed two cups under an espresso machine and pressed a button. Van In told her about the death of Trui Andries, the shooting outside the church, and the alleged rape while Sophie served the espressos together with a tray of cherry liqueur chocolates. She then sat down in an armchair and crossed her legs.

"My ex has made a lot of mistakes in his life," she said with a sparing smile. "I know that he's messed around with his patients now and then, but when it comes to Miss Andries, I can be quite clear-cut. John"—she used his first name—"was only interested in beautiful women, and Miss Andries certainly did not fit the bill."

Van In sipped at the excellent cup of coffee. "So you admit your husband cheated on you."

"He cheated," she said flatly.

Van In detected a sadness in her eyes. "But not with Miss Andries."

"Veerle Andries thought John wanted her. When she got pregnant, she appeared at our door and insisted the baby was his."

"And you didn't believe her."

"We both roared with laughter. You should know that Miss Andries was seriously psychotic. She was so frustrated that she did everything she could to attract attention, and she was prepared to do anything to achieve her goal. Another chocolate, Sergeant?" Sophie treated Guido to a seductive smile. Guido pretended not to notice and took another chocolate.

Van In leaned back in the sofa and tried to digest the new information. The case was getting more complex by the day, and the number of possible solutions was increasing exponentially. "May I ask why you and your husband decided to divorce, Ms. Meerseman?" he asked out of the blue.

The smile on Sophie's lips froze. "These things happen, Commissioner," she said evasively.

Van In changed position, rested his chin in his hands, and looked her in the eye. "Let me put my cards on the table, Ms. Meerseman. A number of people have been killed in the last week and until now we've been fumbling around in the dark. Everyone we've questioned has their own story to tell, and the more people we talk to, the deeper we seem to be sinking into a quagmire of lies. You seem to be an intelligent woman, so I'm hoping for once to hear the truth."

Van In's candidness didn't leave Sophie Meerseman indifferent. She had seen images of the mass shooting on TV. A ninth victim had succumbed to her injuries only the day before, a ten-year-old girl. Three bullets had ripped half her chest away. The close-up of the dying child had moved her to tears. "It's hard for me to say this . . ." Her voice faltered.

"Go on, Mrs. Meerseman."

"I was stretching the truth when I claimed that Veerle Andries wasn't an attractive woman."

Van In nodded. He remembered the photo in Trui's apartment. "So your husband fell in love with her."

Sophie had caught them together in her own bed.

"When she got pregnant, John wanted to move in with her." Sophie Meerseman lowered her eyes. When he'd told her, she had become hysterical and ran out of the house. She got herself drunk and then decided to look up Veerle's mother and have a word. A ten-year-old girl had opened the door. *Come in*, the child had said. *My sister will be home shortly.*

"Veerle and Trui's mother was a devout Catholic. She promised she would talk to her daughter, help her see the error of her ways. She assured me I had no reason to worry."

Van In and Guido were all ears.

"The woman kept her word. Veerle ended her relationship with John."

"And the baby?"

Sophie shrugged. "Veerle's mother didn't want her to have an abortion. The child ended up in an orphanage."

The strength with which magnets were drawn to each other depended a great deal on the distance between them. Sophie Meerseman had maneuvered the magnets into the right position, and they had clicked together. Van In now knew who Jonathan was. He remembered Sister Marie-Louise and her story. Veerle

Andries was the woman who had given birth in a department store restroom.

"What did John think about that?"

"He suppressed the entire affair. Psychiatrists are trained in suppression, aren't they, Commissioner?" A wry smile appeared on her lips.

"Did Richard know what was going on?"

"He was only eight when I left John. The judge granted John custody of Richard. You know how it goes in those circles."

Sophie was visibly upset. After all those years, the pain the divorce and losing her child had caused was still present. Van In thought about his own child and the temptations of Saartje Maes. It was like looking into a mirror that predicted nothing but darkness.

"One final question, Ms. Meerseman."

Sophie smiled joylessly.

"Do you think your ex-husband is capable of murder?"

"I know what you're thinking, Commissioner."

"Perhaps Trui was blackmailing him."

"I don't think so. Trui was raised Catholic like her sister. She would have been more inclined to offer forgiveness than seek revenge."

Van In was reminded of Jonathan's words: "She descended into hell to save us from evil." Trui Andries had discovered that Jonathan was her sister's son. She had taken a job at the orphanage to be close to her nephew.

"Another coffee, Commissioner?"

Van In looked at Guido. The tray with the cherry liqueur chocolates was empty.

"No thank you, ma'am. It's time we were on our way."

The discussion with Sophie Meerseman had brought considerable clarity to the situation. If Jonathan was Veerle

Andries's son, then they had to dig deeper into his past. Sister Marie-Louise had said all she was willing to say. Maybe the janitor had something more. Hadn't he and his wife tried to adopt the boy?

Prosecutor Beekman's house in the country was partially hidden behind a patch of angular pines. It was the ideal place to unwind, far from the bustle of the law courts and in the middle of one of the few areas of natural beauty that had survived in the Bruges region. Beekman was into ecology, not a fanatic ready to take to the streets every time a tree was in danger of being cut down, but the outdoor matter-of-fact type with common sense in abundance. He treasured the portion of nature his parents had left to him and hoped others would do the same with their own inheritance.

Saartje Maes parked her car in the driveway and stepped out. The crunch of her shoes on the gravel was the only sound to be heard for miles. It felt weird, like being on another planet. It had been years since she had inhaled the smell of rotting leaves. She walked up to the door and reached out for the old-fashioned mechanical doorbell. *Dingalingaling.* Its voice was pure, and it traveled through the house like a cheerful song.

In no time at all—ten seconds at the most—she heard a noise inside, someone walking to the door, the footsteps of a woman. A key turned and the door swung open.

"What in God's name are you doing here?"

Hannelore stared at Saartje Maes in astonishment. She had actually been expecting Pieter.

"I want to have a word with you, about your husband."

"Did he send you?"

Saartje shook her head.

"How did you find me then?"

Saartje tried not to smile. Hannelore might interpret it wrongly and she didn't want to cause yet another misunderstanding. "Your mother told me."

It had taken Saartje an hour and a half to convince the hag that she wasn't Van In's lover. "Do you mind if I come in?"

Hannelore had had a miserable night. She had asked herself again and again why Van In had cheated on her, and now the object of her nightmares was standing in front of her on the doorstep.

"You've got a nerve," she said. "If I were you, I'd be ashamed."

"It's not what you think, Hannelore."

"Isn't it?"

"Please give me the chance to explain. If you don't believe me, I promise I'll leave you alone."

Hannelore shook her head and started to close the door in Saartje's face.

"If I was attracted to anyone, it would have to be you," said Saartje in desperation. "I'm a lesbian, Hannelore. Men do nothing for me."

The door slowly opened.

Guido headed off to the police station to pick up Guy Deridder's address, leaving Van In at a covered café terrace on Zand Square. He wasn't in the mood for a face-off with De Kee. He was officially on suspension, and it was better to let sleeping dogs lie. His presence in Hauwer Street would only cause a commotion, and that was the last thing he wanted.

A slovenly dressed waiter brought the Duvel he had ordered. Its frothy head had collapsed. Van In paid the man and made a mental note never to come back. He sipped at the beer and made a face. It tasted of dishwashing liquid, and there were traces of lipstick on the rim. He couldn't help comparing the

Duvel with the case he was investigating: Both left a foul taste in his mouth.

The conversation with Ms. Meerseman had clarified a number of things, but he still didn't have enough to draw conclusions. They needed more information, and at this stage, they were still grasping at straws.

"Deridder has no reason to complain," said Van In as they pulled up to the house an hour later.

Guido pulled on the handbrake and unclicked his seat belt. "He remarried last year," he said with a grin. "A widow with money in the bank."

"Some people always land on their feet."

Van In took a last puff of his cigarette and stepped out of the car. Deridder's villa, a hideous pile of stones with a thatched roof, Flemish ironwork, and oak doors, was flanked on either side by two similar monstrosities in a chic Bruges suburb. A smart town-and-country planning official had had a row of poplars planted to ensure that the residential area wasn't visible from the nearby highway.

"Orphans and widows," said Van In. "Everything pays off if you know how to work it."

The current Mrs. Deridder was a friendly lady in her fifties and matched Van In's image of a rich widow to perfection. She was dressed in a stylish outfit that discreetly camouflaged her rotund figure, and the gold draped around her neck and wrists was worth enough to send an average family on holiday every year for the rest of their lives.

"Could we have a word with Mr. Deridder?"

The woman's ruby-red lips unfolded into a broad smile. "We don't need anything right now, but please, gentlemen, come inside. Who shall I say is here?"

"Pieter Van In and Guido Versavel."

Van In felt like a door-to-door salesman. He wanted to add "Cheese specialists to his majesty the king" but stopped himself just in time. The very mention of royalty would probably have prompted a substantial order. Her husband loved his cheese, no doubt.

"My husband is in his studio. He's a painter, you know. He has an exhibition lined up for next year in the old market hall. Very prestigious."

She floated along the corridor like a quilted wood nymph. Van In and Guido followed. If Guy Deridder didn't achieve success as a painter, he could always write a letter to the *Guinness Book of Records*. After Graceland, his home was the undisputed Kingdom of Kitsch. Pink wallpaper with green leprechauns, gilded telephones, crystal chandeliers, a canary yellow lounge suite, curtains with rhinestones, fluffy dinosaurs, framed jigsaw puzzles on the wall, Greek goddesses and lecherous satyrs, a stuffed poodle with its fossilized snout still stuck in its bowl, a spluttering fountain surrounded by plastic vegetation, Persian rugs *Made in Korea*, a collection of Barbie dolls in an empty aquarium, and two pairs of house slippers with images of Joseph and Mary.

"We have visitors, Guy."

Mrs. Deridder's harrowing voice sounded like the trumpet blast that brought down the walls of Jericho.

"Good afternoon, Mr. Deridder."

The former janitor at Suffer Little Children was wearing a white smock and a black bow tie. Van In placed him in his early forties.

"Good afternoon, gentlemen. How can I be of service?"

Deridder handed his brush and palette to his chubby wood nymph of a wife and turned toward his visitors with the air of a genuine artiste.

"We're from the police," said Van In. "It's about Jonathan Leman."

"Ah. How's the boy doing these days?"

"Not well at all, Mr. Deridder."

"Oh, such a shame."

Van In perused the walls of Deridder's studio. His work reminded him of the leprechauns on the wallpaper, the gilded telephones, and the Persian rugs *Made in Korea.* "We would greatly appreciate your cooperation, Mr. Deridder."

The face of the amateur dauber beamed, but Van In had no delusions. A man who had ripped off a pack of nuns for the best part of ten years had to be smart by definition.

"And I imagine you're also interested in Trui Andries?"

Van In nodded. So much for Sister Marie-Louise's claim that Deridder didn't interact with the other staff.

"Take a seat, gentlemen."

Deridder winked at the wood nymph, and she knew immediately what she had to do.

"Champagne?" she asked.

The wood nymph turned and tiptoed out of the studio like an aging ballerina without waiting for confirmation.

Deridder's interior design skills may have been atrocious, but he clearly knew his champagne.

"Veuve Clicquot, La Grande Dame, 1989. Cheers."

Van In sipped at the pretentious flute, a crystal vase with a gilded rim. "You knew that Jonathan was Trui's nephew."

Deridder nodded and popped a cigarette into a meerschaum holder.

"Trui was a good girl, Commissioner. She wanted to look after Jonathan. After her sister took her own life, Trui applied no fewer than eight times for a job at the orphanage."

"Did the sisters at the orphanage know they were related?"

Deridder puffed at his cigarette. "The sisters finally took her on when she agreed to work for eighty percent of the normal pay. In such circumstances, no one asked any questions."

Van In sipped at the champagne. It was soft, refreshing, with a hint of raspberry.

"And now I'm guessing you'll want to know about Jasper Simons," said Deridder, leaning back in his chair like a Turkish pasha. "Trui persuaded the sisters to give Jasper a job."

"At eighty percent of the normal pay?"

"Seventy-five, Commissioner. Jasper had a psychiatric history. Good deeds had to bring in the bacon, and the sisters knew how to run a business."

Van In liked the man's cynicism.

"I heard that Jasper had trouble with hallucinations. Something about the devil . . ."

"Jasper was a satanist. At least that's what he claimed. When Trui found out, she was determined to convert him, just as she was determined to be a mother for Jonathan. She thought that the social work being done in the orphanage would open Jasper's eyes."

The pieces of part of the puzzle came together seamlessly. Jonathan had told the truth in that respect. Trui had descended into hell to save the ones she loved.

"Do you think she—"

Deridder anticipated the question. "Trui converted to satanism to convince Jasper of the error of his ways. She studied for months on end to be able to refute his arguments."

Van In emptied his glass in one gulp. That explained the extensive library. "And the sisters didn't appreciate it, so they let her go."

"How did you guess, Commissioner?"

Mrs. Deridder topped up the glasses. She clearly knew how to spoil a man.

"One thing still bothers me," said Van In.

"Did I screw the sisters out of three million?"

"That's your business, Mr. Deridder. As far as I'm concerned, you only took what you were entitled to. But didn't you read in the papers that we wanted to question you?"

Deridder smiled. "Have you heard of the Confucian Circle, Commissioner?"

"What does that have to do with it?"

"A great deal, Commissioner. You were fated to meet me. To be honest, I expected you yesterday."

Guido smiled. According to the Confucian Circle principle, when you met someone, you would also meet their friends and acquaintances one day.

"I'm guessing your next question will be about Venex," said Deridder.

Van In heaved a silent sigh of relief. "Do you know him?"

"Venex is a common drug dealer who screws around with young people's heads."

"Is he a satanist?"

Deridder smiled. "Venex is a businessman. He only believes in money."

"Who is he?"

"I don't know, Commissioner. Jonathan told me about him, but when I asked about the man's identity, he clammed up. He often spoke about the legacy of Lodewijk Van Haecke, though, the Holy Blood chaplain."

Guido raised his eyebrows. He remembered the portrait of the satanic priest in the cellar of the Sons of Asmodeus.

"According to reports, the chaplain received a visit around the turn of the century from Aleister Crowley, an occultist renowned in those days as the pope of satanism. The story goes that the chaplain provided Crowley with female company for the night. The girl, a certain Anna Boterman, got pregnant and later gave birth to a son. They say the boy inherited Crowley's fortune."

"How do you know all this?"

"Jasper told me when he'd had one too many. He refused to come back to the orphanage after that."

Van In took a sip of the excellent champagne. It was becoming clear that Venex was the kingpin, the man Trui had written about in her letter, and, in all probability, the brain behind the mass killing. But why? If he wasn't a satanist, then why kill nine innocent churchgoers? And Crowley. Where had he heard that name before?

"So you think Venex had Jonathan completely in his power?"

Deridder nodded. "Jonathan didn't have the financial means to get hold of drugs."

"And Jasper?"

"I don't think Jasper was doing heroin."

"Richard Coleyn?"

"Coleyn? Absolutely." Deridder said the name Coleyn with an element of disdain, enough to draw Van In's attention.

"Do you know him?"

The affable amateur fidgeted nervously with his bow tie. "I know who his father is," he said.

"So you're not a big fan of psychiatrists either," said Van In with a smile.

"No, Commissioner."

"Thank God," said Van In.

Deridder's hand tightened around his glass, and his knuckles turned white. "I imagine you know what happened to my first wife."

Van In nodded. He looked at the wood nymph, but she seemed to be just as upset. Her eyes filled with tears, and she reached for a box of Kleenex.

"Tania"—he hadn't spoken his first wife's name in ages—"was unable to have children. So when Jonathan was brought to the orphanage, we applied to adopt him. Dr. John Coleyn was chair of the committee that dealt with such applications and made recommendations."

Deridder emptied his glass in a single gulp. The wood nymph refilled it immediately.

"We weren't good enough to adopt a child. Our living quarters were inadequate, we didn't earn enough money, and our psychological profile didn't correspond to that of the model family."

Deridder sounded bitter. Dr. Coleyn's recommendation was an insult that had been etched in his memory for eternity. "Nobody said a word about the psychiatrist and all his mistresses."

Guido looked at Van In, hoping the commissioner would learn a lesson from Deridder's words. Van In sensed his colleague's reproachful gaze.

"Did you know that Jonathan is the son of Veerle Andries and John Coleyn?"

Guy Deridder slammed down his glass, and his cheerful expression disappeared. "The bastard."

Silence filled the studio. Van In thought about Hannelore. He had to find her whatever it took and beg her to forget the incident with Saartje, on his bended knees if he had to.

"Interesting conversation," said Guido.

Van In hit the gas. The tires spun and dug themselves into the gravel like hungry trenchers. The Golf shot into reverse and left deep tracks in the neatly leveled driveway.

Guido clicked his safety belt, leaned forward, and switched on the rotating lights. “At least the other people on the road will be able to get out of the way when they see you coming,” he said stoically.

Van In hit the brakes, and the Golf jolted like a badly sprung baby carriage.

“Guido, the queen of bellyaching,” Van In said, crunching into first gear. The sturdy German car accepted the shock and blindly obeyed the foot of its master. Typical German!

“Tell me what’s on your mind.”

Van In slowed down. A police car with rotating lights doing twenty-five brought a smile to more than a few faces on the street.

“I’m going around the bend.”

“Do you suspect John Coleyn?”

“At least he has a motive.”

“So does Deridder, Pieter. I found him a little too smug. Too good to be true. And didn’t he work in a hospital for a while? That gives him a medical background. And don’t forget Mr. Simons. He hated Trui with a vengeance.”

“And what about the shooting?”

Guido didn’t answer. It seemed unlikely that one of the three suspects would have shot eight, now nine, people dead in cold blood. “What do we do now?”

Van In hit the gas. “First I make peace with Hannelore, and tomorrow we make another round of visits.”

“Sounds like a plan.”

“Shall I drop you off at home?”

Guido nodded.

When Van In opened the front door and went inside, he knew immediately that Hannelore wasn’t home. The house was ice cold, and the kitchen was filled with the sour smell of unwashed plates.

He tried to light the fire, and when that didn't work, he turned up the thermostat to eighty degrees. He then raided the refrigerator: a couple of slices of stale bread, a half-empty jar of cheese spread, and a slice of salami that was well past its sell-by date. He gobbled it all down like a starving wolf.

Van In lit a cigarette and punched in the number of his in-laws. He heaved a sigh of relief when he heard his father-in-law's voice.

"Gerard, Pieter here. It's good to hear your voice."

"She was here yesterday to get her things. In and out in half an hour. You know Hannelore. She doesn't want to be a burden."

Van In had suspected as much. Hanne was an independent woman. He was dumb to have thought she'd run home to her parents.

"Is it for me?" someone shouted in the background. Van In recognized Andrea's shrill voice, and Gerard switched to a whisper.

"She's staying with Beekman," he said hastily. "And she loves you."

He heard a commotion on the other end of the line as Andrea pried the phone from her husband's hand. "She wants nothing more to do with you, Pieter. And if I was you, I would . . ."

"If I was you, I'd turn off the heat under your cauldron," said Van In, slamming down the receiver and turning to the window. The man in the moon had a smile on his face. Van In poured himself a Duvel and called Beekman, but the answering machine picked up four times in a row: *I'm not available to take your call. Please leave a message after the tone.*

15

Three Duvels were enough to clear Van In's mind of the crap that had been building up over the last few days. Murders, satanists, drug dealers, and false accusations . . . He didn't give a fuck anymore. The radiators were at boiling point, but instead of turning down the thermostat, he kicked off his shoes, stripped to his underwear, and collapsed on the sofa. He lay on his back and peered at the belly that was blocking the view of his toes. Depression germinated in his head.

Lonely people experienced time differently from overstressed fusspots. When you had nothing to look forward to, you entered another dimension, where minutes seemed to last for hours. There were nine cigarette butts in the ashtray, but Van In still had the impression it was early. The clock in the hall confirmed it. Seven thirty. Another twelve hours to go before sunrise. Sleep made more sense than anything else, and the hope that his dreams might refresh him.

A rusty old lock could sometimes be better than an advanced alarm system. The noise it made was usually enough to wake anyone who heard it, but that only applied to normal people, not lonely drunks who'd passed out after a night on the booze.

"He's home," said Hannelore. She turned the thermostat to sixty-five and threw open the kitchen window.

"You can't leave them alone for long," Saartje said, then giggled.

A cool evening breeze poured into the kitchen like a breath of fresh air. Hannelore took off her coat. The smell of cigarettes and unwashed feet was unbearable. And all that in one single day.

"I think he's in the living room," she said.

"Can I join you?"

"Of course you can." Hannelore threw open the living room door and switched on the light. "Thought so," she said.

Saartje couldn't believe her eyes. She'd rather have a birdbrain with muscles than the thing that was snoring on the sofa.

Van In was in a wooden hut full of naked men and hot steam. He crawled into a corner. The steam hid him from view. The men were a noisy bunch, prattling like American tourists and lashing each other on the back with fine twigs. No one paid any attention to him but he still felt uneasy. Van In had never fantasized about men before and asked himself if he'd landed in one of Guido's dreams by accident. Then a muscular V-shaped specimen suddenly jumped to his feet and threw open the door. An ice-cold wind made him shiver. The men ran outside whooping and cheering and played leapfrog in the snow. Van In wrapped his arms around his chest. His teeth chattered. Two men beckoned him to the door. Why had they left it open? He felt a hand on his shoulder.

"Leave me alone," he screamed.

Hannelore smiled. In his socks and underwear he wasn't much of a Romeo. Saartje looked away out of embarrassment, but only for a second. The picture was too funny to miss.

"Wake up, Pieter. It's me, Hannelore."

Hannelore was a word that had the power to penetrate the clouds of his subconscious mind. He opened his eyes.

"*Ego te absolvo,*" she said.

Van In pictured confessionals and pale-faced priests who gave him severe penances every time he admitted to a sin against purity.

"Saartje explained everything."

Hannelore leaned down and kissed him on the lips. She smelled of pine needles, and her breasts were warm and soft. Someone giggled in the background. Van In groped for the blanket that was lying on the floor beside the sofa and quickly covered his lower body. This wasn't a dream, it was a nightmare. The two women looked down at him. The cold air flowing through the living room door worked wonders. Van In straightened himself up and pulled on his trousers like a bather on the beach, with the blanket held tightly around his waist. Saartje turned and headed back into the kitchen.

"I called you several times," said Van In, his voice dry and hoarse.

"That's sweet of you."

Hannelore gazed at him, her eyes wide and inviting, just like that first time when she massaged his ankles one sultry summer evening.

"I love you, Hanne."

"I know," she said.

Saartje had popped a dish of mashed potatoes in the oven and set the three steaks to sizzling in a pan next to a simmering pot of green beans. She had found all the ingredients in the freezer, and in spite of her lack of experience in the kitchen, she thought she was doing a pretty good job. The wonderful smell in the kitchen reminded her of her childhood, when her mother made roast beef and cauliflower every Sunday without fail.

Van In jabbed his fork into the last chunk of beef and wiped his plate clean.

"That was very tasty, Miss Maes."

Both women burst out laughing.

"Don't pretend you're a saint, Pieter. I'm not planning to run out on you if you use her first name."

Van In reveled in the novelty of the situation. He found it hard to imagine enjoying a meal with his wife that had been prepared by his alleged mistress, and even harder to imagine them gathered around the table talking like civilized human beings.

The topic of conversation was the investigation into the mass shooting, of course, and that led them inevitably to Jonathan.

"Didn't you say you sent him shopping?" Van In asked. "Was he away for long?"

"Onc and half liours, two hours tops. Why d'you ask? I was just getting ready for my nap and I told him he didn't have to hurry."

"Did he wake you when he got back?"

"He didn't want to bother me. I gave him a key and . . ." Hannelore suddenly realized where Van In was leading.

Van In treated himself to a serious swig of Duvel. Now he understood why the fifty thousand francs in the wardrobe had been left untouched. Jonathan had other plans. He'd probably made a copy of the front door key to let himself in later with a bag of heroin to conceal under the toilet rolls. He'd done the same thing to get hold of a key to Muylle's car. Was he the killer? Van In found it hard to believe. Jonathan worked for Venex, and Venex was under investigation by the federal police. The planting of the heroin, the anonymous tip—the entire operation was a stupid diversion intended to get Van In removed from the case. It was an act of desperation, a hasty decision made by someone who felt himself cornered.

"I went shopping myself on Saturday morning," said Hannelore, anticipating his next question. "Someone must have been watching the house."

Van In took another gulp of Duvel. He was slowly but surely coming to grips with the situation. "If you ask me, Jonathan was facing a moral dilemma. Trui's influence made him want to live a different life, a better life, but he was unable to detach himself from Venex. When you sent Jonathan shopping, he turned to Venex for advice, and Venex changed his plans on the spot."

"What plans?" asked Hannelore.

Van In took a moment to think. For one reason or another, he had the feeling that Venex had made a mistake. "The infantile attempt to discredit me suggests that he had reason to believe I was on to him."

"We know he has connections with the federal boys. According to Beekman, they got their information from a snitch, someone reliable who'd worked for them before," said Hannelore. "But Adjutant Delrue refuses to divulge the name of his informant." She scraped the remains of the mash from Van In's plate onto her fork and licked it clean. "He thinks he's getting close to a major drug dealer and he's determined to protect his sources."

"Then it's about time we had a private word with Adjutant Delrue." Van In finished his Duvel and went to the phone. "Hello, Guido. Sorry to bother you so late, but . . ."

"I'm sorry, Father."

Richard had spent the last thirty-six hours in hiding in the house on Raam Street where the fraternity held its regular meetings. Venex usually spent most of his time there, but he hadn't appeared the day before, and Richard had no idea where to reach his master, so he'd waited.

"My neighbor called the emergency services," he said. "There was nothing I could do to stop her."

He told him what had happened and Venex listened attentively. The police were now sure to make the link between Jonathan and Richard, and if Jonathan survived, there was more than a good chance that he would talk. Venex tried to think it through, to be logical. He had to presume that the cops hadn't questioned Jonathan yet. If they had, they would have already been at his door.

"You did the right thing to come to me, Richard."

Venex walked to the phone, looked up the number of the hospital, and called reception. He pretended to be Jonathan's uncle, and in a few short minutes he had the boy's room number. The receptionist then transferred him to the care unit on the eighth floor, where he was informed that Jonathan wasn't ready for visitors. When the night nurse asked for his identity, he broke the connection.

"All is not yet lost, Richard."

Venex smiled and returned the receiver to the cradle. First Jonathan, then Richard.

In the seventies, more than a few Belgians with moderate incomes were given the opportunity to buy their own homes at very affordable prices with the help of government subsidies. Adjutant Delrue, who was still a sergeant at the time, took advantage of the assistance and bought a house on an estate to the north of Bruges.

Van In parked the Golf directly opposite the adjutant's house. Guido surveyed the cheerless facades, all of them identical and each with a TV screen flickering inside. Even the TVs were all in the same place. They got out and crossed the street.

"I wonder how he'll react when he sees us," said Guido.

"Me too, Guido. Me too."

Ding dong.

"Good evening, Adjutant. Mind if we come in?" Van In grinned from ear to ear, and Delrue didn't like it.

"I thought you were suspended," he said.

"There's so much nonsense going around these days. You can't believe everything you hear."

Van In stepped inside. "We won't keep you long, Delrue, just five minutes. Then we'll be out of your life forever."

The federal adjutant was wearing striped pajamas and a cheap pair of bath slippers. His wife was nowhere in sight, which meant she'd probably already retired to the bedroom, where she had a TV of her own—and all the other things she needed to make it through the night. Pressure at work and irregular hours had been the death of many a cop's marriage.

Delrue remained standing in the corridor, determined not to let them come any farther. "Why don't you just bugger off? I see no reason why I should talk to you."

"I've got an offer for you," said Van In.

"Put it in writing."

Delrue stepped forward and placed his hand on the door handle. Van In sensed he was losing the argument. He thought about Sister Marie-Louise. Her weakness was love of one's neighbor. What was the adjutant's weakness?

"What would you say if I told you I could identify the real drug dealer? Think about it, Delrue. Your bosses would be over the moon."

Delrue looked at his visitors. Pressure from Major Baudrin had forced him to be unprofessional. He'd been in too much of a hurry with the search warrant, and the more he thought about it, the less believable it seemed that Van In was a heroin dealer.

"Come in," he snapped.

Guido breathed a sigh of relief, and the smile returned to Van In's face. They followed the adjutant into the living room.

Delrue didn't explain the blanket and pillows on the sofa. He invited them to take a seat and switched off the TV.

"Scotch?"

Van In nodded. Delrue shuffled toward the kitchen. He suddenly looked ten years older.

"What are you going to tell him?" asked Guido.

"No idea. We're inside, and that's what matters." Van In wanted to say something else, but at that moment Delrue appeared with a tray, three glasses, and a quart of Glenfiddich. The label on the bottle had been stamped in red: *For crew only.*

"I didn't know you worked for customs," Van In said sarcastically.

Delrue shrugged his shoulders. Van In and Guido were colleagues. Even his boss drank tax-free whiskey. "I'm guessing that's not why you're here."

"Commissioner Van In's had a tiring week," Guido said, his tone apologetic. "Don't let him get to you."

"We're not the best of buddies, Commissioner, I understand that, and I also admit that the search warrant was a clumsy way to confirm the tip we received, but . . ." Delrue sighed and emptied his glass in a single gulp.

"But the investigation was at a standstill," said Van In.

Delrue nodded. "I was convinced we were almost ready to close the case, but the major wanted immediate results. Our officers have turned into accountants. If we've used up our budget, then we need to move on to a new project and account for the old one. Do you get my drift, Commissioner?"

Van In nodded. He was well aware of the new philosophy. Instead of solving concrete crimes, the Special Detectives Division had been split up into theme-based departments. One focused on people trafficking, others on drugs, computer fraud, the Mafia, selling illegal hormones to farmers . . . They had to infiltrate their own particular underworld and were only allowed to make a move if it suited their federal bosses. That meant when the theme was ripe for media attention. Every crime had its time and place. December was set aside for bank robbers, January for drunk drivers, February and March for the hormone dealers, April and May for the drug dealers . . . and the list went on. There was plenty of crime around, but it was important to introduce order to the chaos. That's what the public wanted.

"So you thought: Let's have a go at Van In?"

Delrue poured himself a second glass.

"My colleagues warned me," he said dryly. "Don't underestimate Van In."

"But you decided to ignore them."

Delrue's resistance dissolved like a sand castle at high tide. The adjutant tossed another glass of whiskey down his throat. "I had reason to believe that the dealer knew our every move in advance, as if someone was providing him with inside information. I'd been convinced for a while that he had contacts in the police, and when your name came up, I put two and two . . ."

"Don't make me laugh, Delrue. You guys don't even trust your wives when you're on an important case. What made you think I—"

"Give me time to explain," said Delrue.

He refilled the glasses and tried to be as succinct as possible, struggling at first to find the right words. The narcotics division had been aware for more than a year that someone was dealing ecstasy and heroin on a large scale in and around Bruges. After months of detective work, they came to the conclusion that most of the stuff was being distributed via the Iron Virgin. They launched Operation Snow White, and two young detectives infiltrated the place but failed to unmask the man behind the scenes. They were also in the dark about the source of the drugs and how they were getting into the country. All they managed to pick up was that the dealer used a pseudonym. Everyone knew him as Venex. Two weeks later, Delrue received an anonymous tip. The unidentified caller claimed that Venex was shifting his operation to the area around Courtrai. The informant suggested they arrest a couple of couriers, but that didn't help. The boys in question had each been recruited for one-off deliveries. They'd been told there wasn't much action in Bruges anymore.

"And in the meantime, the Iron Virgin continued to enjoy protection."

Delrue nodded. "We were convinced that the dealer had moved on."

"I'm guessing you never met the informant," said Van In.

Delrue shook his head.

"Did you ever think he might have been leading you down the garden path?" A picture was slowly forming in Van In's mind, getting clearer by the minute.

"Why would he? His information was always on the ball. With his help we managed to confiscate two kilos of heroin and ten thousand ecstasy pills in a couple of months' time."

"Dealers have been known to betray their couriers," said Van In. Occasionally drug dealers would tip the police themselves and offer up a couple of "innocent" couriers in exchange for some breathing space.

Delrue shook his head, then added, "The consignments were always relatively large. Half a kilo is a lot of heroin, even for a major dealer."

Van In tried to line up four grave pieces of information. One: The drug dealer knew someone in the federal police or the local police who provided him with information. Two: The moment the name Venex raised its head, the federal police received a tip from an unknown informant and large amounts of heroin and ecstasy were intercepted. Three: No one knew where the drugs were coming from. Four: At the first sign of progress in the mass shooting investigation, the informant made a clumsy attempt to frame Van In for drug dealing.

"Do you mind if I ask what happened to the couriers you picked up?"

"We had to let them go."

"Are you kidding? Why?"

"They were all psychiatric patients who were allowed into the city once a week. They were all readmitted to their various treatment centers and kept under lock and key."

Guido looked at Van In. The commissioner was beaming. "One more question, Delrue. When did your informant drop my name?"

"The day before yesterday. He told me he'd spoken to a journalist and that the story was scheduled to appear in the papers even if we did nothing."

"And you didn't consider that suspicious?"

"No."

"Did you contact the journalist?"

"He contacted me to ask if his information was correct."

"And you confirmed it?"

Delrue said nothing.

"Did you confirm it, Adjutant?"

"I didn't deny it," he said with the necessary embarrassment. "Don't get me wrong, Commissioner. A statement in the press is sometimes the only way to put pressure on the magistrates. Don't think the public prosecutor would have done anything if . . ."

"Don't sweat it, Delrue. I'd have done the same in your place."

The adjutant smiled. "I didn't believe the story myself, to be honest. That's why I'm happy you pinned down the dealer, Commissioner."

Guido pinched his eyes shut, curious to see how Van In was going to save himself.

"I thought you were the dealer, Delrue, but on closer inspection I have to admit that I was wrong."

Van In emptied his glass and got to his feet. Guido quickly followed his example.

The adjutant, on the other hand, stayed where he was, staring wide-eyed at his visitors. "They told me you were a bastard," he hissed.

"And they were right, Adjutant. Thanks for the whiskey. See you around."

Van In raised his hand and left the room. He hadn't felt this good in months.

16

The sky above Bruges was a fluffy blanket that merged invisibly with the silhouette of the city. Sharp contrasts made way for grayish contours and shrouded facades. Zand Square was like an urban desert, desolate and abandoned. Van In crossed the square diagonally. He had slept reasonably well the night before, and that was clear to see. He was a happy man. The warmth of Hannelore's body had nourished him the entire night, and the same warmth now protected him from the cutting east wind. Deep in his heart he was certain that everything would work out: the baby and the investigation. The information he had managed to pry from Delrue was exceptionally valuable. Later he planned to tie up the knots and test his hypothesis against reality.

He turned onto Hauwer Street and saw a Golf parked in front of the police station with its engine running. That had to be Guido. The sergeant was sitting bolt upright at the wheel. Van In opened the passenger door and collapsed in the seat. He shook Guido's hand, lit a cigarette, and started to cough.

"Breathtaking aftershave, Guido. I mean literally . . ."

Guido ignored the remark, shifted into first, and hit the gas. There was more than one way to pollute the atmosphere.

Dr. Coleyn's office was dimly lit. A single halogen lamp dangled above his desk, forming an egg-shaped pocket of light. The burly psychiatrist invited Van In and Guido to take a seat as he removed the cellophane wrapper on a new pack of cigarettes.

"We wanted a word with you about your son," said Van In.

Coleyn cut the tax band with his thumbnail. "I heard you paid a visit to my ex-wife." The psychiatrist's voice didn't sound bitter. He still spoke to her from time to time, and if she had news, she would always call him.

"Actually, it's about both your sons," said Van In.

The doctor lit a cigarette, his fingers trembling.

"Richard and Jonathan."

Van In waited.

"I should never have walked out on Veerle," said Coleyn. "How could I have known she would abandon the child as she did?"

Van In was also in the mood for a cigarette, but all the coughing in the car stopped him from lighting up.

"Did Richard tell you?"

Coleyn nodded. His Adam's apple bobbed up and down, and he exhaled huge clouds of smoke as if he could hide his emotions in the haze.

"Richard finally left home a year and a half ago. We'd had another fight. He accused me of being a bad father, and I told him he had no right to judge. Then he told me about Jonathan."

The psychiatrist bowed his head as if the suffering of three generations had suddenly landed on his shoulders. "I should have left Richard with his mother."

Van In felt sorry for the man. *An upside-down world*, he thought. *For once I'm in the chair and the shrink's on the couch.*

"That's something we can't change, Doctor," said Van In.

Guido liked the fact that Van In had addressed the man as "Doctor" for once.

"I insisted he should be like me, like my father and grandfather. But times have changed. I've lost him. I've lost everything: my sons, my wife, and the woman I loved."

Van In waited until Coleyn had finished his story. No one had ever been trained to raise their children. If it went wrong, there was precious little parents could do about it. It wasn't the most cheerful prospect for a father-to-be.

"We suspect Richard exploited a number of your patients, Doctor. He used them as drug couriers, knowing the police would have to readmit them for treatment, rather than hold them in jail. I suspect he plucked his victims from your database."

"You know I can't share that kind of information," said Coleyn.

"At least eleven people have lost their lives, Doctor. The killer may even be one of your patients. I can always ask for a warrant, but I imagine you would prefer to cooperate voluntarily given the circumstances."

Coleyn sighed in resignation, then swiveled in his chair, reached for the computer keyboard, and opened the appropriate file.

Psychiatrists were expected to be a listening ear for people with an ailing soul, and that took time. Dr. Coleyn had two hundred and twelve registered clients. The man worked a fifty-hour week, three thousand minutes in total. Van In figured that if Coleyn spent all his time with his patients and didn't use his phone, attend meetings, or eat lunch, then each of them could count on fourteen minutes a week max.

Coleyn scrolled through the list of names on the screen.

"Masyn. That sounds familiar," said Van In.

"Frederik Masyn is the son of Casper Masyn, the notary who was killed with his wife last Sunday in the church shooting."

"The billionaire."

"That's what they say," said Coleyn emotionlessly.

"What's his problem?"

"Frederik is schizophrenic. He thinks he's the son of Satan."

Van In's penny dropped. Now he had a motive for the church shooting. And it might have more to do with greed than with satanism. Or did they mean the same thing?

"You don't think that Frederik . . ." Coleyn didn't complete his sentence. He remembered lengthy conversations with the boy. The Kingdom of Satan was at hand. The demiurge was soon to rise from the core of the earth and his sons were expected to prepare the way for him. The master needed a palace, cars, jewels, a yacht . . . And that called for money . . . a lot of money.

"He lives close to Saint Jacob's Church, Leeuw Street 13," said Van In. "If he wanted to kill both his parents, he had to make sure he wasn't a suspect. Otherwise he could forget his inheritance."

Coleyn nodded. His stomach churned. After so many sessions with the boy, he'd had to admit that he'd really believed what the boy was saying. "He had to build a palace, come what may."

"What did you say, Doctor?" Van In exchanged a knowing look with Guido. Coleyn appeared to be in a sort of trance.

"I think Frederik staged the shooting to throw us off the scent. A murder can be hard to solve without a motive."

Coleyn nodded once again. If he'd had the boy locked up in an institution, this tragedy would never have happened. Van In got to his feet.

"Are you all right, Doctor? Shall I call someone?"

Coleyn waved the question aside. "Don't worry about me, Commissioner. I have a pile of work to keep me busy."

Coleyn showed them to the door. When they were gone, he slumped into his chair and buried his face in his hands.

"Prosecutor Beekman?"

Van In called from the car on his cell phone. He'd stashed it in the glove compartment a couple of weeks earlier just in case Hannelore needed to contact him in a hurry.

"Speaking."

Van In explained what he wanted. And it wasn't to be sneered at.

"I'll do my best to convince the examining magistrate of the urgency of your request, Pieter," said Beekman.

"Then we'll drive to his office right away."

Van In popped the cell phone in his inside pocket. With a bit of luck, they would soon have a search warrant and an arrest warrant, both in the name of Frederik Masyn. Thirty minutes tops.

"Venex, here we come!"

Guido switched on the rotating lights and hit the gas. "I hope you're right, Pieter."

"I don't want you to leave the building until I get back," said Venex. "Is that understood?"

Richard had just taken an extra dose of heroin. He was lying on the sofa staring at the ceiling.

"Yes, Father."

A dazzling flash blinded him for a second, then all the colors disappeared. He was soon to descend into the warmth of the womb, where he would hide until his daddy took him onto his lap, caressed his head, read him a story.

Venex made his way to the back room. A painting of a smiling Satan graced the wall by the door, but Venex didn't deign to look at it. He opened a drawer in the sideboard, which contained a flat box and a revolver. Venex checked the barrel of the revolver, then stuffed it into the inside pocket of his coat together with the box. He then headed out into the corridor, unlocked the front door, and inhaled the crisp energizing air. This could be the hour of truth. Sink or swim, and he wasn't afraid of drowning. His colleagues had humiliated him long enough. They had laughed at him for years because they envied his talent. And what was talent worth these days? Fifteen minutes of fame? The occasional pat on the back? An article in the papers? No, he was determined to demand respect, permanent respect. And there was only one way to do it.

It took more than an hour to find the secret compartment in the floor. Frederik Masyn spent the entire time in his chair with officers flanking him on either side.

"You would save us a great deal of bother if you would let us have the combination, Mr. Masyn."

Frederik stared at the wall. No one had the right to give him orders.

"It's up to you," said Van In. He removed his cell from his pocket and punched in the number of Tuur Swartenbroeckx. The locksmith promised to be with him in less than fifteen minutes.

"Do you mind if I ask where you were last Sunday morning?"

"None of your business," said Masyn.

"The examining magistrate will be happy to hear it," said Van In as he started to pace nervously back and forth. "Does the name Venex mean anything to you?"

Frederik's eyes sparkled ominously, and his lips curled into a condescending smile. "You shall not take the name of Master in vain," he said in a reprimanding tone. Later, when all this was behind him and the police had realized who they were dealing with, they would offer their apologies and leave him in peace.

Guido joined them in the room and signaled to Van In that he wanted a word. "One of the staff told me that the Masyns have an apartment in Blankenberge. They spend most of their weekends there."

Van In told Guido to contact the Blankenberge police and have the apartment checked out. He then turned back to Frederik. "It wasn't very smart of you to leave the stolen car in Blankenberge."

"Venex is our father, and we are all his children. He brings light where there is darkness and knowledge where there is ignorance."

"Of course he does," said Van In.

He approached the boy and looked him in the eye. "In that case I'm your brother and brothers don't have secrets, right?"

Frederik relaxed. The policeman had finally realized they all had a debt of fidelity to Master. He inspected Van In with a conspiratorial look in his eyes. "Let me show you who I really am," he said and tried to stand up, but the two officers held him back.

"There's no need for that," said Van In, "not now that we're brothers. You can wait outside."

The two officers looked at each other sideways.

"Do what the boss says," said Frederik. He held out his hand to Van In, and they both made their way to the floor safe. Frederik got to his knees in front of the hole in the floor and invited his brother to do the same. He then pulled on a pair of white gloves and entered the four-letter code. The steel door clicked open. A pile of yellowed documents was visible on the floor of the safe in addition to a number of recently typed pages in a plastic folder. Frederik leaned forward, removed the documents, and handed them to Van In.

"I see I'm too late."

Tuur marched into the room, grinning from ear to ear. Guido was right behind him. Frederik turned his head and caught sight of the locksmith's toolbox.

"You dirty Judas," he screamed, throwing himself at Van In

like a wild animal in an attempt to recover the documents. Still on his knees, Van In fell backward and tried to keep the documents out of Frederik's reach. The scuffle lasted no more than a few seconds. Guido grabbed Frederik by the wrist, threw his arm around the boy's throat, and immobilized him. Frederik groaned and tried to free himself, but Guido twisted his arm up behind his back, forcing him to abandon any thoughts of escape. The two officers took over and cuffed him just to be sure. Van In scrambled to his feet, the documents firmly in his grip.

"I'm curious," said Guido, brushing the dust from his uniform.

"It looks like a birth certificate." Van In examined the handwritten lines. "In the year nineteen hundred and one, on December the thirteenth, Joris Karel Frederik Boterman was born . . . Son of Anna Boterman . . . Unmarried. Where did I hear that name before?" Van In knit his brows. "Boterman, Boterman . . ."

"Deridder's story," said Guido. "About the priest Van Haecke and the bastard son of Aleister Crowley!" He grabbed his notebook and checked what he had written the day Jasper Simons committed suicide.

"Take a look." Guido pointed to two words he had circled that day: *Venex* and *owly (oly)*. "Jasper's last words."

Van In and Guido leafed through the other documents. Anna Boterman got married a year later to a certain Adolf Neothère Masyn, bell ringer at the Chapel of the Holy Blood.

"Frederik's official grandfather."

The bundle also included letters from Van Haecke and a report on Crowley's visit to Bruges, all written in elegant, decorative handwriting.

"Who would have thought?"

Van In examined the yellowed pages and suddenly remembered

the folder with the handmade sheets of paper they found at Trui Andries's place.

"Jesus H. Christ."

"What's up?" asked Guido.

"Don't you think the idea of Frederik as a direct descendant of the most notorious satanist of all time is a little bit too good to be true?"

"It's possible. Everything seems to square with the story as we know it."

"Trui Andries was a calligrapher. What if these are counterfeit documents she made herself? What if Jasper told her what their purpose was and she decided to write that letter to State Security? The one that claimed the satanic fraternity she belonged to was planning to commit a terrible crime."

"That's why she was killed," said Guido.

Van In nodded. "I'm guessing Venex found out about the letter. He might even have threatened to kill Jonathan if she breathed a word about the conspiracy."

Van In's cell phone made them both jump.

"Van In speaking."

Guido saw the color drain from the commissioner's face. The conversation lasted no more than twenty seconds, but it was enough to set off a tremor in his boss's hand.

"I'll be there in five minutes," he said with a quivering voice. He snapped the cell phone shut and returned it to his inside pocket.

"That was Saartje. Hannelore's contractions have started. They're on the way to the hospital."

Van In handed Guido the bundle of documents.

"Finish things up here, and call me if there are any new developments."

Before Guido could say a word in response, Van In stormed out of the room like an aging roadrunner.

• • •

"The doctor will be here in half an hour, Mrs. Martens." The friendly nurse handed Hannelore a hospital gown and suggested she put it on while she was waiting.

Saartje unpacked Hannelore's suitcase. This was more exciting than anything she'd experienced in the past few days. Hannelore undressed. In her panties, she looked like a pregnant Venus de Milo, as if she'd just stepped out of an Italian Renaissance painting. Suddenly the door flew open. Hannelore grabbed the hospital gown from the bed and covered her breasts. The two women turned and stared in disbelief at the sweat-soaked monster who had just stormed into the room.

"Jesus, you almost caused a miscarriage," said Hannelore, feigning annoyance.

Van In threw his arms around her and kissed her behind the ear. It melted her.

"But I'm happy you're here."

"Is everything all right?"

"Excellent. What about you?"

Van In gasped for breath. His lungs were threatening to tear, and his heart was pounding like crazy. "Is this it?"

Hannelore dropped her hospital gown. "Take one last look," she said with an impish grin.

Venex made his way into the hospital lobby, its marble walls reflecting his shadow. No one noticed him among the dozens of visitors that streamed in and out of the place day and night. His face was half covered by a scarf, but he didn't take the elevator. That was too much of a risk. He turned left into the stairwell next to the elevator door. There wasn't a soul in sight.

Venex took a deep breath and started his climb to the eighth floor. All was not lost. If he could silence Jonathan, then Richard, no one else would dare betray him.

The two officers bundled Frederik Masyn into their SSV and took him to the police station, leaving Guido behind with the documents found in the floor safe. He sat down and removed the papers from the plastic folder. The words *Last Will and Testament* had been typed on top of the first page. *I, the undersigned, Frederik Masyn, hereby* . . . A list of legal statements followed, together with a detailed inventory of the property and possessions of his parents. *All this I leave to* . . . Guido cursed, threw the will on the floor, raced into the corridor, and grabbed the phone.

The corridor on the eighth floor was empty. Venex followed the room numbers and stopped at 834. He carefully pushed open the door and slipped inside. Jonathan was lying on his back. His eyes were closed, and his breathing was calm. A drip full of clear fluid was suspended from a metal stand at his side, a thin tube leading downward to a plastic flow regulator. The tube ended in a tiny butterfly needle attached to Jonathan's lower arm. Venex fished the flat box from his inside pocket and flipped it open. It contained a syringe without a needle and was filled with a yellowish fluid. He loosened his scarf, took the syringe from the box, and attached it to the plastic regulator.

Dr. D'Hondt had just finished a five-hour operation and was enjoying a cup of tea in his office. He expected the patient to make a full recovery, and in spite of his many years in the surgery business, he still felt good about it. On an impulse, he punched in the number of the eighth floor and asked the nurse on duty if the boy who had almost succumbed to the overdose had regained consciousness. If so, he would like to pay a visit.

"One moment, Doctor?"

The duty nurse put down the receiver. She had five minutes to go before the end of her shift, but that didn't interest the doctors, did it? She rattled down the corridor in her hospital clogs.

Venex heard the nurse's footsteps approaching quickly. He let go of the syringe and wrapped his scarf around his face. Just as he was about to hide behind the bed the door flew open. The nurse looked around the room and was aware in an instant that something wasn't right. Then she spotted the syringe attached to the regulator.

"What's going on here?" The nurse lunged toward Venex.

He was quick to react. He rushed to meet her and punched her hard in the stomach. But she was a robust woman and wasn't easily alarmed. She grabbed his scarf, pulled it from his face, and kicked him in the shins with all her might. Venex growled from the pain and staggered momentarily, but still managed to push the nurse out of his way and limp outside into the corridor.

The duty nurse stood there, bewildered, with the scarf in her hand. But only for a split second. She phoned reception and raised the alarm.

Hannelore was lying on her side. Her contractions had subsided, and Van In was massaging her back, following the rhythm of her breathing.

"I'm thirsty," she said suddenly.

"Do you want me to get you something? There's a vending machine in the corridor."

Hannelore nodded.

"I'll be right back."

The vending machine was located in the stairwell. Van In popped a twenty-franc coin in the slot and pressed the button marked Coke. The can clattered down to the dispenser unit. He crouched. Suddenly he spotted a man stumbling down the stairs.

"Geens. What are you doing here?"

When the crime-scene technician heard his name and recognized Van In, he froze on the spot, wheezing, gasping for breath. A siren screamed in the distance.

"Something wrong?" Van In asked. The laboratory analyst stared at him like a mad scientist who'd just had a eureka moment.

"Hannelore's in labor," Van In said when Geens didn't answer his question. "I'm about to become a father."

"There he is," someone shouted.

Two burly nurses stormed down the stairs. Geens looked left and right like a cornered animal. His right hand disappeared into his inside pocket, and in a fraction of a second he was holding Van In at gunpoint. "This is going to cost you, Commissioner."

At that moment, Van In realized that Raf Geens and Venex were one and the same.

17

If I were you I'd put down the gun, Raf. The place is going to be crawling with police any minute."

Van In did his best to stay calm. He might as well have offered ice cream to a gang of football hooligans if they promised to behave themselves after the match. Geens had nothing to lose, and it was written all over him. His eyes were rolling in their sockets, and a string of foaming saliva was dangling from the corner of his half-open mouth.

"You probably think I'm crazy, Commissioner," said the lab analyst, laughing insanely to underline his point.

"No, actually, I don't," said Van In. "I know you're an intelligent man and that you'll make the right decision in the end."

Saartje spotted Van In at the end of the corridor. Who was he talking to? "Hey, Pieter. Any chance of that Coke?"

She was standing in the doorway to Hannelore's room and was invisible to Geens. Why didn't Van In respond? Hannelore's contractions were increasing in frequency, and she was dying for something to drink. Geens noticed the desperation in Van

In's eyes. He moved a little closer until he could look down the corridor.

"Pretty," he said when Saartje came into view. "So that's where the lady wife is hiding."

Geens gestured with his revolver that Van In should lead the way.

"My wife's about to have a baby, Raf. Let's settle matters here. You've got me, haven't you?"

Geens stood still, and Van In heaved a sigh of relief. Suddenly Geens stretched out his arm, pressing his revolver against Van In's head.

"Actually, I don't need you, Commissioner."

Van In understood what Geens was getting at. As hostages, Hannelore and Saartje were worth a thousand times more than him.

"Wise up, Raf. If you shoot me, there isn't a judge in the country who'll grant you mitigating circumstances."

"Of course none of them would spare me. Don't forget I work for the judiciary. I know how judges reach their verdicts nowadays."

"Let me help you."

"Help me!" he shouted, saliva spattering everywhere. His finger curled around the trigger. A couple of millimeters and the gun would go off.

"Win back their respect," said Van In, fishing for words to penetrate the man's hysteria. He pinched his eyes shut and thought of the baby he would never cherish. Why was Geens waiting? This was taking forever.

"So you want to restore my honor."

Van In opened his eyes. Geens's finger relaxed.

"I wonder if that little wife of yours will think the same."

• • •

Beekman was having lunch in a small Italian restaurant on Saint Amand Square. He'd chosen marinated artichoke hearts and scampi fritti, both dishes he loved. The prosecutor had been a regular for more than twenty years, and he wasn't the only satisfied customer if the number of cover charges was anything to go by. The restaurant was wall to wall every day. One of the waiters—a balding Italian in a red waistcoat, crisp white shirt, and matching tie—served him an amaretto on the house. Beekman gave the man a generous tip, to which he responded with a warm "Grazie."

Beekman's beeper went off just as he was raising the glass to his lips. Now that everyone had cell phones, no one paid the least attention to beepers anymore. Beekman switched it off, pushed the table forward, wormed his way out from behind it, and navigated his way between the diners to the bar telephone.

"Beekman here."

He stood behind the bar and did his best not to get in the way of the hardworking waiters. His face tightened as the conversation proceeded. He spluttered a couple of orders, but the noise in the restaurant forced him to shout.

"Send a car immediately," he roared. "And inform the Diane Group."

The hustle and bustle around him suddenly stopped as eighty pairs of eyes turned to look at him.

Beekman registered the surprise in their faces and whispered, "I'll wait for you outside."

Guido was in the hospital lobby, where a provisional command post had been set up. In less than fifteen minutes, he had managed to muster no fewer than forty officers, and they had hermetically sealed the hospital from the outside world. All he could do was wait until the experts arrived. Sirens wailed in the distance, and from the communication crackling through from his walkie-talkie, he figured Prosecutor Beekman was on his way.

Hannelore was gasping and panting when Van In and Geens entered the room. All the color drained from Saartje's face at the sight of them. She worked her way to the right side of the bed and rested her hand on Hannelore's shoulder.

"It won't be long now," she said. "Your contractions are every five minutes."

Van In turned in desperation to Geens. "Let me call a doctor, Raf. Please!"

"You promised you would save my honor, Commissioner. Babies don't need any help. What if they send a cop in disguise with a teargas grenade?" Geens laughed, smug and superior. "You can call reception, Commissioner. Tell them they have half an hour to clear this part of the hospital. I want you to make sure they follow the correct procedures. If there's still a single living soul in this part of the building in half an hour, your wife is dead. Understood?"

Van In nodded and did what Geens asked. His heart pounded so hard against his lungs that it hurt, and the tension in his head made him dizzy. When the federal officer who had been manning the lines at reception since the start of the crisis asked for more information, Van In shouted at him to obey his orders and hung up.

The maternity unit took up the entire wing of the hospital. The evacuation took exactly twenty-two minutes. Most of the patients were able to make their way to safety without assistance, while officers with semiautomatics kept an eye on things from the end of the corridor. Van In made sure they kept their distance and then explored the other rooms to make sure no one had been left behind or snuck in unnoticed.

"I know what they're up to out there," said Geens, glancing furtively at his watch. Van In collapsed into a chair, breathless and panting.

"At this very moment, a Diane Group platoon is getting ready to move out. If they use a helicopter, they'll be here in less than thirty minutes. The federal boys will close off the area, and marksmen will keep a close eye on any potential escape routes."

He turned to the window and closed the curtains. "They'll install infrared cameras, mount laser-guided telescopes on their rifles, abseil from the roof on climbers' ropes, shoot out the windows and toss in stun grenades, send phony negotiators who'll make me all sorts of tempting suggestions, install directional microphones. If they have to, they'll hire a dwarf and send him in via the air-conditioning."

Van In nodded, still hoping that Geens would realize how pointless his actions were.

"But they'll never do any of that if they know that the hostage taker is in a room with a pregnant woman who's just about ready to give birth. The public would never forgive them."

Hannelore was lying on her back with her knees pulled up, leaning on her elbows, her head tossed back. She groaned as a vicious contraction cut through her belly like a red-hot knife. Geens grabbed a chair, sat down next to her on the left side of the bed, and pointed his revolver at her belly.

Van In stiffened. He started to take shallow breaths, just like Hannelore, in an effort to suppress the feeling that his guts were about to explode. Geens was right. With Hannelore here, no one would give orders to storm the room. There were two possibilities:

wait until Geens made a mistake and try to overpower him, or convince him to hand himself over. In both instances, it was essential that Van In kept his cool.

Suddenly the phone rang. Saartje swallowed a squeal.

"Answer it, Commissioner," said Geens.

Van In walked over to the nightstand and Saartje stepped out of the way to let him pass.

"And repeat every word you hear out loud."

Van In immediately recognized Guido's voice. "He wants to know if Hannelore's okay."

"Who is he?"

"Sergeant Versavel."

"Tell him if anyone dares to attempt any further contact, I'll shoot all three of you on the spot."

Van In repeated what Geens had said and hung up.

"He also asked about your demands."

"Demands. What should I demand? Money? A helicopter? A pardon?" Geens shook his head. "I thought you were smarter than that, Commissioner. First they play for time, then they make all kinds of weird promises, and in the end they shoot you dead as if you were a dog. I explained that already."

Geens was getting upset, his voice agitated and unstable, his finger ever tighter on the trigger.

"Sorry, Raf," said Van In. "That's not what I meant."

Hannelore's body arched in response to a paralyzing shooting pain. She shuddered, started to pant, threw back her head, then collapsed to the bed in exhaustion. Her fingernails clawed the sheets. Van In didn't want to think what was going through her head. Giving birth in circumstances like this was unimaginable. Saartje was frozen to the spot. After Geens had threatened to kill them all, she hadn't moved a muscle.

"It would be a shame if we were robbed of your talents, Raf."

Van In had thought long and hard about what he had just said and he realized the risk he was taking. Geens raised an eyebrow. His trigger finger relaxed.

"Take the Andries case. It was a perfect murder, and all the so-called experts were at a complete loss. Then you came along."

Geens smirked. "You'd like to know if I killed her, wouldn't you."

Van In shrugged his shoulders, taking advantage of Geens's brief inattention to slide his left foot forward by half an inch.

"I have to admit I'm curious," said Van In with a smile. "The experts were scientists just like you, weren't they?" Van In won another half inch.

"That's true, Commissioner."

Saartje started to breathe again, and Hannelore carefully licked her dried and cracked lips.

The hospital lobby was wall-to-wall blue. Visitors had been evacuated together with unnecessary staff. In spite of efforts to clear the hospital grounds, a couple of hundred spectators had assembled at a safe distance, hoping to catch a glimpse of what was going on.

Guido listened in on the crisis meeting going on in an adjacent room. A young captain from the Diane Group was trying to convince Beekman, the governor, De Kee, and a number of other officials that his men could take care of things in no more than two minutes. His plan was simplicity itself. His men had infrared viewers attached to their helmets that allowed them to operate in the dark. They could make their way to within a few feet of the room in which the hostage taker was holed up. All it would take was a brief power outage, a couple of seconds, no more. In the ensuing confusion . . .

The captain vigorously defended his plan, but no one present was prepared to give him a green light. The baby was a sore point. If anything happened to it, the public would demand their heads.

"Let's just say I managed to convince Jasper to continue his relationship with Trui in another world."

"A better world," said Van In.

Geens nodded. "I'm happy you share my vision, Commissioner."

Van In moved his left foot.

"You were their father, after all," he said. "You knew what was good for them."

Hannelore struggled with an oncoming contraction. Suddenly she felt her thighs moisten. Something in her lower belly had snapped.

Geens shook his head, his pistol still pointing at Hannelore's belly. "You think you can distract me with your flattery. Can't you see for yourself how transparent your strategy is? Creeping forward inch by inch, waiting patiently until my attention wanes for a second."

Van In withdrew his foot. The situation was hopeless.

"I had them all in my power, Commissioner. Jasper, Jonathan, Richard, Frederik . . . In the end, they all did what I desired of them."

Van In looked at Hannelore. Plump beads of sweat appeared on her forehead. He could see the terror in her eyes. She also knew that Geens wasn't likely to hand himself over. The man wanted respect. He'd dreamed all his professional life that people would praise him, shower him with the adulation his work deserved. Geens dreamed of immortality and a place in the history books. He wanted to be remembered.

"But Trui threw a wrench in the works," said Van In, feigning confidence.

Geens curled his upper lip, exposing his teeth like a wild animal ready to attack.

"Jasper was in love with her. He wanted to start a new life with her in a better world. I told him that just such a world existed and he believed me. They planned to set out for it together."

Hannelore groaned. She wanted to go to the restroom. The instinct to push was so powerful it was making her dizzy. *Not while he's here*, she thought. *Please God, don't disgrace me.*

"I gave them the recipe for a perfect death," said Geens. "Two measures of tetramethylammonium pyrosulphate. No one would be any the wiser. But the idiot screwed up. Trui took a double dose by accident."

Geens related the entire story. Jasper had mixed the toxin with Coke and left the bottle in the refrigerator. Trui drank the whole thing unawares. Jasper panicked and dumped the body in the ditch.

"Then Jasper paid me a visit. What a state he was in."

Van In tried to follow Geens's train of thought. He had read enough stuff about sects to know that such things happened. According to them, committing suicide was a passage to a better world, to a new and more complete life.

"And you ordered him to cover up his tracks."

Geens nodded.

"They believed in me, Commissioner. Jasper jumped out of a window a couple of days later, then Jonathan appeared with your head on a plate."

"Because you gave them drugs."

Saartje bit her bottom lip. Why was Van In trying to wind this madman up?

The crisis meeting seemed to be taking forever, and Guido was having trouble controlling his impatience. If they didn't do something soon, he would make a move himself. Did those big shots realize they were dealing with a psychopath? Geens had at least eleven deaths to account for and he knew that there was no chance of clemency. If they kept talking like this, Hannelore, Pieter, and Saartje wouldn't stand a chance. Geens would take them all out, then turn the gun on himself.

Guido marched into the room and cleared his throat.

"The drugs part was easy," Geens said proudly.

Van In raised his eyebrows.

"I drew on the supplies Delrue and his men brought in. Every time they asked me to analyze the stuff, I swapped the heroin with sugar and the ecstasy pills with fakes. They were due to be destroyed, after all."

The circle was complete. Van In felt the saliva in his mouth dry up. He realized that Geens's confession had a meaning. The man wanted to be famous one last time. Next step, a bullet through everyone's head, including his own.

"So you were the mysterious informant who tipped off the federal boys," he said.

"Bravo, Commissioner."

Geens's finger curled around the trigger.

"Delrue was onto me and I had to do something to distract him. That's why I told you about the tetramethylammonium pyrosulphate. It put me beyond suspicion. And none of my disciples, not even Frederik, knew my real identity."

"In the meantime, you got on with your plans for the mass shooting."

"Masyn was a billionaire, Commissioner. I did it for the money. And now you've told me Frederik's been arrested. So you took it from me. You shouldn't have done that."

Geens was getting agitated. His hand trembled. As a child he had suffered from hunger and hardship. His God-fearing parents had worked their fingers to the bone to save enough money for college. A degree would guarantee a carefree life for their son, they thought. But his mother died of tuberculosis in 1954 when he was only thirteen, his father two years later, and the juvenile court had entrusted him to the sisters at Suffer Little Children.

One of the sisters caught him with his hands under the blankets one night. She caned him hard on the belly and did irreparable damage. The duty doctor kept his mouth shut, and the sister got away with it. The sisters had humiliated him until he was twenty-one years of age, then they had thrown him out onto the street without a cent. But in spite of everything, he had succeeded in becoming a lab technician. He was good at his job, but to no avail. Like the sisters, his superiors treated him like dirt and gradually robbed him of the last crumb of respect he had tried to maintain. Society spat him out, and he refused to accept it. Only money could soften the pain, but even that had been stolen from him when Masyn was arrested. Both God and Satan had abandoned him. Geens had nothing left to lose. Death was the only honorable alternative.

Van In tensed every fiber of his body. Geens was only a couple of feet away. It had to work.

He threw himself forward. The revolver was all that mattered.

Suddenly the room was plunged into darkness. A shot went off, followed immediately by two loud explosions, a flash of light, and a further two shots.

Geens was slumped in his chair, an expanding patch of red visible on his shirt close to his heart. The revolver was lying beside him on the ground. Four Diane Group officers—like Martians with their infrared viewers—blinked as the neon lights flickered back into service. Van In was on the floor. He had hit the side of the metal bed with his chin. Suddenly Hannelore started to moan.

"They're coming," Saartje shouted.

Van In scrambled to his feet. He thought he was hearing things. *They're coming? Who's coming? They got here already.*

The delivery lasted twenty minutes. When the first little head popped out, Van In's eyes filled with tears. He felt helpless and happy all at once.

"Hannelore didn't want to worry you," said Saartje with a smile. "It was to be a surprise."

Dr. D'Hondt cut the cord and placed the baby on Hannelore's chest.

"It's a boy," he said.

Hannelore smiled at Van In.

"You take him," she said. "I've still got work to do."

The hospital cafeteria was abuzz with cheerful people. Van In lit a cigarette and savored his Duvel. For once it was ice cold.

"Twins," he said, still finding it all hard to believe. "Who would have thought?"

"Ask Hannelore," said Beekman.

Everyone laughed: Beekman, Delrue, Saartje, Pattyn, De Kee, the Diane Group officers, D'Hondt, Guido, and Jonathan. The latter had regained consciousness only half an hour earlier. He was still attached to a drip, but you could see from the glint in his eye that he was on the mend. Van In raised his glass.

"Thanks to all of you," he said with a lump in his throat.

"Thank Guido," said Beekman. "He held us hostage and threatened to call you if we didn't do something. And Geens had said he would shoot you all if anyone tried to make contact. We had to make a move."

Van In got to his feet and walked over to Guido. The two men embraced.

"I sweated water and blood, Pieter. But . . ."

Van In gave him a kiss. "Would you have called?"

Guido shrugged his shoulders. He had aged five years in less than an hour.

"Another round on the house," said Beekman.

Drinks were ordered, and everyone returned to their tables. Van In buried his nose in a fresh, frothy Duvel. The brand-new father was proud as punch. They'd decided on Simon and Sarah. Simon and Sarah Van In.

Mr. Simons heard about the hostage incident on the late news. He took off his glasses, crossed to his desk, removed the crucifix from the wall, and hung it upside down from the metal eyelet attached to the bottom of the cross.

Richard Coleyn awoke from a deep sleep, cold and hungover. He shivered and hoped that Father would be home soon.

PIETER ASPE is the author of the Pieter Van In Mysteries. Aspe lives in Bruges, Belgium, and is one of the most popular contemporary writers in the Flemish language. His novels have sold over one million copies in Europe alone.

BRIAN DOYLE was born in Scotland in 1956 and is currently a professor at the University of Leuven in Belgium. In addition to teaching, he has translated a wide variety of books from Dutch and Flemish into English. In addition to the Pieter Van In Mysteries, his recent book projects include Jef Geeraerts's *The Public Prosecutor* (2009), Jacqueline van Maarsen's *Inheriting Anne Frank* (2010), Christiaan Weijts's *The Window Dresser* (2009), Tessa de Loo's *The Book of Doubt* (2011), Paul Glaser's *Dancing with the Enemy* (2013), and Bob Van Laerhoven's *Baudelaire's Revenge* (2014). He also translates poetry and literary nonfiction.

THE PIETER VAN IN MYSTERIES

FROM OPEN ROAD MEDIA

CPSIA information can be obtained
at www.ICGtesting.com
Printed in the USA
LVOW12s1626180816
500936LV00001B/103/P